MILDRED WINNERLEY;

OR,

THE CURSE OF BEAUTY.

BY THE AUTHOR OF "AMY," "THE WIFE'S TRAGEDY," &c.

LONDON:

PUBLISHED BY E. LLOYD, 12, SALISBURY SQUARE, FLEET
STREET, AND SOLD BY ALL BOOKSELLERS.

MILDRED WINNERLEY;

OR, THE CURSE OF BEAUTY.

No. 1.

INTRODUCTION.

IN the great metropolis of England, in that proud place which may justly be entitled the emporium of the world, amidst its vastness and its magnificence, amidst its greatness and its gaiety, centred in the midst of its princely palaces, located amongst the homes where the children of fortune and fashion dwell—in the very heart of the laughing, waltzing, flaunting, giddy, luxurious town—there exists, and has existed for some years, a fearful mystery—a mystery such as no other capital in Europe can parallel; which, were it known to the dissipated throng around, would thrill that throng with horror; and which, were it revealed in any of the adjacent ball-rooms, would bring the merriment to a stop, pale the cheek of beauty, pall the heart of youth, paralyse the limbs of the dancers, and plunge the listeners in gloom. It is well for the sons and daughters of folly that to them the tale is unknown.

London has but one such mystery; and the story has been told to few. The mystery illustrates a sad and terrible chapter in the history of the human heart; and the story, fearful as it is, is never forgotten by those to whom it is once related.

It matters not how the story was learnt by me; it is not requisite that I should detail how I became acquainted with the facts. Perhaps it would have been well for my peace and happiness if I had never acquired the particulars; for when I have told the reader all, he will comprehend why it is that I shudder whenever I meet a form of surpassing female beauty, and why it is that I tremble with fear when I chance to see two lover sauntering lovingly together.

There are certain persons who must not read this story.—Let all who are in love, and have that love returned, refrain from reading another chaper. I will tell you why—but wait a minute.

Let every fair girl, and especially yourself, my rosy-cheeked, blue-eyed beauty, hesitate before turning over another leaf. Perhaps you wish to know for what reason I give you this caution. Well, you shall be informed presently; in the meantime, if you possibly can—take my advice.

The mystery, then, is not to be pried into by lovers, neither are young ladies who are decidedly pretty to read another page. Young men, if they are handsome, are to remain ignorant of all that I have to tell. And married people, if they are not jealous, had better stop at this paragraph, and go no further.

Well, now, you wish to know what there can be in the story itself to warrant my giving this advice. Do you think I am going to answer you in the very first chapter? Certainly not. I have good reason for cautioning you as I have done; knowing as I do the mystery which I propose to tell, and being very solicitious about your peace of mind. However, if you will act contrary to that which I advise, and will seek to be wiser than I wish you to be, you must take the consequences.

But the mystery, you say—let us have some inkling of the mystery; we begin to suspect that you have no mystery after all!

Have no suspicion, good reader. The mystery is this—

There stands in one of the sombre, select-looking squares, at the west-end of the metropolis, a large mansion of somewhat imposing appearance. The square itself is doubtless well-known to the reader, and the house to which I refer, has in all probability attracted his attention. It is a stately, spacious building, with a heavy portal and old-fashioned mullioned windows. Pilasters of red brick support an architrave cornice of cumbrous masonry, and give to the house the appearance of being striped like the nether garments of a livery servant. An air of drowsy dullness pervades every brick, and speaks forth in every stone. The great oaken door looks torpid and inactive; while the window-panes are dim and dingy, like the eyes of waning age when the glitter of their youth is gone. Over the steps of the doorway is an iron arch sustaining a lamp of antique construction. There was a time when this arch had a more pointed and gothic shape, when it was festooned with iron ornaments, and decorated with gilded finials; but the gold has worn away, the ornaments have dropped off one by one, and the arch itself has lost its airy spring, and become round-shouldered and obtuse with age. Then, the lamp which it supports is not lit by gas, but by oil, after the fashion of old. And when it burns, it does so with a sluggish flame, as if it were half asleep; and is chary of giving light, as if it thought it had given enough in its time, and longed to rest from its labours. Good light, bright, merry light that lamp has given, having shone upon beauty stepping from her carriage, gaiety going to the ball-room, and the bride setting forth upon her journey. Upon these has that lamp-light shone—ay and upon other scenes besides. It has lit in the undertakers with the coffins, and illuminated the way to the hearse; it has shone upon the babe taken out to its first visit, and upon the corpse carried out to its last home. And now the old lamp burns dimly, drowsily; the flame glows dancingly no more. And if you look up at the house itself, and view its faded aspect, and scan its mouldering walls, and mark its gloomy windows, you cease to wonder that the old lamp gives so dusky a light, and that the oil burns so faintly. Dejection and sadness characterise every door-post, and every window-pane; life, that is but the mockery of death, existence that is but the semblance of annihilation, may be discovered in each particular of the stately, sombre mansion. People live in that house—it is inhabited; but if you post yourself against the iron railings of the opposite enclosure, and watch those windows from dawn to sunset, you will fail to descry a human countenance looking out through the dusky panes. Gloomy figures, darkly-habited, you may at times discern, moving slowly from room to room; but if you listen you will hear no sound of music, no voice of song, no tread of merry footsteps. Perchance you will see a black coach drive up to the door, and persons pass out of it, and enter the house. Those persons will be clothed in mourning—they all wear mourning who dwell within these walls. You will never see the balcony fitted-up for a ball, you will never perceive a link-boy at the door. If you observe that mansion, as I have done—if you watch it as I have watched it, your curiosity will become excited, you will pant to know with what tragical story it is connected. It is not improbable that you will imagine beauty and wealth to have once suffered some fearful misery in those apartments, and there you will imagine rightly; but it is also not improbable that you will think the sufferers to have been of high birth and noble lineage, yet in that you will think wrongly. The mystery has to do with beauty and with poverty, with exalted rank and with the children of toil. When you know what is *inside* the house, in addition to that which is outside, your wonder will be doubly increased.

Look up, and you will perceive one room in that house—the top-most room—the windows of which have their curtains always drawn down. Go, and watch at midnight;

and then, as the clock strikes twelve, you may chance to discern a lady, clothed in black, slowly ascend the staircase, and with a lamp in hand enter that room. In hat room there will be a light when all the other apartments of the mansion are dark and silent.

The light remains in the room for one hour. The lady then takes the lamp in her hand and descends the stairs.

It is known to the inhabitants of the square that every night the lady ascends the stairs, and that every night she stays one hour in that room.

What can that apartment contain? Why does the lady visit it every night?

In those mysteries are involved the story of the CURSE OF BEAUTY.

CHAPTER I.

HAMLET.—Do you see nothing there?

THE QUEEN.   All that is, I see.

                                                    HAMLET.

THE LADY WHO FOR EVER SITS BEFORE THE LOOKING-GLASS.

THE door of the room into which every night the lady goes, is always kept locked during the day. That door is painted of a deep plack hue; the keyhole is covered over on the inner side; so that you cannot see through into the apartment.

They who live in that house as servants of the lady, have a suspicion as to what that room contains. None of them are correctly informed on the subject; but they have become used to the mystery, and do not now—as they once did—try to penetrate the secret.

Some years since, one of the domestics, unable to restrain his curiosity, procured a key to fit, and proceeded to unlock the door. As, however, he was turning the key in the lock, he started at perceiving that the cover of a small box, fixed in the wood-work of the door, slowly opened, and disclosed to view a small bell, which immediately commenced ringing. Terrified, and fearful of being detected, the man attempted to withdraw his key, and close the cover of the small box. To his increasing terror and surprise, he found it impossible either to do one or the other—the key was firm in the lock, the cover of the box would not close, and the bell continued to tinkle. On the stairs, as the man was hastily making his descent, he was met by the lady who every night visits the room.

Since the day on which the occurrence happened, the man has never been seen in that house !

What, then, can the mystery be? Why is the room kept so carefully closed? Does any one know the secret besides the lady who nocturally visits the apartment?

Yes; the secret is known to me. I have never told the story, save and except to one person; and were I to offer that person the worth of worlds, I do not believe that she would consent to look at all which might be shown to her in the top apartment of that old mansion.

And yet there are no ghosts nor hobgoblins there. This story has not to deal with anything of the sort. It is not a romance to terrify; it is a tale of truth, which may instruct.

Well, are you prepared to know what the mystery is ? Listen, then, and I will tell it to you.

There is in that room—that strange mysterious room, something which the lady goes every night to look at—something which she deems it her duty regularly to visit No other apartment in all the other large mansions of the neighbourhood contains anything similar.

If the door of that room be opened to you, and you enter, you immediately perceive that the walls are hung with black, and that the carpet on the floor is of the same dismal colour. Various small objects meet your view ; but there is something in the centre of the room which immediately arrests your attention. You look at nothing else until you have examined that.

In the middle of the room stands a looking-glass of large dimensions, and before the looking-glass sits a lady. You walk straight up to the mirror, and that which strikes you as being strange is, that you do not see the lady reflected in the glass ; *you see something else* !

The lady always sits as there you see her. Years ago she was seated there, and she sits in the same position now ; she is sitting there even as I write and as you read.

She is very beautiful ! Never was there a human shape of more perfect mould. All the fabled excellences of a fabled Venus you may descry in that faultlessly-symmetrical form. Her attitude is graceful ; her figure is elegant ; the contour of her limbs is full and free, and flowing. If you look at her countenance, you perceive that her features are cast in the highest style of beauty—they are marvellously beautiful ! The face is that of a young woman in her twenty-first or twenty-second year. She sits looking towards the glass, and her right hand is employed in arranging a tress of her hair ; the left hand is partially concealed beneath a lace scarf. On those hands, and that hair, you could not gaze without a feeling of rapturous admiration. The hair is glossy, and its tresses are of a raven hue. The neck which those tresses shade is of dazzling whiteness, and is so stately in its shape that the head sits on it with an air of majesty. Never had shoulders a more graceful fall ; never were arms more exquisitely fashioned ; never has sculptor seen a bust more excellently modelled. The hands are small, the finers are tapering and white. The nails of those fingers are not long and narrow, as in people who lack mental energy, but broad and large as in those whose will is strong, and their determinations firm. Then, if you pursue your examination of the countenance, you find that the features are well defined, that the eyebrows are broad and well-marked, and that the forehead is open and expansive. The lips are perfect in the beauty of their outline ; the chin is delicately moulded ; the teeth resemble pearl rather than ivory. A voluptuary would die with delight gazing on that incomparable form ; the most austere of men would become a devotee before the shrine of such transcendant loveliness. For the face is not one that you could look upon, and then turn away, to go forth into the busy crowd and forget that you have seen it. No ; the gleam of those dark eyes, if once gazed upon, will haunt the gazer through eternity. If you mark well the expression of that countenance, you perceive that winningness is there mingled with command—that those eyes so fit for beamings of love, are also the eyes which can dart glances of scorn. Look steadfastly, and you will read something more than love in those eyes and on those features. That brow bespeaks ambition, those lips betoken pride. Turn your gaze towards that hand, and you at once discern in the peculiar bend of the wrist, the desire to reign, the passion to make conquest. Undoubtedly there is sweetness in that face; but look at it long, and you begin to tremble as you involuntarily think of the fate of her upon whom you gaze. Something tells you, that beauty so exquisite was destined to bring sorrow to its owner: something inpresses you with the belief that no child of mortality could inherit such beauty without also inheriting a full shall of earthly woe. In vain you wish it otherwise, you read the destiny too well. And as you mark he blush upon that roseate cheek, the smile upon those vermeil lips, the sparkle in those lustrous eyes, you become sorrowful; for beneath the blush, within the smile, concealed by the sparkle, you perceive misery lurking, like a demon waiting to claim its victim. Then it is your wish to know the lady's story, the history of her joys and sorrows, and why she for ever sits before that mirror.

All that you desire to know you shall learn presently. But now go nearer; touch that delicately-tinted skin, and look deeper into those meaning eyes. You do; and you find that which you touch to be cold, and you find those eyes to be fixed and life-less. Another minute's examination suffices to inform you that the figure, perfect as it seems, is made of wax.

Yes; it is wax, but wax so exquisitely modelled, that imitated appears to surpass created beauty. You almost fear to raise the flowing drapery; but you do so, and you perceive that the bosom does not heave, that the figure is rigid as carved marble. You start back, and ask yourself—Whose work of excellence is this? Was there ever a living, breathing form, that was the original of this surpassing loveliness?

There was such a being. She is dead now. But before you learn her history, you must become better acquainted with the room containing the waxen image.

Step up behind the waxen figure, and look over its shoulder upon the same mirror at which the image is gazing. Ha! why do you start—why are you terrified? Is it because the mirror reflects that which you did not expect to see?

Nothing can be more startling. Whoever stands behind that image and glances at the looking-glass, naturally thinks to see the reflection of the image there. You see nothing of the kind. That which you behold is the reflection of a skeleton, with the under-jaw hanging down, and the hand-bones stained with blood.

If you move to the left of the waxen image you lose sight of the skeleton, and perceive the countenance of the beauteous lady; but if you stand behind the figure, and look upon the mirror in the same line of direction as that in which the figure itself seems gazing, you cease to see the lady, and have before you the hideous skeleton.

Therefore, the lady remains ever seated in the chair, ever gazing in the looking-glass; but never seeing herself, always gazing upon the eye-less skull, and upon the blood-stained bones.

This is strange; this is mysterious! Look around the room and you see other things which increase the mystery.

Against the wall hangs a picture in a black frame. One moment's glance suffices to inform you that the picture is a portrait of the lady whose waxen effigy you have examind. Very beautiful is that portrait; for it represents the lady as she was in the first blush of womanhood, when youth, and health, and joyancy were with her.

The black hair trails gloriously over the alabaster shoulders; and the dark eyes seem fixed upon you, enchanting you as with a spell. Still, in the expression of the portrait, as in the expression of the image, you read the existence of passions which must have wrought sorrow and misery to her in whose bosom they lodged; you see that the portrait is very beautiful, but you almost suspect that even behind that portrait some skeleton must be concealed.

Over the mantle is suspended a coronal of faded flowers, such as might have graced beauty at a ball or at a *fête*. Below the coronal is a blue ribbon, the tint of which has lost its brightness. On the shelf beneath is a bundle of letters, together with a ring, a lock of hair, and various minor articles.

Look now to the wall between the windows, and you perceive something shrouded from view by a black veil. Remove that veil, and what do you behold? A portrait of a man, the original of which, your instinct tells you, must have been known to the lady whose history you wish to learn. He is represented as a young man, of dark complexion, and with a reckless, though unamiable expression of countenance. His attire is that of a gentleman; but the more you examine the face the more puzzled you become. You know not whether he was a man of rank or fortune, or some desperate and clever highwayman. That the countenance is in some degree handsome, you cannot deny; there is something in the gay, dashing air which pervades the portrait, that enchants you at the first glance, but causes you pain on further reflection. It is impossible to become divested of the idea that the original of the portrait was at bottom a cold-hearted villain; for the expression of the mouth declares as much. You now begin to wonder what his villanies were, and you feel curious to know in what manner he was connected with the beauteous lady. You feel that her fate had to do with his; you have an impression that her joys and sorrows had their origin in him. And you let fall again the veil over the picture, knowing that you have some strange story of love and its trials to learn.

Now walk round the room. Pass behind the mirror, and approach the door by which you entered. You start! you are afraid! It is no wonder that you manifest such fear; for before you is a recess of the wall, and behind the door, you perceive the skeleton, the reflection of which you saw in the looking-glass.

It is a real skeleton. Convince yourself of that fact by touching it. The bones are hard and dry. Smell them, and you find that they have an earthy odour. The hands stained as if with the stain of blood. Look well, and you discern that the attitude in which the skeleton is placed is the same as that in which the lady sits.

The thought which now suggests itself is—Can this be the skeleton of the man whose portrait is hidden by the black veil, and do the blood-dyed hands indicate that he was the murderer of the beauteous lady? No. Examine the skeleton well, and you find that the smallness of the extremities, the smoothness of the long bones, and the breadth of the haunch-bones, clearly prove that the skeleton is that of a woman. What woman?—you naturally ask. Surely not the skeleton of her whose portrait you have been viewing? Surely not that of her who was so beautiful? And yet the skeleton and the waxen effigy are both of one height, and both are seated in the same posture!

You now understand why in your former position you did not see the reflection of the lady in the glass. That glass is placed obliquely in relation to the two objects which it reflects.   Place yourself a little on one side of your looking-glass at home, and let some person occupy a seat at a short distance on the other side of the mirror. You will then find that you see the image of the other person in the glass, and not the reflection of yourself, while the other person will fail to discern his own likeness, but will behold in the glass the image of you. This is very simple. It is an exemplification of an optical law with which every one should be familiar. When you have tried this experiment you will understand why it is that in the upper room of that gloomy house a person standing behind the waxen lady sees a skeleton in the looking-glass ; and how is it that if you place yourself before the skeleton, and then look in the mirror, you see the reflection of the beautiful image.

Silent and motionless ever sits that form of beauty, gazing at the hideous symbol of mortality. By night and day, from dawn to dawn again, through winter and summer, in spring and autumn, when the flowers are in bloom, and when the snow is on the ground, even gazes the lady in the looking-glass, but never beholding herself. The skeleton for the lady—the lady for the skeleton !   What can the mystery mean ?

People move onward through the square, and know not of the mystery so near them. Every day laughing children, merry youths, and smiling maidens pass that house, you have passed that house, people are passing it even as I write ; but who, of all who go past it, entertain a suspicion of the strange secret which it contains ; who thinks that in the topmost room, where the blinds of the window are always drawn, a figure so beautiful is ever gazing at a form so frightful ?   The tale has never been told until now.

And what, then, is that tale ? and why do the skeleton and the lady thus sit looking at each other in the mirror ? and wherefore every night does the owner of that house ascend the staircase and visit that lonely room ?   It must be for some purpose

And the picture beneath the veil.—Did the original of that portrait wrong the lovely being whose image in cold wax is so irresistibly beautiful ? did he deceive and betray her, did he act the seducer's part, and did she fall the seducer's victim ? or were they both participators in one common crime, and did each meet one common punishment ? You burn to know the mystery ; you are anxious to undertand the secret.

There was a time, reader, when I would not have revealed that secret ; but I will reveal it now.

You ask if beauty can be a curse. I answer that it can be both a curse and a blessing. You wish to know how it can prove so. Listen to the story of Mildred Winnerley, and learn !

CHAPTER II.

He climbs the crackling stair—he bursts the door,
Nor feels his feet glow scorching with the floor,
His breath choked, gasping, with the volumed smoke,
But still from room to room his way he broke.—BYRON'S CORSAIR.

MILDRED AND MARION WINNERLEY.—THE CHEST AND THE SECRETS THEREIN.

THREE-AND-TWENTY years ago the events related in this chapter happened. The place was a village in Hampshire ; and the occurrences befell on a summer's day.

Do you know any of the Hampshire villages, good reader ? do you know how beauteous and how English-like they are ?   For the most part embossed in green hills, and dotted down here and there in lovely valleys, always pleasantly situated, and always affording charms to the lovers of the picturesque, they vie with the fairest scenes to be

found in this fair land.   There is not one of them but what would enchant you at the
first glance; that is, if you are fond of roses and honneysuckles, if you have any liking
for pretty gleaming rivers, and partiality for old-fashioned, ivy-mantled church towers.
Green downs and sunny uplands are everywhere in view; while if you are disposed
to seek quiet scenery, you could not find better, were you to search the kingdom, from
the Land's End to John o' Groat's.

Nevertheless, you are not to suppose, that because the Hampshire villages are beautiful, there is anything like Arcadia to be found therein.   The inhabitants are not all
happy shepherds and gentle-minded maids; neither does their employment consist only
in keeping sheep and making love.   Beautiful as those villages are, sadsome scenes
often happen in them; and in their soft retreats, as in every place besides, the tragedy

of life is mingled with the pleasant comedy. The incidents of the present chapter of our story will prove the truth of this last assertion.

Twenty-three years ago, then, in the front room of a small Hampshire cottage, there sat a blooming, beauteous maiden, before her looking-glass. The time was evening ; and the window of the room was open to allow the cool balmy breeze to enter at its own sweet will.

The maiden was very beautiful. She had large dark eyes, black as jet, and bright as diamonds. Her features were elegant rather than pretty ; and her figure was dignified and queenly. The curl of her dark upper lip, and the slight frown which sat upon her gracefully-curved eyebrows, told that she was not unconscious of possessing such rare beauty, while the care which she was displaying in making her toilet, revealed also that she wished to use that beauty to advantage. Her glossy locks fell in large ringlets upon her shoulders, and the dark richness of her hair served to bring out in its full purity the dazzling pearliness of the skin.

At the further end of the room, remote from where the beauty sat at her looking-glass, reclined in her chair an elderly, benevolent-looking woman, who, from her appearance, was suffering under an attack of illness. As a sudden pang of pain shot through the frame of the invalid, she turned her gaze in the direction of the beauty, and knocking her crutch stick on the floor, cried—

"Mildred ! Milly !"

The beauty either did not hear, or refrained from noticing the call. She continued her operations before the mirror ; now untwisting one obsinate ringlet, and then giving a slight twist to another equally as obstinate a one, as if she deemed the proper disposition of those exquisite curls to be the most important affair in the universe. It was a foolish thought, if she did think so, for nature had made those locks beautiful enough, and art could not add to their beauty.

Again the invalid rapped her stick upon the floor.

"Come hither, Milly—come child! I am ill—I am dying."

But the maiden paid no attention to the call; she did not even turn her head in the direction whence it came. Still she continued before the looking-glass, still that pleasant portrait in the glass had enchantment for her eyes. The portrait was that of herself, and a more glorious picture she could not have looked upon. But she was very well aware of that; and accordingly, she deemed that time could not be wasted, if spent in gazing on anything so delightful. First she surveyed her countenance in full ; then she made an effort to view it in profile ; this was followed up by an attempt to see how her back-hair was disposed ; and finally bending her head so as to recline her cheek upon her hand, she surveyed her general appearance when assuming that pretty coquettish attitude. A third time the invalid struck the floor smartly with her stick.

"Will you let me die, Milly—will you let me die, and not come to me?"

"Why, what do you want, grandmother? how tiresome you are !" said the beauty, turning round, but not looking at her relative, being busily engaged in fastening a brooch into her dress.

"My—my physic, child. I—I cannot reach it with my hand; and I am in pain—in great pain."

"There now, grandmother! if you haven't made me break the clasp of my brooch. I wish you'd let one dress oneself without being so troublesome."

" Troublesome, Mildred—troublesome did you say, child? It is a day I never thought to see when I should become troublesome to those whom I have always treated with kindness. But well, well; don't come near me, child. I can do without you, I an bear my pain, I can bear it. You——"

" Now do be quiet, grandmother! Here is your physic. You know in what haste I am."

" Haste for what, girl? where are you hastening to ?"

" The ball, grandmother—the ball at Squire Bannerton's. Have you forgot the ball ?"

" I, child ? what have I to do with balls and dances now ? There is death in my heart already, and my brain seems to be on fire. If you love me, Mildred—if you thought about me, child—you would stay with me to-night—you would stay at home."

" What, not go to the ball grandmother ! when Squire Bannerton has invited both of us, though Marion says that she will not go, because—because—I don't know what ; but she will stay to keep you company. Oh ! grandmother, I would not miss the ball for anything ! The whole village will be there, and oh ! there will be such doings!"

" Well, well, mark me, Mildred—mark what I say ! with your gay doings, and your fine things, and your dances, and your ball, you have grown proud and upstart ; such as I never thought to see you grow. And you will suffer for it—you will suffer, mark my words ! Your fine looks, and your finery will be your misery. I am sorry for you, child. I—I—but go—go away ; do not stop here with your old grandmother, go, Mildred Winnerley—go !"

" Why, really, grandmother ! I never——"

" What is dear grandmother angry about ?" inquired a smiling girl, who at that moment bounded into the room.

" She don't know herself, Marion," replied the beauty. " It is merely because I am going to the ball to-night, and grandmother is putting herself in a passion about—about—I'm possitive I don't know what it is about, for there cannot be any harm in my accepting the squre's invitation."

" Oh, dear Mildred, I'm sure grandmother isn't angry about that. Dear grand-mother cannot object to your going to the ball, if I stay at home to keep her company. And you are looking so beautiful this evening, sweet Mil. I declare that I don't know when I've seen you look so handsome. Besides, Gerrard Chester will be here pre-sently to fetch you, and poor Gerrard would be so disappointed if you were not ready to go to the ball with him."

" Why should he be disappointed, sister Marion?"

" Why, gracious me ! Milly, how coldly you speak of poor Gerrard! one would almost think——"

" Well, Marion ; what were you going to say ?"

Marion took her sister's hand, and looking in her face, said—

" You love poor Gerrard—do you not ? I am sure that he loves you, dear Mildred."

" It is very kind of him, no doubt, dear sister, but——"

" But what, Mildred ?"

"I—that is—Gerard Chester is very poor; and I never gave him any encouragement; I have never told him anything about loving him—have I, sister?"

"Told—never told! But you know, sister, you——"

"There now, Marion, say no more. Grandmother will wonder why you are talking so much about Gerrard Chester."

"Ay, ay, Mildred, child," observed the invalid, "I hear what Marion tells you. And Gerrard Chester is a good man and a worthy one. But he is not fine enough for you, nor rich enough either. He's not 'my lord,' and he can't make you 'my lady' by marrying. Well, well, he's better without you. Fine as ye are, with your proud looks, there's no such beauty in your heart; no, God grant there were! Master Gerrard can find a truer love if he choose to look, and one who would not give him so many haughty words. May be, Mildred, child, a day will come when you will humble your proud front to Gerrard Chester."

"Why, grandmother! what can be the matter with you? I have never said anything against Mr. Chester, except—except——"

"Hush, Mildred!" exclaimed her sister; "here is Gerrard coming to fetch you. And he looks so gay, and happy, and handsome, poor fellow! that I would not for the world you should make him sorrowful by any appearance of coldness, or any reluctance to accompany him. Is he not good-looking, sister? So noble in his walk, so gentle in his manner, so fond—so very fond of you, dear Mildred. Oh, sister, you ought to love him!"

"Hush! Marion, he is here."

The door opened, and Gerrard Chester entered the cottage. Never were commendations better bestowed than when Marion Winnerley spoke in praise of the gentle youth who was the recognised suitor of her sister. He was handsome, as she had said him to be; he was noble-looking, as she had positive declared. But although Gerrard Chester had dressed himself in his best attire, and had put on the very best coat which he possessed, his humble garments bore unmistakable evidence to his poverty. Little favour, therefore, found he in the eyes of Mildred. It was not because he wanted good looks, not because he was too young or too old, that she received his attentions with coldness, if not with disdain; but because he was poor and lowly—because he had not broad lands and the title of squire. And every day as Mildred stood before her looking-glass, and beheld how beautiful she was, she felt less and less inclined to become the wife of Gerrard Chester. She had heard of girls who on account of their beauty had become countesses, and she had read stories telling of handsome maidens who had risen from humble conditions to be the wives of lords and dukes. Why, then, thought Mildred, should I throw myself away upon a poor farmer's son, while I have the chance of one day becoming a lady in the land? Such a question, Mildred had but one way of answering, and that was by looking coldly at poor Gerrard, and then gazing in the mirror, to see how her beauty had increased within the last few months. Now, however, Gerrard Chester had come to take her to the ball at Squire Bannerton's. For the squire having-arrived at his fiftieth birth-day, and being a strong, hale, open-hearted, benevolent man, had thought fit to give an entertainment to all parties in celebration of the anniversary of his birth. To this festival the Winnerleys and Mr. Chester had been invited, and poor Gerrard had indulged in the fond hope that Mildred would be pleased at his undertaking to escort her. He knew it would be an honour, and he felt that it would be a pleasure. He had brought a coronal of the most beautiful flowers for Mildred to wear on her head, and he had brought her also a large nosegay which he had gathered with his own hands.

Mildred allowed the coronal to be placed on her brow. She saw that the red roses contrasted delightfully with her dark tresses, and because the coronal added to her beauty, and not because Gerrard Chester had brought it to her, she was pleased, and in the excess of her pleasure condescended to thank Gerrard for his gift.

"Oh! how beautiful you look! dear sister—how very beautiful!" ejaculated kind, generous Marion. "I am sure, sister, that you will be the beauty of the ball. Everybody will admire you—that they will. And you will be so happy, dear Milly—so very happy, I hope!"

"And why are you not coming as well, Miss Marion?" asked Gerrard Chester.

"I cannot," replied the open hearted girl, without manifesting any regret at the hindrance. "Dear grandmother would have no one to take care of her were I to go with sister."

"But you would go if Mildred were to stay with your grandmother?"

"Oh, yes; then I should, certainly. But I would not keep sister Milly at home on any account, that I wouldn't! I am always more happy when I know that she is enjoying herself than I am when I go out on my own pleasure. Sister Mildred is so beautiful too—so very beautiful!"

But Mildred Winnerley did not require her sister Marion to apprize her of the beauty which she possessed, albeit the honest flattery of that gentle sister was accepted by her with a secret sense of delight. The cloak was placed on the beautiful shoulders, the straw hat upon the decorated head, Mildred Winnerley took the arm of Gerrard Chester, and thus accompanied, proceeded to the festival.

Never, in all her after-life, did Mildred Winnerley forget the occurrences of that evening!

But Mildred was gone, and Marion was alone; for Marion had followed her sister to the door, and had remained gazing after her as she went up the village.

"Marion!" cried the aged woman, from the inside of the cottage.

The maiden closed the door, and flew to assist the invalid.

"Is she gone, Marion, child?"

"Mildred, grandmother, do you mean? Oh yes; she has gone away so happy; and she will be happier still among all the bright merry company. You are not vexed because sister Milly has gone to the ball—are you, dear grandmother?"

"Sit ye down, child—sit ye down, and I will talk to you. I am dying; I can feel that I have not long to live."

"Oh! grandmother—dear grandmother! do not say that!"

"I am, child. My head pains me, and my senses wander; sometimes I lose my memory and forget where I am, and who you are; I forget your names—forget that you are Mildred and Marion. Heaven bless you both, children! I shall not be with you long."

Marion turned aside her face to weep.

"Tell me, child, what did Dr. Hughson say about me—what did he say was the matter with me?"

"He said that it was apoplexy, dear grandmother, which caused you to fall down in the fit the other day. I scarcely know what apoplexy means; but Dr. Hughson said, after he had bled you, that there was no fear of your having another of those frightful fits."

"And yet Marion, my child, I feel as I did then. My brain is hot, and at times everything seems whirling around me. I see fire flash before my eyes. There is a noise in my ears like the roar of the distant sea. I shall die soon; but before I die, I must tell you all—all which you do not know."

"What is that, grandmother? You have told us often that we do not know everything which we shall know some day. Our mother—we do not remember her. You have told us that she was more like sister Milly than myself, and we know by that she was very beautiful."

"She was. But draw nearer to me. Give me your hand, Marion. You are the child whom I have loved. You shall know the secrets."

"But sister Milly, grandmother, is she not to hear them too? Dear Mildred is always saying that she knows her father was some great person; and she thinks on some day to come, she shall have a large fortune, and a beautiful house, and I don't know how grand. As for myself, dear grandmother, I never want to be a great lady, I'm sure; but I should like to see sister Milly happy."

"Listen to me, child, Mildred has fine looks, and they have made her proud; she is beautiful, and her beauty will bring her sorrow. I am afraid of her; I am afraid to die and leave her."

"Afraid of Mildred! grandmother?"

"Yes; I—I could not tell her what I may tell you; I could not trust her with the secrets. There is no fine house for her—no riches as she thinks; but—well, well, I've got the papers in my chest up stairs, and I will show them to you presently."

"Are they in the old black chest, grandmother—the old black chest that is so strong, and all bound round with iron?"

"They are. In that chest, too, is something else, something for you both?"

"And what is that, dear grandmother?"

"It is money—money-notes, saved to keep you both when I am dead; till you can shift in the world, and find out the person you will read of in the papers."

"What papers, grandmother?"

"The papers in the chest. They will tell you who you are; and all the history that I have never told you yet. Mildred must not know; I cannot give them to her; but you shall have them; you shall have them, Marion; for you are good, and have a kind heart, and are very beautiful."

"I! grandmother—beautiful?"

"Your face is not like Mildred's; but there is beauty in your heart, my child. You shall have the papers—have them in your own keeping. When I am dead you must seek him out."

"Who, grandmother, seek out who?"

"I—I will tell you presently. Light the lamp, child—light the large lamp."
Marion did so.

"Now, let me lean on your arm. There, that will do. Give me my stick, and then take the lamp in your hand. But close the door first, child—close the door."

" What are you going to do, dear grandmother?"

" To open the chest—the black chest. There are bank-notes ir. it ; and papers too. You shall have them both—you shall have them all. Lead me up the stairs, lead me gently. The black chest has not had a key turned in it for years."

Marion Winnerley obeyed these directions, and assisted her grandmother to mount the staircase leading to the upper room of the cottage. In that room was a dark-coloured chest, placed in a recess, and with the key-hole towards the wall. Marion moved the chest into the middle of the room, and her grandmother handed her a key, with which she bade her open the lock.

The maiden stooped down, and attempted to unfasten the old chest. To do this was by no means an easy task, for the lock had grown rusty with age and disuse, while the massive lid resisted poor Marion's first efforts at lifting it up. At length this feat was accomplished, the rusty bolt was turned back, the chest was opened, the papers of which the aged woman had spoken were disclosed to view.

It was at this moment that Marion looked up in her grandmother's face; she saw that her eyes glistened strangely ; she saw that her hand grasped the lamp in a convulsive manner.

" The papers, child—the papers in——"

Suddenly the invalid ceased from speaking ; her eyes became fixed and staring ; the lamp trembled in her grasp ; and before Marion could start up and put forth a hand to save her, the palsy-stricken woman fell forwards into the open chest !

" Help—help !" shrieked Marion.

But at that moment, the lamp having fallen among the papers, a bright flame arose, spreading from paper to paper, from floor to ceiling, from the dress of the fallen woman to that of the frightened girl. Marion grasped the waist of her grandmother, and attempted to drag her out of the burning chest. But Marion's strength was small, and the weight of the aged woman was great. Higher and higher rose the bright flames— higher and higher towards the ceiling. From the chest they spread to the bed-furniture ; from the bed-furniture to the wood-work of the room, hissing and crackling.

" Help ! oh, help !" again shrieked the terrified girl.

Then, exerting her whole strength, she once more made an attempt to save her grandmother from being burnt to death, and by a strong effort succeeded in dragging the insensate woman to the door-way of the apartment. But what was Marion to do ? She could not carry her grandmother down the stairs; she could not leave her in the burning room. And round them both the flames were gathering, round them both the furnace was heating. And now the dense smoke and the scorching air were become overpowering; the flames were spreading more fiercely; the fire was advancing nearer and nearer to claim its victims !

" Help—help me ! God help me !" cried Marion. But as the last word escaped her lips, the hot smoke rolled forward, her strength failed her, she made one step, and then fell prostrate on the ground !

The fair girl and the aged woman in the burning room, both fallen, both insensate, both helpless !

And the bright flame came curling towards them, and the red fire glowed vividly on the walls around !

CHAPTER III.

CALIBAN.   No, 'pray thee ;—
I must obey; his art is of such power,
It would control my dam's god, Setebos,
And make a vassal of him.—TEMPEST.

THE MASTER AND HIS MYSTERY.

IN a deep dell, about a mile distant from the village, a party of gipsies had that night pitched their tents.   They were few in number, and had apparently arrived in that part of the country for some other object than that of making money at the village festival. What that object was the reader will presently know.

Pleasant and secluded was the spot which the gipsies had chosen for their halting-place.   The dell was situated on the skirts of an adjoining forest ; tall trees waved their boughs over its margin, and between those green boughs the silver moonlight streamed softly upon the tents beneath.   Those tents were composed of a number of bent sticks fastened in the ground, so as to form a loose framework, over which a few coarse coverings were thrown.   A light-built but commodious cart was placed in the rear of the tents, while in the foreground an unharnessed horse was feeding to his satisfaction on the green juicy turf.   There was a huge, black iron pot hanging over a wood-fire.   An old woman, was busily employed stirring the savoury contents of the kettle, and near her a rough, swarthy-looking man, whose bushy beard and long tangled hair contributed to give him a very unprepossessing appearance, was actively engaged in breaking up sundry pieces of old fence wood, with which, from time to time, he supplied the fire beneath the kettle.

The evening was closing in ; the tall trees threw their broad shadows across the dell, and the fire-light shone upon the gipsies, as they sat on the turf around, employed in various occupations

Apart from the rest of the tribe, and in a distant corner of the dell, where the light of the fire did not beam upon their faces, two men had taken up their seats on the grass, and were engaged in deep converse together.   One of these men had the true gipsy cast of countenance, and appeared to be the leader of his band; the other was a man of less swarthy complexion, but with loose, straggling hair, and with features that were intensely villanous in their expression.

Standing in the shadow of one of the tents, and with her eyes directed to the place where the two men were seated together, was a young and handsome-looking gipsy girl, whose age might have been about twenty summers.   She was tall and erect as a young palm tree; whilst the attitude in which she stood partook of an air of wild grace, which was fascinating in the highest degree.   Her bright eyes, glimmering like stars through the dusk of evening, were intently fixed upon the two men in the distance, and her arms being folded across her bosom, indicated that she was indulging in a meditative mood.

For a few minutes the gipsy girl remained in the same position.   Then casting a glance around her, and perceiving that she was not observed by any of her tribe, she crouched down upon the grass, and crept stealthily towards the spot where the two men were seated.

In order that they might be the better concealed from the view of their associates, the men had thrown themselves on the turf behind a large furze-bush, the bush intervening between them and the camp, and thus secluding them from observation. On the opposite side of this furze-bush the gipsy girl concealed herself. She crept thither noiselessly, and crouched down against the bush so that she might hear every word which the speakers uttered.

The gipsy girl listened.

"I tell you what it is, Jasper, you are too bold in this matter; and I don't clearly see the use of our running such a risk," observed the leader of the band to his companion.

"What have we come here for then, Pharold?" returned the other man.

"Why, yes; if we could manage the affair nicely, and were sure of getting off without noise, it might be done; but I have my doubts. I——"

"Come, come, Pharold. It's an easy job—easier than you think for. The trunk is in the front room. I had a look at it last night, and saw it there myself. Inside that trunk is all we want."

"Are you sure of that?"

"I am. They are all there."

"What—the papers?"

"Yes; and there is money besides. I take the papers and you the money."

"Do you think there is much money?"

"Bank-notes. The old woman has been very saving of late years, and she has riches in that iron-bound chest. This night it must be done."

"But how many are in the cottage, and what are they?"

"Women. There were three, but one has gone to the dancing. It is the old woman herself and a young girl who are left behind. We can gag them both, or if that won't do, we can use our knives."

"No, Jasper," said the gipsy, grasping the arm of his companion. "We must not have murder. We can do without that."

"Are you getting frightened at blood-work, Pharold? Why, what is to be done if resistance is made, and an outcry raised?"

"Do you not know how to prevent both from happening?" asked the gipsy.

"No," replied Jasper.

"Then you are ignorant of the chief secret of our tribe! Listen! We have an art which we have practised for ages. In late years our art has been partly discovered by our enemies, and they take to themselves the honour of inventing it. Fools that they are! It was the art of our tribe when they dwelt at their home in Egypt; it was known to the forefathers of the Zingari before the pyramids of their land were built. By this one art we conquer without the use of sword or fire-arms, go where we may. In it is our strength; in it is our power. Where—in what part of the world are there not gipsies? Everywhere, go where you will, the Zingari are there, and this art is known to them all; by this art they hold communion with one another; through this art they resist their enemies and cannot be destroyed; with this art they will in the end gain back their rights, and inherit their land again."

"Why, what are you jabbering about, Pharold—are you talking of the fortune-telling?"

"I am, and know you what that which you call fortune-telling is? Know you how the cast-out gipsy is able to look into years that are to come, and tell what will happen in those years."

"I don't know; and I have but one opinion on the matter."

"And what is your opinion, Jasper?"

"It just amounts to this, Master Pharold. Fortune-telling does very well to make fools of those who believe in it; but I should like to see a man among you who could tell what my fortune is to be."

"It has been told already," answered the gipsy in a serious voice.

"Well, I should like to hear it. What is it, Master Pharold?"

"Death—death—death!" replied the gipsy chief; uttering the words slowly and distinctly.

Jasper indulged in a hoarse laugh.

"What! three deaths, Master Pharold?"

"Not three deaths, but a death that will be thrice a death," answered the Zingaro.

The outcast turned round his head and stared at his companion, as if startled at the strangeness of the announcement. For the space of a minute there was a deep silence; then, Jasper laid his hand on the arm of the gipsy chief and asked—

"Who was it told my fortune—tell me who?"

"It was Isis."

"Isis!" repeated Jasper, putting on a ferocious look. "I do not like that girl; I am afraid of her. Hark ye, Pharold. She has a trick of learning secrets which she has no business to know; and she is not so well disposed either to you or me. Would it not be better if she were out of the camp?"

"What has she done? How would you cast her out?" inquired the Zingaro.

Jasper paused a moment and then answered—

"By this."

The gipsy girl peeped through the furze bush, and saw the glitter of an open knife, which the ruffian held in his hand. She shuddered, for she knew that it was herself of whom Jasper had spoken, and she knew that his enmity towards her was great. As, however, she continued peering through the interstices of the furze bush, her dark Egyptian countenance assumed an expression of deep scorn; and her large dusky eyes rolled wildly within their orbits.

Pharold jerked the knife out of the hand of his companion.

"Tush! Jasper," said he; "talk not as if you were a fool. Why would you harm the girl?"

"Because—" and Jasper approximated his lips to the gipsy's ear.—"Because she hates us both, and will one day do us harm."

"Perhaps so," returned Pharold. "Be that as it may, however, no hand must be raised against Isis. You do not know her; you do not know that she is the seeress of our tribe."

"She's a good hand at fortune telling, I know that. The girl is clever enough at getting the silver pieces from the fools to whom she tells the lies."

"Isis never tells lies," rejoined the gipsy chief calmly.

"Well, have it as you like about that; but I've kept a sharp eye on her, and understand a few of her tricks. I've saved your life once, Pharold; and I'd do it again if you'd let me, by getting rid of those who have no good-will towards either of us."

The gipsy-chief grasped the hand of his companion, and replied—

"Listen, Jasper! There must be no harm done to Isis; you must not so much as lift your little finger against her. Beware! I owe you much; but I should be your enemy if hurt came to that girl through you."

"Are you so fond of her, then, Pharold?"

"No; it is not that. Isis is our seeress. You have lived long with the tribe; but you do not yet understand the mystery of our art. From you our secrets have been hidden, and you know not the means by which we read the destiny of each man or woman who desires to learn the future. Into that future Isis can look; her eyes can see the years that are to come, as easily as as they can look back to see the things which have passed."

"Can the girl really tell such secrets?"

"She can. It is our art.   Now, come, let us to the tent, and there prepare for our visit to the cottage."

Isis crept stealthily from her hiding-place, and disappeared in the darkness, while the two gipsies directed their steps towards the encampment of the tribe.

On their way thither they passed a small turfy bank, and as they did so, the sound of footsteps on the opposite side of the bank attracted the attention of Pharold.   Both he and Jasper ascended the eminence, and beneath them, looking upward at the moon, stood a young man and a maiden.

The moonlight illuminated the countenances of the two intruders ; and Jasper beholding the face of one whom he seemed to recognize, rushed forward, and seized the arm of the young man.

"Ha!" he exclaimed, "you must be his son ! You are like him—much like him; and we have met."

"What man are you ?" demanded the companion of the maiden.

Jasper approximated his lips to the ear of the young man, and whispered a few words.   Then, drawing forth his knife, he added, in a harsh, guttural voice—

"You know me now; and you, who are his son, I can now strike dead to the earth."

The gipsy uplifted his knife ; the maiden darted forward and threw herself upon the breast of her companion.

That maiden was Mildred Winnerley, but who was he to whose neck she now clung ? Was Mildred with Gerrard Chester ?

CHAPTER IV.

To you my soul's affections move,
      Devoutly, warmly, true ;
My life has been a task of love,
      One long, long thought of you,
                          THOMAS MOORE.

THE PREDICTION.

As Gerrard Chester and Mildred passed up the village on their way to Squire Bannerton's, the young man remarked that, although his beauteous companion appeared to be in excellent spirits, she spoke but few words to him, and answered such questions as he put to her in a manner so curt and careless, that it seemed as if she wished not to answer them at all. In vain poor Gerrard addressed her respectfully; in vain he sued to her lovingly. He wished her to lean with more force upon his arm ; but she persisted in only touching the sleeve of his coat as lightly as she could ; he wished her to walk slower; so that they might have the more time to converse, but Mildred hastened onwards, and seemed eager to reach the place of merriment.

"We shall be too early for the first dance, dear Mildred," said Gerrard. Let us climb the stile, and take a walk through the meadow."

"No," replied the maiden; "it will be out of our way, and the grass is damp."

"The grass damp, dearest Mildred? Why you forget that there has been no rain for a week past."

"Yes; but the dew—the dew is falling just now," returned Mildred.

Gerrand was silent. He remembered a time when Mildred Winnerley had wa lked arm in arm with him through the moonlit meadows, caring not for the dew upon the grass, nor for the dampness in the air; he remembered also—for what does love forget? —that in that by-past time he had heard Mildred say how much she enjoyed a ramble through the green fields at evening, and that nothing, to her, was so delightful as to walk along the path skirting the copse wood, and listen at dusky eve to the nightingale's song. The moon was shining brightly as ever, the song of the nightingale was still to be heard in the copse wood, there were as many gay flowers in the grass as there had been in summers gone by; yet Mildred was afraid of the dew, Mildred would not saunter along the meadow-path, Mildred cared not to listen to the nightingale's song Gerrard felt how changed she was; he felt that she who walked by his side was not the Mildred of other days. And, oh! when love makes a discovery so fearful as that—when it finds that the loved being whom it is willing to adore, whom it believes to be faithful, whom it has placed trust in for years,—when it finds that idolized being to have become changed—to be no longer the same, how great is the agony, how inconsolable the despair. To meet the averted face where you have been accustomed to behold the gladsome smile, to encounter the cold look from eyes which once beamed upon you in soft love, to hear the freezing monosyllable reply to questions which affection had formerly answered in burning words, this is misery, this is woe, exceeding all other torture which earth can furnish, or which demons have the power to invent. Gerrard Chester felt such to be the extent of his misery, such to be the depth of his anguish, now that he had found the Mildred of his love to be no longer the Mildred she had been. Beauteous she was as ever—poor Gerrard thought that she was even more beautiful still, but with that thought came the chilling. soul-destroying consciousness that the beauty which he beheld, the heart which he prized, the love which he valued, was not for him! Yet for that love he would have waged war with any danger; to have been the owner of that heart he would have given all that he had to give, he would have sacrificed all else that he had been accustomed to hold most dear.

"Dear Mildred, why are you so sorrowful, so sad?" asked Gerrard Chester, address-sing his companion in an affectionate tone.

"Sad, Gerrard? Oh, dear no, I am not sad. How could you think me to be so?"

"You do not speak; you do not seem as if you wish to talk with me."

"Why what do you want me to talk about? How unreasonable you are, Gerrard We are going to the ball—are we not?"

"Yes, Mildred, yes." But Mildred had charged Gerrard with being unreasonable and that charge had sunk deep into the lover's heart. That charge told him—alas! too plainly—that love had entirely drooped, faded and died away in the breast of the fair-girl who walked by his side. Poor Gerrard knew that to love—real love, nothing is un-reasonable, nothing is absurd. He knew that foolishness appears as wisdom, if uttered by the lips of those we love; but the most intricate sentences which those lips may utter become plain and distinct if love be at hand to prompt an explanation. Yet Mildred had charged him with unreasonableness; Mildred, whom he had loved so well, had declared that though silent she was not sad.

"You will dance with me at the ball, dear Mildred?" asked Gerrard; his voice failing as he spoke.

"Perhaps," was the reply—"perhaps I may, Gerrard."

And Mildred began humming a little melody which her lover had heard her sing in years gone by. He spoke not; he did not press her to converse with him further. That song recalled the memory of a happier time, and woke up reminiscences of former years. he reminiscences were bright ones, but the feelings they engendered were those of sorrow; the past which memory recalled seemed to have been all a sunny time, yet though summer was around him, poor Gerrard felt that in his heart it was winter now.

They entered the ball-room together. It was a large tent which had been erected in the grounds of the Bannerton estate. 'Squire Bannerton was the chief man of the village, open-hearted, affable, and benevolent, as the squire of an English village should be. There was not a better huntsman in the whole country, and none, even among the light-weights, could take a horse over a five-barred gate in more splendid style. To the farmers 'Squire Bannerton knew how to talk concerning crops and cattle; with Mr. Oldham, the vicar of the village, he could discourse on matters pertaining to the church, being perfectly familiar with the works of St. Chrysostom, St. Jerome, and the rest of the Old Fathers; if Dr. Sanguinis, the physician, chanced to pay him a visit, he had a word or two to say about diseases organic and constitutional, chronic and acute, while if he chanced to hold controversy with Mr. Hibblewaite, the lawyer of the place, every remark that he made afforded demonstrative evidence of his being the best interpreter of Blackstone, Littleton, Coke, and Fearn, that could be found anywhere within fifty miles round. But with all these accomplishments 'Squire Bannerton possessed a still better claim to respect in being the staunch friend of the poor, the readiest reliever of the needy, and the most upright magistrate who was ever yet appointed to fill such an office. Healthy, happy and beloved, he had lived on till his fiftieth birth-day had arrived; while it so happened that on that very day his daughter, who was his only child, attained her twentieth year. The 'squire wished to celebrate these two important events in the best manner he could. The subject had been cogitating in his mind for many weeks previously, and now he had brought his cogitations to a close by deciding that a grand festival should be got up, that the whole village should be a scene of merriment, and that every villager should have a holiday, together with the means of making himself as happy as he could possibly be. The day had arrived. the feast was prepared. Merrily rang the bells of the old church; gaily flaunted the gaudy flags on house-top and on garden-gate. Full well the 'squire knew that people cannot be merry on an empty stomach; so an ox was roasted, and beer-barrels were brought forth, and a real, true, substantial banquet was prepared. And after the banquet there were merry games; and after the games there were pleasant parties; and after the pleasant parties came the evening and the dance. Great preparations had been made for that dance by every youth and maiden who had received an invitation. It is impossible to say how many new dresses were manufactured for the occasion, how many gay ribbons were bought, or how many beautiful nosegays were made up. And now the time had arrived to don the finery, to put on the best looks with the best dress, and to help in promoting a festal commemoration, such as time should never cause to be forgotten, but which should be remembered with pleasure by those who took partnership therein, when age should have coined silver in their locks, and when decrepitude should have caused them to find comforters in crutches.

Such was the entertainment to which Mildred Winnerley and Gerrard Chester had been invited. Poor Gerrard had looked forward to that evening with a fond hope that it would prove one of the happiest occasions of his life. Now, however, his hope was destroyed, his dreams were dissipated. Mildred accompanied him to the ball, dressed in her best attire, and wearing ornaments which had been presented to her by himself. But Gerrard felt that she wore not those ornaments for him, that not for him had Mildred arrayed herself in those garments which became her so well. They went to the ball together, they were partners in the first dance; but poor Gerrard remarked that Mildred had no smiles for him, and that her eyes wandered over the apartment as if in search of some other object.

The first dance was concluded, and the youth and the maiden mingled themselves with the company. At length Gerrard pressed Mildred to take a seat; wite reluctance she consented, and having found an unoccupied bench, they sat down together.

Still Mildred did not look at her lover, neither did she answer any questions addressed to her by him. Gerrard Chester folded his arms, hung down his head, and in silence mused upon the strange change which a few months had wrought.

Minutes flew by, and still Gerrard Chester remained musing and motionless. His heart told him in each beating how his deep love for Mildred Winnerley was, and told him at the same time that she whom he loved so well no longer cared for him. Fearful is it when the heart makes such a discovery, sadsome is the sight that the wide earth then presents to the weary eyes. No wonder that poor Gerrard was sad and gloomy, no wonder that he failed to take notice of the gay faces around him, and paid no attention to the merry words which were whispered in his ears. Long and fondly had he cherished the sweet delusion of believing himself to be loved with all that deep affection which he deemed his own love to deserve; long and fondly—for many months and for many years—had he sought delight in that entrancing thought, in that blissful though delusive dream; but now that dream was fast fading away, and the bitter truth was in progress of discovery. Mildred Winnerley cared not for the love of Gerrard Chester—cared not for the love of him who, to win her love, felt that he could part with all things else that he had become accustomed to cherish and hold dear.

Brooding over this fearful discovery, absorbed in the depth of his sadness, poor Gerrard sat silently upon the bench where he had seated himself beside Mildred. And as the sorrowful youth thought over his dreams, and mused upon his blighted passion, even though his eyes were closed, and his head bent down, the image of his Mildred rose before him—his Mildred in her peerless beauty! How radiantly lovely she appeared! so like the bright form which love had fashioned her to be, so graceful and so elegant in the possession of those rare gifts with which by nature she had been endowed. A phantom of delight—an image of perfection stood the beauteous form before him; and as Gerrard gazed, the image of Mildred in her loveliness appeared to smile even as

Mildred herself had deigned to smile upon poor Gerrard in the earliest days of his courtship. Enraptured by the vision which his fancy had evoked, the young lover turned round to gaze upon the reality—upon that fair form which imagination had painted so brightly and so beauteously. He turned round, but upon whom did he look? Where was Mildred—his Mildred, whom he had believed to be seated by his side? No Mildred was there. It was the face of a happy girl who was holding converse with her faithful and attentive swain. How long poor Gerrard had remained in this abstracted mood he knew not, nor could he form any satisfactory idea of how much time had elapsed since. he last saw Mildred sitting beside him. He arose and looked around the apartment No Mildred could he see. Everywhere merry parties met his gaze—everywhere he discerned smiling beauty and mirthful manhood; but she—she whom he strained his eyeballs to descry, whom he panted with eagerness to behold, was not amongst that throng. And without her, devoid of her presence, the gay and merry scene became worse than a desert to Gerrard Chester. He moved forward, he drew his hand across his eyes, he staggered, paused, and clutching the shoulder of a person who stood near him, muttered in an indistinct manner and with palid lips—

"Mildred—where is she?"

"Do you wish to know where to find Miss Winnerley, Mr. Chester?"

"Yes—tell me where—where?"

"She passed out at the door yonder, with Mr. Hargrave Manners, not two minutes ago."

Gerrard Chester rushed towards the door, and looked out, expecting to see Mildred in company with Hargrave Manners. He was disappointed. There was an open lawn before him, and strolling over that lawn, where two parties of lovers, who had left the thronged ball-room to enjoy the society of each other upon the moonlit greensward; neither of these parties consisted of Mildred Winnerley and the companion with whom she had been seen to leave the ball-room.

Where was Gerrard to look, whither was he to proceed in quest of Mildred? All was silent and calm around him, save the sounds of merriment that now and then floated to his ear from the tent of the dancers. Above him the bright moon was sailing placidly along the heavens, and before him in the distance were clusters of dark trees with the tops silvered by the moonbeams. Mildred was not to be seen ; Mildred answered not to the calling of Gerrard Chester, as faintly, and with much effort, the youth endeavoured to articulate her name.

And still the forsaken lover stood lonely and disconsolate upon the open lawn, still his gaze wandered over the silent scene before him, vainly endeavouring to descry the form of her whom he so fondly, madly loved. At length his attention was arrested by the appearance of something moving beneath a group of trees far away to his left. He fixed his glance in that direction, and shortly became satisfied that the figures he saw moving were those of a man and a maiden. Onwards he crept towards them. A suspicion stole into his mind that he was about to discover the objects of his search. As he approached nearer, that suspicion acquired strength, and ere long ripened into certainty. It was Mildred whom he saw—Mildred Winnerley and Hargrave Manners! Gerrard knew his Mildred by the sash which she wore around her waist, and which had been given to her by him. And on that sash rested the hand of Hargrave Manners—rested without repulse!

MILDRED PREPARING FOR THE BALL.

Silently, creepingly, watchfully, Gerrard Chester followed in the footsteps of the two ramblers; he hid himself in the shade beside them to watch their actions, he stole close-ly behind them, attempting to overhear their words. They proceeded onwards until they reached the dell in which the gipsies were encamped.

"Whither are you leading me, Mr. Manners?" asked Mildred.

"Why ask the question, sweet one? Wherefore are you afraid? Would Mildred Winnerley, the beauty of the village, rather go back to the ball and dance with Gerrard Chester?"

"Oh! no—not with him," replied Mildred.

The question and the reply were both heard by Gerrard himself. He pressed his hot hand to his brow, drew a deep, though noiseless inspiration, and trod onwards in the footsteps of the maiden and the youth.

And now Mildred and her companion passed on into a shady part of the dell, where the huge black shadows lay far-outstretched upon the grass, where the tall trees above stood calm, motionless, and dark in the quiet moonlight, and where all seemed so silent and so secluded that it was wondrous fair Mildred walked on so fearlessly as she seemed to do. Presently, however, the indistinct muttering of some parties near at hand caught her ear and caused her to pause.

"Hush!" she exclaimed—"there is some one near us, dear Hargrave."

"Your fears deceive you, sweetest," replied her companion. "No one is here save ourselves. Let us proceed a few yards farther, and then we will take a seat upon yonder bank."

Hargrave Manners clasped the waist of the fair girl more tightly, and urged her forwards; scarcely had he taken three steps before two men darted from out of a recess formed by a slight curvature in the bank, and seized the arms of the wanderers, at the same time blocking up their path. Those two men were Pharold and Jasper.

"Take your hands off, sirrah!" exclaimed Manners, making a violent effort to free himself from the grasp of the gipsy.

"Who are you—what errand has brought you here?" demanded Pharold.

"The questions are such as I do not choose to answer without a better knowledge of my interrogator," replied Manners. "If I be not mistaken, I have less right to be accounted a trespasser in this place than he who chooses to put his questions in so bold a manner."

For a few moments the gipsy scanned the countenance of the intruder with a sharp inquisitive gaze. Then, loosing his hold of the young man's arm, he said to his companion—

"Take away your hand, Jasper. This man is known to me; he is the nephew of the 'squire who lives at yonder hall."

Instead of obeying the command, Jasper continued to detain Mildred, regarding her at the same time with a dark, malicious look, that approached to a stare.

"Are you moon-struck, Jasper, man?" demanded Pharold. "Release the girl, I say!"

Still unheeding the command, the gipsy drew forth his knife, and grinning demoniacally at the maiden, grasped her arm more tightly, and growled forth—

"Your name—tell me your name?"

At this moment the knife of the outlaw was struck out of his hand, and Gerrard Chester, stepping forward, confronted the questioner.

"Her name is Mildred Winnerley. It will be at your peril if you touch her again with a single finger."

For a few seconds the gipsy lost his presence of mind and was irresolute how to act. Approaching nearer to the maiden, however, he peered into her face, and in a voice, the tone of which was somewhat tremulous, said—

"Her name is Mildred—Mildred—and—and her other name is——"

"Winnerley," replied Manners, "you have already been told that by Mr. Chester."

"Are you sure that that is her name—has she no other—none?"

"Mildred Winnerley is my name," said the maiden, "Mr. Manners and Mr. Chester have told you the truth."

Jasper released the arm of the fair girl; and accompanied by Pharold, moved aside, so that the party might have room to pass; he then muttered in a low tone—

"She is like—she is very like!"

"Like whom?" demanded Pharold.

"Like—" but here the gipsy paused and said no more.

It was now that Mildred turned her eyes towards Gerrard Chester, and blushing as she spoke, said in a faltering voice—

"I thank you much for your attention, Mr. Chester; but why have you followed us here?"

"Followed!" ejaculated Gerrard, "Mildred—Mildred Winnerley, I—I—we are friends—are we not?"

"Yes, Mr. Chester, we have always been so—true friends, I believe."

"And lovers too, one would be led to conceive from Mr. Chester's behaviour at the present moment," observed Hargrave Manners, sarcastically.

Gerrard drew himself up to his full hight, fixed a look of defiance upon the last speaker, and in a voice, the tones of which were indistinct through the turbulence of passion, rejoined—

"Ay, and lovers too, Mr. Manners! Why do you sneer? What mean you by your remark? Beware, sir! I have told you that I loved Mildred, I tell you now that you, nor any one else, shall dare to thwart me in that love without the risk of life. I am not afraid to tell you this, Hargrave Manners, though you are the squire's nephew, and I the farmer's son. The love that I bear for Mildred Winnerley has lasted long, and although it has been strangely requited this evening, it is the same still!"

"Ha! ha!—ha! ha! ha!" laughed some one who was hidden amongst the brush-wood, near to where the party stood. Gerrard Chester turned round to discover from whom the laugh proceeded, and at the same moment the hand of a dark, tall, and aged gipsy-woman was laid upon his wrist.

"Do you talk of love—love for her?" demanded the gipsy, pointing with her out-stretched finger towards Mildred.

"I did, woman—I do," returned Gerrard, in a husky voice; at the same moment taking the right hand of the maiden in his clasp.

The gipsy tore apart the arms of the youth and the maiden; then, pushing Mildred aside, she turned towards Gerrard Chester, and allowing a grin to play upon her countenance, said—

"See! I have parted you. Touch her not again; talk no more of love for her!"

"What mean you, woman? Why these words?" exclaimed Gerrard tremblingly, as he again made a movement towards Mildred.

"Back, I say!" shouted the gipsy. "Will the hound go and play with the lioness? Will the stag seek company with the tiger's mate? Ha! ha! ha! You talk of love—love for what?"

"For her, woman—for you, dear Mildred. Be not afraid of what this wild creature says."

The gipsy approached Gerrard Chester, and placed her face in contact with his.

"Be *you* afraid!" she said; "it is you who have cause to fear. Go, love her if you will—love death—grim death—red blood and dark old death! Love her, boy—love her, and love pride, and murder, and death?"

"Pride, and murder, and death," repeated Gerrard.

"Ay, love her now—love her now! Ha! ha! ha!" shouted the gipsy, as she sprang back and disappeared amongst the brushwood.

Hargrave Manners had not offered one word of comment upon all that the gipsy-woman had said; retaining the clasp of the left hand of Mildred, he had been a silent spectator of the scene. Now, however, addressing Gerrard, he observed—

"I shall be sorry, Mr. Chester, if it so turn out that the strange words of this crazy woman cause you to have unpleasant dreams to-night. Will you not also share with me in my sorrow, Miss Winnerley?"

Mildred was silent, Gerrard advanced, and once more took her hand.

"Shall I see you home, dear Mildred?" said he.

There was a minute's pause, and then Mildred answered—

"Thank you, Mr. Chester. I am not going home just now, I shall first take a short walk with Mr. Manners, who, I have no doubt, will afterwards allow me to trouble him with the task of seeing me safely home to the cottage. For the present, Mr. Chester, you will permit me the pleasure of wishing you good night."

The parting adieu was not responded to by Gerrard Chester. He looked at Mildred, he saw that she leaned for support upon the arm of Hargrave Manners, and that no expression of sorrow or of pain was visible upon her countenance. Wildly and fearfully were the glaring eyeballs of poor Gerrard directed towards the form of her whom he so madly loved; and as Mildred turned from him to accompany the 'squire's nephew, and as she separated from him without one expression of tenderness, without one glance of love, his heart sank within him like a leaden weight, his chest seemed bound round with leathern thongs, his brain whirled within his head, he clasped his hands to his cold forehead, and stood like a statue in the deep agony of his grief. Minutes passed, and he still remained in this position. Suddenly, however, feelings of a more vengeful nature sprang up within his breast. Who was Hargrave Manners, that he should thus act the rival with impunity? Would it not be right and proper and manly to follow him at once, stop him in his path, demand from him an explanation of his conduct, and in the event of that explanation being refused, or proving unsatisfactory, to challenge him to combat there and then, to provoke him to the contest, and by such means to seek reparation for the deep injury which poor Gerrard felt Hargrave Manners to have wrought? A few minutes of hasty thought, and then Gerrard was decided. Yes; he would do so; he would at once follow his rival, demand that he should relinquish the hand of Mildred Winnerley, and strike him to the earth if that demand was met with a refusal. The excited man was about starting in the pursuit, when his arm was again grasped by the old gipsy-woman who made her appearance from amongst the brushwood.

"Where would you go, man—would you go to kill?" she asked in a hoarse muffled voice.

"Yes—to kill him," answered Gerrard, mechanically.

"And why do that? Wait, wait, and *she* will work your revenge. There will be murder yet—murder with *your* hands clean. She is fair and beautiful, she has bright eyes, white teeth, and long fingers; but wait. Red blood and dark death have their work to do without you—they will do it."

Gerrard Chester suddenly seized the gipsy, and dragged her forward to where the shade cast by the adjoining bank fell more darkly across the path.

"Tell me, woman," he exclaimed, " is there meaning in your words or not. Are you a fortune-teller, and if so, of whom is it that you speak ?"

"Of your heart's love, your bright beauty, your peach-cheeked darling. What will she do? What is her fortune to be? Listen, boy, and 1 will tell you. I told it years ago when she was young—when your beauty was very young."

"Quick, woman ! It is to be—what?

"There is a double line, and that is blood; there is another double line, twice crossed, and that is death. Pride for beauty, blood for pride, death for blood. The bright eyes and the dark heart, the fair brow and the foul soul. I have said what will be; shall I tell you what is now ?"

"Yes, Mildred——"

"I will tell you where to find her. Yonder—in the dark wood, she is there. But stay ! do not follow her—do not follow him ! Look to the right. Do you see—do you see the red glare staining the sky? Ha! and what are those ? Do you think them stars? They are no stars ; it is fire—red fire and bright sparks."

"Fire !" ejaculated Gerrard in amazement.

"Ay, and at the home of your beauty. Go hasten there. You will find one there who is more beauteous than your beauty—more fair than your darling. She is in the flames—the red laughing flames. Go to her quickly."

Gerrard Chester saw the vivid glare which illuminated the clouds above the burning cottage of the Winnerleys; he was about to hasten in that direction at his fullest speed, when he suddenly paused, and turning his face towards the distant copse-wood, said—

"I must find Mildred first—I must take her with me."

"No !" exclaimed the gipsy, again seizing the arm of Gerrard Chester, and preventing him from carrying out his intention. "Leave her—leave your beauty now. Rare things—strange things must happen to-night. Care not for your beauty ; she wishes not for you."

And as the gipsy-woman spoke, a flash of light rose upward to the sky from the burning cottage, and Gerrard Chester thought that he heard a shriek of distress borne to his ear through the chill air of evening. No longer hesitating, he detached himself from the grasp of the gipsy, gave one look in the direction of the copse-wood, and then hastened forwards at full speed towards the cottage.

"There will be strange deeds to-night; years will work to their end ere the sun of to-morrow shines," said the gipsy, laughing to herself. "Ay, by the stars there will be sweet tales soon to be told ! Ha! ha! ha!"

What the gipsy meant—what the strange things were—and why the wild woman had cause to laugh, the story soon will show.

———

CHAPTER V.

THE WORDS SPOKEN BY DEATH IN THE LONELY ROOM.

THE fallen lamp had set fire to the papers in the old chest at the cottage of the Winnerleys, that fire had communicated to the apartment; Mrs. Winnerley herself had stumbled amidst the flames; and Marion, overpowered by the heat, and faint with excess of fear, lay prostrate by the side of her aged relative. Every moment the heat increased in intensity, every moment added to the fierceness of the fire. Round and round, over and over, curled the bright flames as they danced around paralysed age and prostrate beauty—as they leapt in their fiery gambols over the stricken woman and the senseless girl. In their madness they burst out at the window, and showed themselves to the light and to the stars; in their fury they licked the floor and then shot upwards through the roof to revel amongst the old thatch; in their recklessness they swooped down from the hot ceiling upon the frail form of gentle Marion; and in their savageness they hurried through the old doorway and planted themselves upon the staircase, to bid defiance to those who should attempt to deprive them of their victims. Thus so madly, thus so furiously, thus with such recklessness and in such savage mood did the bright flames play in that lonely room, where age and beauty prisoners were—age succourless and beauty reft of power.

Still more fiercely the fire burned, still brighter grew the blaze. The ceiling was crumbling to pieces, the walls were hissing with the heat, the floor was charring and rapidly becoming black. Within those walls, beneath that ceiling, upon the floor lay Marion and her grandmother. Fire around them, flame above them, and a burning floor to rest upon. What chance was there that they should escape the doom which threatened them? What hope was there that the bright eyes of Marion would ever smile upon her sister Mildred again?

There was no chance, no hope. The flames grew larger, the fire grew brighter, the doom became more certain. And now the frame work of the ceiling gave way; there was a large mass about to fall upon the senseless victims, and bury them beneath the ruin.

The beam cracked; the plaster loosened; the ceiling was about to fall!

Just then, footsteps and voices sounded in the room below, light feet trod upon the staircase, the slender figure of a girl entered the burning room, and behind the girl followed a tall stalwart man. One second more, and Marion was caught up by the strong hands of the fearless maiden, while the paralysed woman was at the same moment borne from the apartment in the hands of the tall swarthy man.

Many minutes passed before Marion Winnerley recovered herself sufficiently to scan the countenances of those who stood around her, when she was able to do so she looked up, and the first face which met her gaze was that of Isis, the gipsy girl.

"Where am I?" inquired poor Marion, faintly.

"In safety—in perfect safety," replied Isis. "I have saved you from the fire, dear."

"And my grandmother—where is she?"

"She also is safe."

"Let me see her, let me know that she is so! No, no; she cannot be—she is in the fire."

"You think wrongly, dearest. See!" and Isis assisted Marion to where a number of villagers were gathered round the door of a cottage. "Look in that room. Your grandmother is there. She is saved from the fire, as you are."

"And by you too—by you?"

"Yes, by me. Here is the man who rescued her; but it was I who led him up the stairs to find her."

Marion eagerly seized the hand of the gipsy girl, and imprinting upon it a hasty kiss, said—

"You are good, you are kind for having preserved my grandmother. I must know who you are. Tell me your name."

"It is Isis."

"But your other—your Christian name?"

"A Zingaro has no Christian name, she has but one. Call me Isis."

Marion would have continued expressing her thanks to the gipsy-girl, had not the surgeon of the village at that moment entered, in order to tend upon Mrs. Winnerley. Disregarding the slight injuries which had happened to herself, poor Marion bent over the bed on which her grandmother lay, attentively watching every change in the expression of the doctor's countenance, as he examined the various injuries which had happened to the aged woman, and endeavoured to rally her prostrate energies by the use of such simple medicaments as he happened to have at hand.

And now while the surgeon is standing by the couch of the sufferer, and Marion is lingering there also, we will go back to the burning cottage, and narrate the course of events as they happened there.

Most of the villagers having gone to seek amusement at the 'squire's festival, it was some time before the flames issuing from the cottage window were noticed by any of the neighbours. A throng soon collected, however, when the alarm of fire was once raised. Numerous as this throng speedily became, there was none, even amongst the sturdiest of those who were gathered together, that dared attempt the rescue of Marion and her grandmother. The lower room of the cottage was entered and examined, but no one being found there, it was generally concluded that the maiden and the aged woman must be in the upper room. The stairs were ascended, the villagers applied their ears to the door; they heard the crackling of the burning wood, they heard what they thought to be a groan, they perceived something dark on the floor of the room, and they believed Marion Winnerley to be in that apartment, a prey to the ravenous fire. Not one of them, however, had the courage to rush in, to dare the flames, and attempt the deed of bravery. It was at this critical moment, that Isis, the gipsy-girl, arrived at the scene of action. She paused only to hear the vague hints of a maiden and an aged woman being shut up in that burning room, she hesitated only while the crowd moved aside to allow her to pass. Her foot was on the staircase, her hand was upraised to dash aside the flames, when she felt herself grasped by the shoulder, and turning around, perceived that Jasper had hastened after her, and had reached the cottage nearly as soon as she had done, albeit she had used her utmost speed.

"Where are you going, Isis?" asked the outlaw.

"Follow!" returned the maiden, grasping his hand, and dragging him after her into the burning room.

Obeying the instructions he received from Isis, Jasper caught up the insensate body of the paralysed woman, while the gipsy herself seized the frail form of poor Marion.   No time was lost in performing these feats, no time was lost in hastening from the room and seeking a retreat from the cottage.   Marion and her grandmother were saved from the flames, their saviour was the gipsy-girl.

But what was that which had caught the eye of Jasper as he stood within the burning room? why was it that having deposited his burthen, he now returned to the scene of ruin, approached the cottage and glanced at the stairs by which he had descended but a few minutes since?

Jasper had seen the old trunk, he had caught sight of some of the papers which it contained, those papers he expressly wished to get into his possession, and those papers were now surrounded with flame.

For a second only Jasper paused to consider. He saw that the staircase was on fire in many places, and knew that it must soon fall.   Nevertheless, nerving himself for the performance of the feat, he rushed forward, trod his way over the creaking steps, and once more dashed into the flaming room.   Before him was the old chest still unconsumed, and at the bottom of that chest he could dimly perceive some papers which the fire had as yet but slightly touched.   He sprang forward to seize them; his hand was put forward to grasp them, when, hearing a crackling noise above his head, he looked up, and saw that the roof had given way and was just about to fall.   He plunged his arm into the chest, he touched the scorched paper with his fingers; then darting back, he had but time to reach the door before a mass of the ignited roof fell upon the floor and barred up tne entrance to the apartment.   Of all the papers which that trunk had contained, Jasper had gained possession of only one.   With that one rolled up in his hand he sped from the ruin; and nearly suffocated by the dense smoke, scorched by the intense heat, and bruised by the falling of sundry heavy fragments, he reached the outside of the cottage, worked his way through the crowd that were assembled there, and retreating to a secluded spot where he thought himself to be free from observation, proceeded to examine the paper which he had stolen from out of the old chest.

But Jasper was mistaken in thinking that his actions had passed without observation; there was one by whom they were noticed, one whose vigilant glance had not allowed a single movement of the outlaw to escape unobserved since the moment of his re-entering the cottage to attempt gaining possession of the papers.   That one individual had followed him through the flames, had stood behind him in the smoke, had crept after him to the spot where he now stood.   The watcher was vigilant, and that watcher was a woman.

Taking advantage of the shadow cast by an old tree, the outlaw unfolded the paper, preparatory to examining its contents.   Fold after fold he carefully opened; and as he did so, the woman crept closer to him, and uplifted noiselessly a thick stick which was bulky and heavy at the end most remote from her hand.

The last fold was opened, the outlaw raised the paper to his eyes.   Swiftly as speeds the lightning, the uplifted stick descended upon his head, he staggered, reeled, and fell senseless beneath the blow.

"Ha! ha! ha!" laughed the woman, as she snatched the paper from the feeble grasp of the prostrate.   "You knew not who was behind you!   You knew not who has been near you so often, nor who it is that knows you so well.   Time will tell you—time will tell you!"

The woman who had now gained possession of the paper was the same old gipsy who

had given such strange warnings to Gerrard Chester only a few minutes previous. Having secured the paper, she proceeded with it to the light, and glancing at it for a moment, appeared suddenly startled.

"Ha!" she exclaimed, "this is useful—very useful! Who would have thought of my lighting upon this?"

Then, thrusting the paper into her bosom, the old gipsey stooped down, and examined the countenance of the fallen man. She saw that the pupils of his eyes were dilated, and heard his breathing to be stentorous and deep.

"He'll come to, there's life enough in him yet," she observed, as placing her hand in her bosom to feel if the paper was safe, she arose, and took her way in the direction of the burning cottage.

The flames were making rapid progress, the walls of the once pretty tenement had fallen in, and the fire had now communicated to the flowers and shrubs in Marion's little garden. But Marion was not there to see the destruction, yet where she was, there was greater destruction still. She stood beside the couch whereon her grandmother lay; she watched the surgeon, as he exhausted the resources of his knowledge to give aid to the aged sufferer. And as she saw how silent and how motionless her grandmother was, as she caught a view of the fearful injuries which the sufferer had sustained, she turned deadly pale, trembled, and grasping the surgeon's arm, said,

"Tell me, sir, tell me—is my grandmother dead?"

"Not yet, my good girl," was the reply.

"But she will die soon—she is dying now?"

The surgeon hesitated before he replied to the question. As he was about to say further to Marion on the subject, he observed his patient move; and at the same moment Marion heard a faint breathless voice articulate her name.

"I am here, dear grandmother—here by your side," she exclaimed, as she bent her ear to the patient's lips. "Do you know that I am here, dear grandmother?"

"I do," replied the sufferer, feebly pressing the soft hand that was placed in contact with her own.

Marion looked; she saw that her grandmother's eyes were turned towards her—that she was recognized—that she still had a relative, whom a few minutes since, she thought that she had lost for ever. And as she felt the slight pressure of her grandmother's hand, and heard the faint whisperings of that well-known voice, she turned her face towards the surgeon, and in a tone of anxious hope, said,

"My grandmother will live now! Oh, tell me—tell me that you are sure she will live?"

The surgeon was silent.

"Speak, sir?" said Marion, clasping the surgeon's arm, "I—I can listen to you. I am prepared—quite prepared to hear all—to hear anything. Speak, sir, tell me?"

After a moment's deliberation the surgeon drew Marion aside.

"My good girl," he said, "it would be wrong of me if under present circumstances I were to attempt at deceiving you. Your grandmother has not only had another attack of paralysis, but she has also suffered great injuries from the severe burns which she has recently received. So great is the shock which such extensive injuries communicate to the system, that even if your grandmother were less aged than she is, I—"

"Do not be afraid to tell me, sir. Go on I—I can hear you."

"Were my patient a young woman, I was about to say, the result of injuries so extensively received would almost inevitably be fatal. In the present case I regret to say that recovery is perfectly impossible."

No word, no shriek, no sound escaped the lips of Marion; All that the surgeon had said she had listened to, all that he had hinted she had comprehended. And now the terrible truth was plain to her in all its appalling ghastliness. There was nothing left to hope, nothing left to cling to. The future—the dreary desolate future, with none to trust to, none that she could call " parent " upon earth, opened itself to the view of poor feeble Marion. She turned round, she threw herself upon the bed, she pressed her pale lips to the cheek of the dying woman.

"Mar—Mar, child, what has Mr. Venner told you?" asked the sufferer; who had watched the conference between her grand-daughter and the surgeon.

"Nothing, dear grandmother. Do not ask. Are you in pain? let me know if you are in much pain."

"In death's pain, Mar. I am dying—dying now."

Marion started up,

"Where is Mildred?" she exclaimed—"where is my sister? has no one been to fetch her?"

"Yes; but we cannot find her," was the reply.

"Not—not find her! where is Mr. Chester—where is he?"

"He has gone to seek after her. She is not at Mr. Bannerton's, but Gerrard Chester has gone to find her," replied one of the villagers.

Minutes passed away, and still Mildred came not. What could it mean? The clock ticked, the patient groaned, Marion waited.

"Where is Mildred—what has happened?" she ejaculated.

A party went forth in search of the missing girl, they distributed themselves over the village, they made inquiries at every house.

Still the time passed on, hour after hour fled by. The fire was extinguished, the smoke was curling over the black, smouldering ruins, there were two or three loiterers around the scene of destruction, but it was the dead of night, and all was silent.

"Mildred—my sister—my own—my only sister!" ejaculated Marion as she pressed her hand to her heart, and crept across the apartment towards the window.

Marion looked out into the night. There was the pale moon smiling placidly in the heavens, there were the stars glittering on their thrones.

No Mildred came!

The dying woman called Marion to her couch.

"Where is she? why does she not come?" asked the sufferer.

"I know not, dear grandmother. Heaven grant that no harm has happened to dear Mildred!"

Marion trembled as she spoke.

A few minutes more passed, and still silence reigned around There were many watchers in that quiet room; but none moved, none spoke.

Suddenly the aged sufferer arose in her bed, she grasped the shoulders of Marion, and in a hollow voice inquired—

"Is all burnt?"

"Yes, dear grandmother, but do not tr   e about that."

"And the chest—the old chest up stairs, where is that?"

"Burnt, grandmother—burnt to ashes."

The patient fixed her dull glassy eyes upon the countenance of the maiden, and said,

"Mar, listen to me, Mar. I am dying and must leave you. God help you and your poor sister! God preserve you both when I am gone!"

"He will, dear grandmother. Fear not for us. Mildred and I are young and strong. We can work, dear grandmother—we can work, and we shall not want."

"Not you, Mar, child. I am not afraid that you will have God's help; but —"

"You are weeping, grandmother! You are fretting when you should not do so. There! let me wipe your eyes; let me place your head upon the pillow."

The dying woman tightened her grasp of the maiden's shoulder, and looked still more fixedly at her, with those strange, death-like eyes.

"Marion," she said, "I shall die soon, but I have much to tell you first. I—I am in pain, and cannot speak loud. You must listen."

"Wait, dear grandmother—wait till Mildred comes."

"No!" exclaimed the sufferer, speaking in a louder tone—"not to her! It is to you. Let them go away; let there be no one in the room but you and death."

"And who, grandmother?"

"And death, child. We will be alone together. Tell them to go."

The attendants were about to leave the apartment.

"Must all go, dear grandmother—must we be quite alone?"

"Are you afraid, Mar—are you afraid of talking to death? Tell them all to go. There must be none to listen."

Marion obeyed her grandmother's command, and requested her friends to withdraw. The request was granted.

"Now, Mar," said the dying woman, "are they all gone?"

"Yes, dear grandmother. We are alone."

"Hold me, then—hold me and listen! I should have told you this before, I might have told it to you, but not to Mildred."

"What is there, dear grandmother, that my sister should not hear as well as I?"

"This—it is the secret which I have kept from you so long—the secret of your birth, Mar—of your's and Mildred's. I am weak and cannot say much. If the old chest were not burnt I could spare myself the trouble. God help you, my poor Mar, that I should set fire to those papers!"

"There is no cause why you should regret that, dear grandmother. They are burnt."

"They are—they are! And you—oh! pardon me, God—pardon me!"

"Why do you ask God to pardon you, grandmother? What is it that troubles you? You have wronged no one."

"I have wronged you!"

"I?"

"Listen, child! Your name is not that which I have called you by, and I am not your grandmother."

"Not—not my grandmother?"

"I am not, child. Death tells you truth."

Marion was overcome with amazement, and knew not what to believe, nor how to act. Was it truth which the dying woman had proclaimed, or was it but the raving of delirium—the phrenzy of death?

"But Mildred, grandmother——"

"She is your sister; and I have deceived her as I have you."

"Lie down, dear grandmother, lie down and do not speak. You are putting yourself in pain."

"Ha!" exclaimed the sufferer—"you do not believe me, Mar—you doubt me. Listen—listen!"

"To what, dear grandmother?"

"To the story. Your father, Mar—your father was a bold man when he ran away with his pretty bride from her rich home.   He was poor and she had plenty; he loved her, he asked her to be his wife.   Your mother had proud parents; they denied him their doors.   It was a bold thing to do, but he stole from them their child, and married her.   They had two children in years afterwards, and those two children are Mildred and you.   Your father loved his wife; she brought him no riches, and yet he loved her and was happy.   At length—at length——"

"You shudder, dear grandmother!"

"Listen, child!—At length your mother left her husband—left her home—left you. Beneath the roof of another she sought greater happiness than that which she had found in her home—do you understand?"

"Yes, grandmother, I do.   And—and——"

"Listen further.   You, Marion, child, and your sister, were deserted by her who should have had the love to cling to you, even if she left her rightful home.   Take my hand, child, press it hard.—Is it cold—quite cold?—I have not told you all.   You have to hear how your father came to hate his children—how he, too, left them, and died in another land.   The papers in the old chest you say, are burnt; your story therefore, you will never learn from them.   Listen, then, to me,—listen before life goes from me, and I am deprived from telling you that which else you will never know. Hold me, wipe the dampness off my forehead.   There, there, now—now!   My breath is becoming short; my heart has stopped from beating.   Bend down your ear.   Is all still —all still?"

"Yes, dear grandmother."

"There is no one near us—no one listening?"

"No one, grandmother.   It is so silent—so silent!"

"I will tell you now your mother's name.   I will tell you the rest of the story.   It was a dark night child—a dark night in a dreary winter, when the wind was blowing coldly, and the rain-drops were pattering fast as they fell from the eaves of the houses. A man sat in a lone room, holding a letter in his hand; he read the letter—read it in that lonely room at midnight.   Listen my Mar—my child! he read that letter— he crushed it to pieces in his hands; he sat for many minutes speechless and motionless, with one hand clasped to his brow, the other pressing on his heart.   Then, rising from the chair in which he had been sitting, he glanced at the fragments of the letter, moved across the room, stole gently, silently across it, to where a knife lay in a drawer.   The man took the knife in his hand, and grasped the handle of a door which opened into the bed-chamber of two sleeping children.   Do you hear me, Mar?"

"Yes, yes, dear grandmother; but I am so cold, so chilly.   Do not tell me more til sister Mildred comes."

"No, Marion, child!   Death will not tell it to her; it is not for her to hear.   Hold me—hold me closely while I tell out the story.   Why are you looking about the room, Mar?   Will you not hear me—not hear death, child?"

"I do, dear grandmother—I—do."

"The man entered the room where the children slept—he crept to the bed-side—the moon-light fell into the chamber—it fell upon the fragments of the letter in his hand —he looked at that, then at the knife, then at the children.   They were young children, and they slept, the elder clasping the younger.   The man up-lifted his knife, turned away his head that he might not see—and—and—the man, Mar, was your father—your own father! the children were—were—I am faint now.   I can say no—no more !"

"Grandmother! tell me—tell me what my—my father did on that night!   Oh, tell me grandmother! that I may know before you die."

The sufferer made an effort to speak, stretched out her cold hand to draw poor Marion closer to her, and in a faint, half-articulate voice, replied,—

"You must know, child.   I should have told you before.   Prop me up, prop me gently.   There—there!   Death can talk now, death can tell you, that—that the man was your father ; the children were—were—the reason was—your father—mother—I —press me—hold me !"

"Grandmother—dear grandmother!   Help—help !"

"No, child—not yet, do not call them yet.   Is all silent, quite silent, Mar ?"

Marion replied by informing her grandmother that no one was present in that room except their two selves.   The glazed eyes of the dying woman wandered wildly round the apartment endeavouring to descry if it were as the watcher beside her bed had told her that it was ; and when those death-dimmed eyes had performed the weary duty, their dull gaze again settled on the countenance of the maiden who stood weeping beside the bed.   It is a fearful contrast—that of beauty—life, with wrinkled age in death !   It is one of earth's most melancholy sight's when the lean hands press upon the plump fingers—when the ice cold palm comes in contact with the warm vel- vet skin, and eyes that are full and bright meet the glance of orbs that are about to close upon the world for ever !   So was it in that lonely room at midnight's most dreary hour ; so stood fair Marion beside the couch of death.

The couch of death !   Oh, phrase of saddest import !   In the pages of Eastern story we read of the magician's chest which bore those who sat upon it wheresoever they wished, and to what land they pleased.   There is more of such magic in the silent, gloomy death-bed ; it can transport to a greater distance, it carries its load to the most remote of all climes.   Death has a talisman more powerful than ever Eastern enchanter wielded—more potent than Arabic tale-writer has ever described.   Through earth, through air, through opening sky and vasty space, the magic chest of death bears its all-helpless burden, the journey is swift and the destination is quickly reached. Almost, ere the start is taken the goal is won ; almost ere the talisman has begun to act, the spell is woven and the work is done.

So Death and Beauty stood in the one room together—Beauty weeping by Death, and Death with its lank fingers clasping Beauty.   Marion shrunk not from the grasp, her lips were pressed to the cold cheek of her grandmother, and then they were withdrawn only to whisper words of affection's deepest sorrow.

And the dying woman looked upon the weeping girl, struggling as she looked, to speak the words which her palsied tongue refused to utter.   A faint, inarticulate murmur was all that broke the silence—was all that intimated how age had secrets to tell, and death was giving his denial to their being told.   There was deep stillness in the room—silence that was made deeper by the faint murmur of the dying, and the subdued weeping of the sorrowful.

"Grandmother, can you not speak louder.   I cannot hear you now.   Shall I never hear you more ?"

The sufferer made a single effort to reply, but the syllables faded from her lips, her sad eyes told how much the struggle had cost her, and her head sank upon the pillow, while the hollow rattle sounded hoarsely in her throat.

"God have pity on me!" ejaculated poor Marion. "She is dead—she is dead!"

At that moment the door of the room opened, three persons hastily entered the apartment, and made their way towards the couch of the dying. Marion turned round, beheld her sister, Hargrave Manners, and Gerrard Chester.

"Where have you been, sister Mildred. Take my hand—see!"

The younger sister drew the elder closer to the bed of the dying woman.

"Look, sister! Oh, why have you been away so long?"

Mildred bent over the dying woman, and addressed her in a tone of affectionate solicitude. No answer was returned to that address. The sufferer allowed her gaze to rest for one moment upon the face of Mildred, then closed her eyes, and with an effort, turned aside her head.

"Oh, why do you not speak to me, dear grandmother? I am Mildred. Do you not know me? Yes, yes, you do; but why do you press my hand so tightly, yet refuse to look at me?"

A faint "God bless thee, child!" was all the reply that the dying woman made to the enquiry. It was strange why the sufferer, recognizing as she did the countenance of the poor girl, should not have taken more notice of her, and have endeavoured to say more than she had said. Strange indeed, that at that fearful time when the angel of eternity was waiting to escort his charge, that there should be tears, and kind looks for the younger sister, but none for the elder. Why was it so; what did the preference mean?

Mildred turned aside to converse with her sister, and Hargrave Manners took her hand, while in a tone of seeming sympathy he addressed to her such words of condolence as at the moment he could command with readiness.

Hargrave Manners pressed the hand of Mildred Winnerly, and Gerrard Chester was a spectator of that scene!

And now it was that an incident occurred which never in all her after-life—never through the course of many troubled years did Marion—bright Marion forget; in the days to come it haunted her as a vision, in the nights of the future it was ever and ever re-acted to her in dreams. There was none of those now standing together in that room who failed to remember that which happened when the two sisters looked upon each other in the dreary chamber of death!

Hand clasped in hand stood Mildred Winnerley and Hargrave Manners. Their backs were towards the couch of the dying, and they could not see how the dull eyes of death were gazing at them, they could not see how strangely the glare was mingled with the gaze; they were not watching when the head of the sufferer turned slowly upon the pillow, and her glazed eyes moved in the direction of where they stood, they failed to perceive the sudden start which accompanied that look; they saw that death had discovered a secret, and they knew not that to death a mystery was known.

The glance of the dying woman was arrested by beholding Mildred and Hargrave standing together with their hands united. Strange it was that the dying gained strength at the sight; strange it was that she who was so near to death, and unable but a few minutes before to move without assistance, now upraised herself in the bed, moved aside the coverings, sat erect and firm, as if bidding defiance to death, as if endued with new and sudden life.   Her eyeballs first rolling in their sockets, then becoming fixed in a wild and ghastly gaze.   Her fingers clutched the bed-clothes in a convulsive clasp; her ashen lips quivered as they gave utterance to faint inarticulate sounds.   Noiselessly she rose from the bed, stood upon the floor, and moved towards where Mildred and Hargrave were standing with hand locked in hand.   The step of death was firm; the form of death moved over the floor without trembling.   It advanced, it glided forward spectre-like and silent; it laid its cold moist fingers upon the hands of the maiden and the youth, separating with one hurried movement the one hand from the other, and putting them assunder with strange and mad-like energy.

"Apart—stand apart!" exclaimed a hollow voice,

Mildred and Hargrave Manners, startled by the strange command, loooked quickly round, and their gaze fell upon the form of death.

"Apart—apart!" again cried the voice of the dying.   Then, while youth was still gazing upon age, while life was still wondering at death, the eyeballs of the aged woman became fixed and motionless in their sockets, her lips separated, her breathing ceased to be audible, and with her hand still upraised to bid Mildred and Hargrave stand apart, she sank back and fell a corpse upon the floor.

"Grandmother! dear grandmother!" shrieked Marion.

There was one in that room to whom the shriek passed unheard, one from whom the cry of agony awoke no response.   Ears that death had shut up for ever, could not hear the shriek, and lips that had already kissed the grave could not answer to the call.   In vain poor Marion's grief, in vain her exclamations of woe.   There was cold flesh before her, growing colder every moment.   The one sole|being who had been her protectress for so many years, the one kind spirit that had hitherto led her through the labyrinth of life, was for ever separated from her now.   Fatherless and mother-less, the sisters were alone in the wide and desert world.

The corpse was placed upon the bed, the cold hands being outstretched upon the coverlid.   There was no breath, no pulse, no movement, no struggle, and no life.   Yet how strange was the incident which happened in that silent, gloomy chamber—which happened there when the two sisters approached to look upon the form of death!

Strange indeed; for as Marion and Mildred bent over the corpse, touching its chilly flesh, pressing its pulseless fingers, gazing at the gazeless eyes, what cause had they to suspect that death knew how they stood, or how they gazed, or what they touched? Yet death must have known, death, must have seen, or that which happened could not have taken place.

The sisters had seated themselves beside the bed, their backs being towards the corpse.   Hargrave Manners had placed himself by the side of Mildred, while Gerrard Chester stood silently looking on at some little distance.

"Your loss is great Miss Winnerley," said Hargrave, taking the hand of Mildred, "but do not suffer any fear for the future to weigh upon your spirits.   Bereaved though you be of so kind and loving a relative, doubt not there are others still remaining in the world who will account it a pleasure to become the protectors both of you and your sister."

Mildred trembled, looked up timidly at the countenance of Hargrave, and faintly uttered,—

"My grandmother, did you hear—did you hear her words?"

"What of them, Miss Winnerley? Why do you refer to the ravings of delirium at this moment?"

"I know not—but—but——"

"Surely, Miss Winnerley, you attach no meaning—you cannot attach any meaning to words uttered at such a time, and under such circumstances?"

"I—I—it is no matter. We are friends," replied Mildred hesitating as she spoke, and using a tone that approached almost to a whisper.

"I will be the friend of yourself and of your sister. Let me have the pleasure of knowing Miss Marion, that you accept my friendship," said Hargrave, stretching out his hand to the younger girl.

Marion shuddered and was silent.

"Sister cannot speak. I will answer for her, Mr. Manners. She knows that you will keep your word."

"And you believe so likewise?"

Mildred hesitated for a single second; then, with much fervour she replied, clasping the fingers of Hargrave as she spoke—

"I do; I must. I have promised to trust to you—for ever."

But hardly had the words escaped Mildred's lips, before both she and Hargrave Manners felt something cold and clammy suddenly come in contact with their fingers. Each started and looked round. A white hand—a white pulseless hand had intruded itself between them—had laid its ashen fingers upon their own. A shudder crept over both. Involuntarily they each turned round; involuntarily each threw a timorous glance at the bed behind them, and the corpse which lay thereon. Could it be possible, or were their eyes deceiving them? Upright in the bed, seated erect as if endowed again with life, sat the form of the dead woman. There was no motion in her glazed eyeballs, no movement of her colourless lips. Her face was turned towards Mildred and Hargrave; her hand—the hand of death, was placed in contact with the hands of the youth and the maiden. No shriek, no startled cry of amazement broke the silence of the scene; no one had strength to step forward, and separate death from youth and beauty. And still the cold hand lay outstretched upon the warm ones; still the pulseless fingers clasped, or rather clutched the hands of Hargrave Manners and Mildred Winnerley. A pause—a pause of a few seconds, and then the hand of the dead woman pressed apart the arms of Mildred and her companion, separated the one from the other, and by one expressive movement indicated that the maiden and the youth were to sit no longer in company. And as Mildred started up in her fright, and recoiled from Hargrave, and as he leant back in his chair to avoid contact with the fingers of death, a faint sound escaped from the lips of the dead woman, and the corpse fell back rigidly upon the bed.

"Away, sister—come away!" exclaimed poor Marion. "There is meaning in this."

"What—what meaning?" stammered Mildred.

"Touch not the hand of Mr. Manners again this evening. I pray you not to do so, dear sister. I know not what it means, nor why such strange thoughts come over me; but touch not his hand?"

"His hand?"

"Ay, his hand," returned a voice from the further end of the room.

All turned their eyes in the direction whence his voice proceeded, and perceived to their astonishment that the old gipsy woman had entered the apartment.

"Why have you come here? why have you dared to enter this room?" demanded Gerrard Chester, as he stepped forward, and laid his hand upon the gipsey's shoulder.

"To talk of death, and woe, and evil in the proper place," replied the intruder. "The beauty is afraid of death, and yet, see! Give me your hand—your own hand, my fine lady. Handsome, as you are, you would of course like to know your fortune; let me tell it to you to-night."

"Not here—not now—not in this room!" interposed Gerrard Chester, as the gipsy was about to seize the wrist of Mildred.

"I can tell it to you to-night; and would you like to lose the chance, my handsome lady? Come, I have rare things to tell you, and this is the place and time."

"Sister—sister Mildred! what are you about to do?" exclaimed Marion, endeavouring to prevent her sister from holding out her hand to the gipsy.

"I am not afraid, Marion. We have the world before us now. Let us hear what our fortunes shall be."

Mildred stretched forth the palm of her right hand to the gipsy, who, grasping it eagerly, drew Mildred towards the bed, and placed the hand which had been given her in contact with that of the corpse.

"A dead hand and a live hand together. Ay, ay, we can tell brave things now! Be still and let me read the lines. That will do. Now take the dead hand and press it against your own. Bravely done! All that shall be is now written where it can be read with ease."

So while the deep silence was kept, while the spectators stood aghast, terrified by the unholiness of the scene, while the corpse lay on the bed, and the dead hand kept its contact with the living one, the gipsy read for beauty the mysteries which the future had in store. In that room, where the silent thing upon the couch—that form now chilling into rigidness, told of the fearful past, youth and beauty, eager in desire and reckless in their daring, waited to hear revealed the mysteries of the still more fearful future. The lights were burning low in their sockets, the night-wind was howling around the cottage, now and then the forked lightning flashed in through the holes in the window-shutters, peal after peal the growling thunder rolled along the distant heaven. Pallid, even as the face of the silent form upon the couch, were the countenances of those who had gathered round the gipsy and the maiden.

Was it madness that possessed Mildred? Why had she chosen at that particular moment to favour the gipsy's wish? She had given her consent with readiness, she had even expressed a more than common eagerness to hear that which the gipsy had to tell; and yet she gave her hand mechanically. She uttered the words of consent in a voice which scarcely seemed to be her own. It might have been doubted whether it was Mildred herself who wished to hear the future read, or whether some malicious spirit had taken unto itself the form of Mildred, and acted for her in so strange a manner. But still the gipsy remained gazing upon the palm of the living and of the dead: still the listeners waited to hear that which the reader of the future should reveal.

"Is your cunning at fault, or can you make out anything that is worth your while to tell?" asked Mildred.

"Much—I can read much," was the reply.

"And it is—what?"

The gipsy looked up, fixed her dark eyes upon the countenance of her interrogator, and in a grave voice replied—

"Here are deep lines here, and deep lines which have much meaning in them too. I have read them—read all they say, and all they mean. Dare you to hear what they tell, my handsome beauty?"

"Yes, yes," answered Mildred.

"Ay, ay, you may say 'yes' easily; but listen while I read you what your fortune shall be," said the gipsy. "Here is pride, and you have beauty; pride and beauty work together, and they make death. Do you understand me?"

"No," stammered Mildred.

"Handsome as you are, you will before long. Pride, misery, and death, that is what the deep lines say.   Remember, too, this is the thirteenth night of the month ; six months will pass away, and then on the thirteenth night do not forget the words—pride, misery, and death ! Six months more will pass. away, and again on the thirteenth night it will be well that you think over the same words then !   But six months more will pass, and on the thirteenth night returning, I warrant you will remember well the words the gipsy told you;—pride, misery, and death !"

"Why—why shall I remember them then ?" asked Mildred, anxiously.

"Because—" and the gipsy's voice assumed a graver tone, "there will be no fortune then which it will want a gipsy to tell.   The last of the thirteens will have arrived ; and there will be nothing more to read upon your soft white hand.   Wait till the time comes, my handsome beauty.   Six thirteens one after another, and when they have been three times told there will be no fortune to tell !   Yours is a silky hand, and the lines are deep. Pride, misery, and death !   There are four words which I read ; but one I will not tell you now."

All present heard the prophecy, all who stood in that chamber of death heard what the deep lines had to say. Slightly and only slightly did the colour pale upon Mildred's cheeks as she listened to the words of the gipsy woman ; but poor timid Marion felt a sensation of faintness creep over her as the fearful prediction fell upon her ears, and as over and over continuously and continuously, a chorus of voices seemed to chant around her the dirge composed of those sadly-meaning sounds—pride, misery, and death.

Pride, misery, and death ! pride, misery, and death ! that was the chorus which the invisible choristers sang ; that was the reading which the deep lines had given. And Marion saw that her sister was beautiful, and knew that she was proud.   Pride and beauty were to work the misery, and then—then, there was to be death !

The gipsy woman was about making her exit from the gloomy chamber, her hand was on the latch of the door when her further progress was intercepted by Gerrard Chester, who grasped her by the shoulder, and drew her aside to one corner of the room.

"Stay, woman !" said he, " you said that four words constituted the fortune of the maiden whose destiny you have pretended to make known.   Three of those words you have told us ; the fourth is—what ?"

"I will not tell her. I will not shock the handsome beauty.   Time—time will tell her what the fourth word should have been———"

"You will not confide that word to her, you say. What objection have you to telling it to me ?"

For a few seconds the gipsy gazed earnestly, yet wildly, at the countenance of Gerrard Chester.   Then, grasping his hand suddenly, and throwing a single glance at his palm, she muttered—

"Yes, yes, it is right for you to know—right for you to remember what the fourth word is.   But you will keep the secret—you will promise to do that ?"

"I promise you that I will tell no one what the four words are. One of them is pride, the second misery, the third———"

"Stop !" cried the gipsy. " The third has not been told you yet. Pride and misery make the first two, and the fourth one is death ; but there is another which comes between the second and the last."

"And that word—that word is—is——"

"Murder."

"Murder!" repeated Gerrard—"murder! And—and who is the murderer to be?"

The gipsy raised her right hand, and extending the fore-finger, pointed towards where Mildred stood erect, with gentle Marion clinging to her side.

"Her! do you mean her?—do you mean Mild—Mil—"

"Ha! ha! ha!" laughed the gipsy, as escaping from the grasp of Gerrard Chester she flung open the door, and rushed out of the cottage.

And there, motionless and silent, stood Gerrard, gazing upon the form of her towards whom the gipsy had pointed. The corpse lay on the bed; Marion was clinging for support unto her eldest sister; and again the right hand of Mildred Winnerley was clasped in that of Hargrave Manners. Still the strange prophecy was ringing in their ears; still did fair Marion fancy that she saw the arm of her dead grandmother upraised to separate Hargrave and her sister; still did proud Mildred stand gazing at the line on her soft white palm; and still in the silence—the deep solemn silence, did Gerrard Chester hear the word "Murderer!" muttered to him by unseen lips, while shadowy figures pointed to where the haughty beauty stood, and strange presentiments arose within his brain.

Pride, misery, *murder*, and death! Those were the words of mystery; that was what the deep lines had said.

So, let the six months pass; let love and sorrow, joy and woe, beauty and pride work on, to weave the web of destiny and work the patterns therein. The first six months pass away and again the thirteenth evening has arrived.

Will beauty work its curse? Will the prophecy of the gipsy be fulfilled?

———

CHAPTER VI.

THE FIRST SIX MONTHS PASSED.—HOW THE PROPHECY BEGINS TO BE FULFILLED.

SIX months had passed by since the day of Mrs. Winnerley's decease. Mildred and Marion had both seen the earth thrown upon their grand mother's coffin; but deeply felt her loss, and as deeply had experienced the sad feeling of utter loneliness which follows when the last friend is laid in the grave, and the old familiar face that smiled upon the infant and beamed in benignancy upon the child is veiled for ever from further view by the green turf and the cold moist sod. Lonely as the two sisters were left, there were yet some kind hearts who were willing to befriend them; and when, after their relative's funeral, they turned away from the grave, not knowing where to seek a home, the father of Gerrard Chester laid his hand upon the arm of the weeping Marion, and requesting her and her sister to accompany them, took them both to his own dwelling, showed them a room in which he and good Mrs. Chester had fitted up on purpose for their reception, told them he had respected their now dead grandmother, that he regretted her death, that he wished to evince his respect for her memory by acting kindly toward those whom she had left behind ; and then, assuring Mildred and her sister that he had always regarded them both as two good and deserving young women, the worthy farmer desired them henceforth to consider his house as their home, and to make themselves as comfortable therein as they possibly could.

" Ye be foine girls, both of ye," said the honest man ; " and though they do say Miss Mildred is a bit freaksome and that like, I've no doubt she'll do her best, now her poor grandmother's laid in the church-yard. There never was a detter dame alive than she was, poor old creature ; and I know she did her best to bring you both up as honest, dutiful dirls. I've heard her say at times that she hoped to see you holding your heads up in the world a little higher some day or other ; and may be if you mind what she said, and do as ye ought, you both will be foine ladies.   Same time though, I don't want to put any fly-away thoughts in your head, seeing that they get quick enough into the brains of all our young folk ; but be good, and well--conducted, and industrious, and then if you beent both happy and comfortable some day or other it will be wonderful strange. Of one thing you need have no fear so long as ye be what I say, you'll never want a friend, either of you. I've got children of my own, and now you've come to live in my house, you'll be on the same footing with them. I'm a good father, I believe, to those I've brought up under my roof, and if you be as prudent and well-disposed as they, you'll find farmer Chester to be as good a friend as he is known to be a father. I can't say more than that, girls ; and all I had to say I've said. There's a room for you both ; there's a table to work at, a table for you to read at, and here's Jane and Bessy, and Gerrard too, all to have a chat with you. Give me your hands, both. There ! God bless you and make you happy ! and now I'll go and see if Roger's got out the team."

So Marion and her sister were installed in a new home—in the home of Gerrard Chester ! when she whom they had deemed their only friend went to the silent grave, when the wide world opened upon them in all its cold, chilly, freezing loneliness—and cold and lonely enough God knows it appears when the wanderer is without a friend !—when they know not whither to go, whose aid to seek, what course to pursne, the father of the man whom haughty Mildred had despised, the father of him whom she had rejected in her pride and her ambition, came forward to welcome them to his home, to offer them shelter beneath his roof, to hold out to them the open hand, and give them the pledge of friendship.   To his home they went, under his roof they took up their abode, and Gerrard Chester met Mildred Winnerley every morning at the breakfast table, and every evening at the time appointed for prayer. Surely Gerrard had now an opportunity to press his suit, to win the love of the haughty beauty ; but poor Gerrard took no undue advantages of the circumstances under which he was placed.   Mildred was as holy to him while under the roof of his father's dwelling as she had been when in her own cottage home. Never once did he by word or deed allude to her dependency upon others ; never did he attempt to lower her pride by referring to the change which had taken place in her condition. If to tend assiduously upon one fair being, to anticipate her every want, to strive unremittingly to procure her every enjoyment—if gentle demeanour, courteous attention, anxious solicitude, and ceaseless adoration be wooing, then was Mildred Winnerley wooed more sincerely by Gerrard Chester than ever before gentle woman was wooed by earthly lover. Yet seldom was it that even a smile repaid the poor youth for his assiduity, seldom was it that she to whom he paid such homage noticed it with other than the most common place acknowledgment. Still, for all that, the haughty maiden was well pleased to see herself the idol of a worshipper whom she had determined should worship in vain; her vanity was flattered, her pride accepted the homage as rightful tribute paid by a vassal to his sovereign. And every morning Mildred found a fresh bunch of flowers laid upon her work-table, and every evening she made her own selection as to what tunes Gerrard should play her upon his flute; the flowers she placed in the vase appointed for them, and as for the tunes, when they were played she thanked the player, telling him at the same time that she was fond of music, but liked the violin better than she did the flute.

And six months passed away, summer faded into winter, the trees tired of their long service, threw off one by one their green liveries, the sun wearied with shining so fiercely, grew lazy and rose up later and later every morning, endeavouring to shirk a portion of his work on each succeeding afternoon; the old dial upon the church tower didn't care to labour so hard and make so many hours as it had been doing; the grass took the liberty to look up beneath the old tree which formed the trysting-place for all the lovers in the village, wondering where they had all gone to, and why they didn't come and sit there as they had been used to do; the flowers availed themselves of permission to depart; the fruit fell from the boughs; the rats rubbed their sides to see the stores of new corn placed in the barns; the partridges looked at one another sorrowfully, and puzzled themselves to make out where all the rest of their race had gone to; people were perplexed to decide if the autumn had passed and the winter had begun; the fires began to get jolly, the candles underwent most heroic martyrdom; the wind got into a bad habit of whistling; the rain took up with all manner of mad freaks and showered, drizzled, poured down, beat down, and drove about without any regard to propriety; the days grew shorter, the nights grew longer to make up for it; there were intimations abroad that Jack Frost was expected down by the next stage; nobody knew what had become of old Michaelmas, whether he had gone onward to welcome his friend Christmas, or returned home again to chat with sunny Midsummer. Amidst falling leaves, and closing flowers, and rain, and wind, and candle-light, the six months came to their end; and Marion and Mildred had almost forgotten the gipsy's prophecy.

It was night—a dark, gloomy, dreary night. In a room of farmer Chester's dwelling the two sisters sat listening to the sighing of the wind as it lurked amid the old trees which surrounded the farm. As yet the hour was not late, but Marion had been busily engaged during the day, and her eyelids felt heavy, and a drowsy sensation was stealing over her which she found it impossible to resist. So, while Mildred sat by her side, and while they were both listening to the night-wind, Marion closed her eyes and allowed her head to droop forward upon her bosom. Mildred started as her sister's handkerchief fell into her lap, and turning round to restore the article to its owner, perceived that Marion was asleep.

"Marion?" she whispered.

There was no reply.

What could it mean? Why was Mildred so gloomy? She did not raise her head to wake her sister, nor did she again attempt to rouse Marion from her slumber; but rising up and stealing softly across the room, the proud girl seated herself upon a chair near the window, drew aside the curtains and looked out at the dark clouds and the starless sky.

So still, so silent did Mildred Winnerley sit, peering out upon the darkness as if she traced faces in the gloom.   There was no moonlight to play upon her rich tresses; there was no candle burning in the apartment to reveal the exquisite beauty of that handsome countenance : yet as the clouds swept by, and as now and then a partial gleam entered through the uncurtained window, a looker-on might have beheld an expression of woe visible upon that countenance which ill accorded with the rare beauty it possessed, and the proud haughtiness that sat enthroned upon the brow.

Silent—all so silent ! the maiden sleeping in her chair, and the sister gazing at the dark winpow.   And the solemn minutes sped on, while the clock in the tower of the old church marked those minutes as they passed.   Never once did Mildred turn her eyes towards her sleeping sister ; not a single word escaped her lips to break the lonesome silence.   But, beautiful as she was, and haughty as she was, and proud as the gleam of her dark eyes shewed her to be, there was yet something which caused her sorrow, something which induced her to press her hand against her heart, and wife the tear-drops from off her cheeks.   Ay, there were tears upon the cheek of haughty Mildred, there was misery written there in the darkness upon her proud countenance.   Why was that ?   What could the meaning be ?   Was the gipsy's prophecy in process of fulfil-ment, were the words of mystery already proving themselves to be the revelations of doom ?   Oh ! Mildred Winnerley, in the silence of the dusky chamber, why is it that thine eyes are red with weeping, and why does thy white bosom heave so heavily beneath the pressure of thy hand ?

The first six months were at an end.   It was the night of the thirteenth.   Pride and misery were evidently in that one room together ; but something more than misery and pride had been prophecied in the gipsy's prophecy !

Whether it was that Mildred wished to feel the cold wind fan her burning brow, or whether it was that she found the darkness of the night congenial with her troubled spirits, need not be told ; but rising from her seat, and still holding her hand pressed to her bosom, she crept across the room, passed along a short passage, and unfastening a door in the rear of the house, emerged into the air.   She had scarcely taken a dozen steps before she felt her arm grasped by some one behind her, and at the same moment a handkerchief was placed upon her mouth.

" Keep silence, and no harm will happen to you," said a strange voice in her ear.

And before Mildred had time to make a struggle, or could look around to see who it was that had spoken, she was lifted from the ground, and carried away in the arms of her capturer.   In vain she attempted to utter an exclamation ; in vain were her efforts to free herself from the strong grasp by which she was held.   The farm-yard was crossed, a meadow in the rear was passed over, a small copse was threaded, and then, scarcely five minutes having elapsed from the time of her seizure, she found herself placed upon her feet, and her capturer standing before her.

" Do you know me ?" he asked.   " There is no moon to-night ; but there is light enough for you to see who it is that talks to you now."

" I—I—help ! help !"

" Silence, girl !   Do you not know who I am ?"

" No, no," stammered Mildred.

"Do you forget Pharold the gipsey, who once saved you from being drowned, who brought you presents when you were a mere child — do you forget him?"

"I—I—no. You—you are he," replied Mildred.

"Pharold the gipsey-chief talks with you now. Listen to him—listen to him, Mildred Winnerley. You are a proud girl; you cannot love those who are only of the same station as yourself. Your heart is ambitious; you long to possess gold—bright gold, to be the wife of one who has title, riches, and power. Listen to me! I have all that you seek. I am a chief, and therefore I have power; I am a king, and therefore have a title. Money is mine, if money you covet. I, Pharold the Zingaro, choose you for my wife—choose you, because like myself you have a proud mind and a bold heart.

Answer me—for I have brought you here this night to hear the answer from your own lips—will you accept the offer, will you be the gipsey's bride? Think, Mildred Winnerley, before you speak."

The novelty of the scene, the strangeness of the question, so far overpowered the frighted girl, that she could not summon strength enough to utter a single word. It was true that the gipsey had once rescued her from death; true that he had often acted kindly towards her; but that he should now, and in such a manner, propose so strange a question, and demand so hasty an answer, that he—outcast from society as he was— should seek to wed himself to the haughty maiden who had rejected so many offers, was a mystery indeed.—Silence was preserved by both parties for some minutes, then, again pressing the hand of Mildred, the gipsey said,—

"You wonder at my words; you are surprised that I should put such a question to you. Hear me, Mildred Winnerley! Pharold the gipsey can love you—love you because, like him, you are proud, bold and ambitious. You wish for power; you wish for wealth, you wish for honour. Power you may have, for I can make you a queen; wealth you may have, for wealth is at my command, and as for honour; who is there among my tribe that would dare to act with disrespect towards the wife of their chief? You hear me. I wait for your answer"

"Not now—I cannot give it you now," replied Mildred.

"It must be now—it must be this night and this hour," returned the gipsey. "I will explain to you more. It is the law of our whole race that if the chief of one tribe die, leaving a daughter, and the chief of another tribe be without a wife, the tribe to which the girl belongs can offer her to him in marriage, and he dares not refuse to accept her, unless some other maiden comes forward and swear that he is under a promise to wed himself to her. Ten nights ago the chief of the tribe next in rank to our own, was laid in his grave, and to-night they bring his daughter to us for me to take her as my wife. I have seen her, and though she has enough of beauty, I like her not, and would rather that some one else should be her husband. They are waiting for me now; and they have brought with them the girl that I dislike. Answer me then, will you go with me, will you accompany me to the tent; and when they demand that I take for my wife the daughter of their tribe, will you step forward and swear the oath that you have pledged yourself to be the bride of Pharold! Consider—consider well. And now—your answer."

"1 give it you. Even if I loved you—which I do not—do you think that I would forget myself, and consent to be a gipsey's wife?"

"A gipsey's wife! Ay, and why not, girl? Is it well for you to be so proud—you who know not who your own father was, who know not if he was not a villain whose name it may be wise to hide? Throw off your pride now; hear, and reply—will you save me, or must I marry her whom they would have me to wed?"

Mildred curled her lip, and was silent.

"You hate me, girl! you hate me, or you would speak now."

"Have I not a right to love when I please, and hate when I please?" said Mildred, after a short pause.

The black eyes of the gipsey glittered with a strange brightness, as he replied,

"You have, girl—you have. But listen to me, now—mark me! I saved your life once, I have loved you for years since then. Now, were you to give me your hand the next moment, I would not accept it—I would fling it back. The gipsey either loves or hates; and if hate be given him he returns it with interest. Go—go, and remember this night. When your pride has worked your misery, when you are other than you are now, remember this night! And when you are rich and wear fine clothes, as will one day be the case, fear then the answer that you gave to Pharold, the gipsey. Come, I will lead you to your home, I will lead you to where I brought you from; and when you next meet Pharold the gipsey, he will not ask your hand, he will not talk to you of love again. We shall meet, Mildred Winnerley; but it will not be here, it will not be where I shall ask, and you in your haughtiness deny."

So saying, Pharold led Mildred to the door of the farm-house; and then uttering the words, "Remember this night!" glided from her, and disappeared among a cluster of trees at a distance.

Some time passed before Mildred could command strength enough to press open the door and enter the house. When at length she was able to do so, she crept silently along the passage, and entering the room which she had quitted some half-hour since, perceived that her sister was still sleeping in the chair. Not wishing to awake her, she stole noiselessly across the apartment and, re-seated herself upon the seat before the window.

Mildred had resumed her seat; but she did not gaze into the dark night, she did not look out, as she had done before, upon the gloomy sky. In silence she sat, brooding over the strange event which had just happened to her, and the strange words which the gipsey had uttered at parting. And as Mildred so sat and brooded, as she sat in the darkness musing on the gipsey's prediction, she thought that she heard a slight noise behind her. For the moment she was afraid to turn her head; but again hearing a movement in the room, she looked round and perceived, by the aid of the faint moon-light which had just made its way into the chamber, that Marion had woke from her sleep. A strange wild light glittered in Marion's eyes; and her cheeks were so ashen pale that Mildred was afraid to look at her sister. Marion did not speak, did not beckon; but slid gently off the chair upon her knees, and with her eyes fixed upon Mildred, and with her mouth wide open, crept across the floor towards her. So fearful did Marion seem that Mildred shuddered with fright as the pale figure of her sister drew nearer and nearer. Not Marion herself, ut the ghost of Marion did the figure resemble; so wild was the expression of its eyes, so white its countenance, so silent its movement. And when it crouched beside Mildred's lap, and laid its fingers upon her hand, she felt them to be cold, and she felt that they trembled as they touched.

"Mildred—sister Mildred!" said a voice which did not sound like that of Marion.

Mildred did not reply.

"What does it mean, sister—what has it been all about?" asked the same voice, while the cold fingers clung more tightly to Mildred's hand.

"I—I—Marion! sister! why do you look so strangely?" exclaimed Mildred.

The pale figure drew itself nearer, breathed more quickly, and with trembling arms and quivering lips, crouched yet more closely beside the haughty beauty.

"Listen, sister—listen!"

"I am listening now, Marion. What is it that frightens you? Why do you tremble so, and why are you so cold?"

"I have had a dream, dear sister—oh! a strange, terrible dream. I see it now. I see it all going on, and I hear them speak—hark! hark!"

"To what am I to listen, sister Marion?"

"To—what day is it, sister—what is the day of the month?"

"The—the thirteenth, Marion."

"Ha! It is—it is! I—I am faint, sister—very faint. I—"

"Good heavens! dear Marion, what can be the matter! I will call Mrs. Chester and Elizabeth; they—"

Marion seized the hands of her sister.

"No, dear Mildred, no. Do not call them, do not let them come. I am better now. Wipe my forehead for me, sister; it is so damp, so wet. There, there, I am much better now, much better than I was, sister.

Marion reclined her head against Mildred's bosom, and Mildred encircled her waist with an affectionate clasp. No word was spoken by either for some minutes; but gradually the eyes of the younger sister resumed their usual expression; her respiration became more easy, her lips regained a portion of their wonted colour. At length looking up, and gazing fixedly at Mildred's countenance, she said in a grave and solemn manner,

"I have had such a fearful dream, sweet sister; a dream that I shall never forget; and it was you that the dream was about, it was you that I saw with—"

Marion paused.

"With what, sister?"

"Not now, Milly—I will not tell you now. But this is the thirteenth day; and on this night six months dear grandmother died. Do you remember, sister Mildred, all that happened on that night?"

"I do, dear Mar. Speak not of it now."

"Yes, sister. Do not be angry with me. Oh! how many, many times I have thought over that gipsey-woman's words! I have heard them whispered in my ears again and again, sister, and seen them written on the dark sky when at night I have looked out at my chamber window. I heard them, sister—I heard them just now in my dream."

"Do not be foolish, dear Mar."

"I am not foolish, sister. Remember! it was not till after dear grandmother had parted you from Mr. Manners that the gipsey said the words. You will not be angry with me, dear—will you—for saying that my sister Milly is proud? You are so, sister, and perhaps you cannot help it. But the gipsey-woman said that misery would come after pride; and I do not wish to see my sweet sister miserable. Oh! they were strange, frightful words, sister! And that—that was a strange dreadful night."

"It was, dear Mar. But let us forget about it if we can; let us think no more about it."

"I cannot do so if you can, sweet sister; and I wish—I wish—"

"What is it you wish, Mar?"

"That you had never seen—never known Mr. Manners—Hargrave Manners, sister. I wish it from my heart—from my very soul!"

"But why, Mar—why have you such a wish?"

"I—I—you love him sister—you love him because his father is rich, and is a baronet; you see him often, sister; you are always together; and yet—yet you remember how grandmother placed her hand between you and him on the night she died. Already Mr. Manners has offended his father, and is compelled to seek refuge with his uncle. His father is ill, and cannot live long. I know what you think, sister—you think that Sir Walmsly Manners will soon die, and that his son will come in for the property; but suppose, sister, Sir Walmsly should disinherit Mr. Hargrave—suppose that when Hargrave Manners does obtain the property he should no longer care for my poor sister. Dearest, I see you are looking angry, I see that you do not like me to talk so; but I have been dreaming, sister, I have had a frightful dream. And in my dream I heard the gipsey-woman's words repeated over and over again. 'Pride, misery, and death—pride, misery, and death!' I saw you too in my dream, sister; and I dreamt that the three six months had passed away—that dear grandmother had lain in her grave eighteen months, and that the thirteenth of the month had come and was passing. I saw also the old gipsey-woman, and I dreamt that she took me by the arm and said, 'Look!' and then I looked, sister, and saw you—you, my own sister—my one only sister, a—a—no, no; let me never tell you—never say to anyone what I saw!"

"Why do you say that, Mar? How very foolish it is of you to allow yourself to be frightened by the words of a mad woman, and by a silly dream. I thought my sister Mar had more courage."

"I have courage, sister; but—"

"Why, look at me, Mar. Do I fear the gipsey's words? Think you that anything so absurd could make me timid, or nervous?"

"Remember!" said a deep, hollow voice, which seem to proceed from outside the cottage.

Mildred started, and looked up. There was a man's face at the window, which vanished so soon as she turned her eyes in that direction. Whose face it was she knew not; but from a glimpse which she had of the slouched hat and dark hair of the individual, she was induced to suppose him to be none other than Pharold the gipsey. Rising up, Mildred gazed through the glass and out on the dark road. Everything seemed motionless there; the wind had become lulled, the rain had ceased to beat among the old trees, there were no passengers to be seen.

"What was it, sister—whose face was that?" inquired poor Marion, timorously.

"Face, sister; there was no face; nothing—nothing whatever, save the dark night and the lone road."

"The dark night and the lone road," repeated Marion, to herself. And, as the words hung upon her lips, the drama of her own and her proud sister's future life seemed to unclose itself before her; and far, far away in the future, where the eighteen months were at an end, and where crowding shapes stood beckoning with their spectre-like arms—far, far away in the future, where the gipsey's prophecy had its fulfilment, where destiny was waiting to award the doom, sad Marion saw nought with her visionary eyes, save the dark night and the lone road; ever through the toilsome journey—ever onward stretching far, the lone road wound, while ever over it hung the shadows of night —gloomy shadows deepening with the lengthening way.

So again silent, speechless, thoughtful, sat the two sisters in the dusky room. Arm entwined round arm, side pressed to side, the head of the younger resting against the bosom of the elder, so did beauty in its gentleness, and beauty that was more dazzling still in its proud haughtiness sit together in the silence and the gloom!

"Sister Mildred, I have a question to ask you," said Marion, looking up towards the dark eyes of her sister with a tender, yet an earnest gaze.

"Ask it, dear Mar, let me know what it is about."

Marion was silent for a moment. Then, raising herself up, she twined her right arm about Mildred's neck, and looked more intently into those proudly beauteous eyes.

"Dearest," said she, "you are my sister—poor Marion has but one sister in the whole world, and you are that only one. Were harm ever to happen to you, were I to see you miserable, I should feel your sorrow more deeply than if it were my own. I would rather—ten thousand times rather—suffer any pain, endure any privation than see you, dearest, miserable for a single day. You know that I speak in earnest; you know that I but express that which my heart feels; so you will pardon me—Milly will pardon her sister for asking the question, if in her heart — her very heart, Mildred Winnerley believes she is loved by Hargrave Manners? Sister, is such your belief?

Marion waited; the old clock in the next room continued to tick, the clouds passed one by one before the pale crescent of the moon.

"You do not answer me, sister; you are trembling. I can feel your pulse beating hard against my fingers. Do you fear to answer me, sister?"

"No, Mar—no."

"In the sight of Heaven, sister, and on that night of the month which saw our dear grandmother die, do you believe that you are sincerely and truly loved by the man whom I know has proposed love to you, and in whose words I am afraid—afraid, dear sister, that you have placed too much trust!"

"Sister Marion is very kind to night," said Mildred, a little tiffed at being submitted to such an interrogatory. "Really, one would be led to suppose from hearing you talk, sister, that your experience in matters of the heart had been on a scale extensive enough to warrant your discriminating powers being regarded as valuable by poor simple maidens like myself."

"This is unkind—unjust; it is unlike my sister," returned poor Marion. "I did but speak to you in love, and you have answered me in anger. My question was one that a sister may put to a sister, the reply scarcely seems to be one that Mildred Winnerley would give to her sister Marion."

"I did not wish to say anything unkind, dear Mar; though I must confess that your inquisitiveness occasioned me some slight vexation at the moment. As to your inquiry, I think it to be almost unnecessary for me to tell you that Hargrave Manners is a gentleman, and that his word may be trusted."

"'His word,' sister; and has he told you that he really loves you—loves you in truth and honour?"

After a pause of a few moment's duration, Mildred answered, "He has."

"And you believe him, sister—you do not doubt him?"

"I do not."

"You see no reason to distrust him, you have no cause to suspect the sincerity of his professions—the reality of his love?"

"I have not."

"Then he will marry you—he will make you his wife. Once the wife of Hargrave Manners, and in time my poor sister will bear the title of a lady. Oh, how proud sister, you will be then!"

"Would it not make you happy, Mar, to see me married to Hargrave would you not? like to have it in your power to say that your sister is Lady Manners?"

"No, Milly—no; not if you were miserable."

"Mercy me, Mar! what nonsense you talk! Why, in the name of wonder do you associate the position of a fine lady with the idea of being miserable? What strange whim can you have got into your head? When I am Hargrave's wife, sister, will not the people look up and ask favours of me, will not hundreds of those who scarcely speak to me now wish to court my company then? Oh, sister, it will be delightful to be rich, delightful to be the wife of a man who will one day have a title and broad lands of his own. I shall be so happy then, sister—oh! I shall be so happy then—so very, very happy!"

"Remember!" again said the strange voice outside the window.

Once more Mildred started from her seat, and gazed hastily through the casement; once more too, she fancied that in the gloom around the cottage she discovered the moving figure of Pharold, the gipsy-chief.

"What do you see, sister?"

"Nothing, Mar—nothing but the dark night and the lonely road."

And oh, with what strange significance did those words again fall upon the ear of poor trembling Marion. She spoke not, she moved not, but her thoughts were—"What if the gay life that my sister has pictured should prove to be but a dark night and a lonely road? What if instead of dwelling amidst sunshine as she dreams to do, there shall be nothing for her save night—dark night, through which, and on a lonely road she must journey to the yet darker night of the grave? Heaven keep my poor sister from misery and woe."

And again the sisters sat together in silence, until at length Mildred rose from her seat.

"I am going to fetch a candle, sister, and see what time it is. I will also fetch a letter that I received from Hargrave two days ago, some parts of which I wish to read to you. I shall be back to you very quickly, dear Mar."

Mildred departed, and in proceeding along one of the passages of the house met one of the domestics who was carrying two candles in her hand.

"I was about bringing you a light, Miss Mildred," said the woman. "It never struck me till just now how you and Miss Marion were sitting all alone in the dark. I begin to be fearsome about missus and the old man. Roger told me the other day there was no trusting the old crittur; she's not at all sure on her legs as she used to be. Deary me! see what the time is—eleven o'clock, I declare! and they not come home yet! Well, I'm sure I should be all in a fever about them, if young master wasn't with them, and Mr. Gerrard knows how to get the old mare along as well as Roger himself doos. But as for master, I'm sure, I don't know where he has gone to. He came home about two hours ago, and went out again about half an hour afterwards; Roger says that he saw him as he came down the village taking the way to 'Squire Bannerton's; but what he can have gone there for at this time of night, when the

'Squire and Mr. Hargrave are both away is quite mysterious to a body like me. Poor master didn't look very well either when he went out. I was fearsome of his going into the cold air, and then to be so late, and ——"

" He will be back soon, I dare say, Susan," interrupted Mildred, " and as for your mistress, Mr. Gerrard and his sisters, we were told not to expect them home earlier than eleven. It is a very long ride, Susan; and it will not do for Gerrard to drive too fast on so dark a night."

" Well, all I hope is they'll come home soon and not catch any colds or rheumatizzes, and as for master, I'm sure if he'd asked the advice of a poor body like me, I should have advised him to keep in doors and get his cough well, not to go tramping about at such an hour of the night all in the damp and the fog. Only to think of his going out just as I'd got his gruel ready, and made him a nice fire, and put his baccy and his pipe all on the table ready for him. I'm quite fidgetty about him—that I am, and—Heaven bless us! there's all his gruel boiling over into the fire, I declare!"

Susan ran away to see to the gruel, and Mildred taking one of the candles in her hand, proceeded up-stairs to fetch the letter which she had promised to read portions of to her sister Marion.

Of nothing at that moment did Mildred Winnerley feel more sure, than that she had placed the letter she now wished to find, within her work-box, and fastened the lid of the box with her own hand; yet now—strange to say—no such letter could Mildred discover in the place where she was certain of having deposited it. In vain she turned over her needle-paper, her balls of cotton, and the various other little items appertaining to a lady's work-box; in vain she looked between the lining and the lid, in vain too she took each article out singly and examined each piece of paper separately. No letter like the one she looked for could she find. And now her cheeks turned of a deadly paleness, her hands trembled as she replaced the articles in the box. Evident enough it was, from the demeanour of the poor girl, that the letter which she sought for was one of more than common importance, and one which she feared to think had fallen into the hands of any one else in that house. Not knowing how to account for its disappearance, she seated herself upon a chair, pressed her hands against her brow, and endeavoured to recall her thoughts so as to assure herself whether she had to a certainty placed the letter in the box. Yes, she was certain—quite certain; she called to mind how she had taken a pin-cushion out of one of the divisions to make room for it, and the difficulty she had afterwards in locking the box, owing to a portion of the letter having been placed between the lid and the hinge. How then could the letter have disappeared? by whom had the box been unlocked? by whose hand had the missing article been removed? These were questions which at the moment poor Mildred could not answer to her satisfaction. Suddenly, however, she remembered that a little cousin of Gerrard's, had been on a visit at the house during the early part of the day, and that she had sent her up stairs to fetch a reel of cotton; this much at least was certain. But what had the child done with the letter? What had been her object in taking it out of the box, and where had she since put it? Mildred searched every corner of the room, and then proceeding down stairs examined all the toys with which the child had played. Still no letter could she find. What was she to suppose? Had little Jessy carried away the letter in her pocket? Such in all probability was the case. What

then if it should fall into the hands of the child's parents. Poor Mildred quivered with
agitation as the probability of such a mischance having occurred suggested itself to her
mind. Hope, however, came to her aid, and she consoled herself by trusting that the
missing epistle was still reposing in safety at the bottom of little Jessy's pocket; and
that she should be able to recover it on the ensuing morning. Comforting herself with
this belief, Mildred returned to the room in which she had left her sister.

"To-morrow will do, dear sister," returned Marion. "Is it not getting very late?
Where can Mrs. Chester and the family be?"

"Hark! Mar, is not that some one at the door?"

"Yes," answered Marion, "Susan is pulling back the bolt. Who can it be?"

" At that moment Mr. Chester entered the house. The sisters heard him ask the domestics if his wife and daughters were come home, and then make inquiry as to whether Miss Mildred had gone to bed. No sooner had he received answers to these questions than passing on into his own room, he closed the door, and turned the key in the lock. Not many minutes had passed before Susan entered the apartment in which the two sisters were.

"Heaven save us, Miss Winnerley and Miss Marion!" ejaculated the good woman, "there's something the matter with poor master which neither you nor I know anything about. He looks so downsome and miserable-like, one quite grieves to see him. He wasn't so this morning, and it's only come in the evening. I asked him if he felt himself very ill, but there was no getting him to say. And then his gruel for the cold which he has, I've made it three times over for him to-night, and when I told him just now it was all ready for his supper so soon as missus and young master comes, he said as how he didn't want it, and hadn't any appetite to eat it. Not but what that's very foolish of him; for I haven't the least morsel of patience with people who go and lose their appetites, and do such silly things as that. As for my part, I— but, hush! I hear wheels on the road; they are coming nearer, that's the old mare's trot, ay, and that's Boxer's bark, too. Look, Miss Marion, do you see them? I'll go and open the door, and tell master they're here."

Five minutes had not passed before the old mare trotted up to the door, and Mrs. Chester and her daughter, together with Gerrard, alighted from the clumsy vehicle in which they had been journeying. A very short time was sufficient for all to disencumber themselves of their travelling attire, and then Susan led the way into the room where supper was laid, snuffed the candles, stirred up the fire, and tripped off to see whether her master's gruel had taken another industrious fit, and boiled over again in height of its zeal.

The supper was on the table, the younger members of the household were gathered around the board. But where was Mr. Chester and his wife, why had they gone upstairs together, and on what subject could they be so deeply engaged in conversation as to forget the waiting meal, and the late unseasonable hour.

Gerrard was about going to see where his father was, when the door of the room opened, and Mr. and Mrs. Chester entered. No one present could help observing that the countenance of both were very grave, and that something had occurred to divest the hearty old farmer of his usual cheerfulness, rendering him so thoughtful and taciturn as he now appeared to be.

The meal was partaken of in silence. The reserved manner of their father so far influenced Gerrard and his sisters that they forbore to talk, and made no reference to the events that had occurred during the day. A strange sad supper to it seemed to Mildred and Marion. Poor Marion knew not how it was that she felt so disinclined to eat, nor did she know why presentments of some boding evil floated upwards through her mind. Similar feelings seemed also to affect the elder sister; for more than once when Mildred was raising her fork to her lips, her hand trembled, and the fork fell from her grasp. As she was about to drink, her fingers missed their hold of the glass, and allowed it to fall upon the table, while, in attempting to snuff the candle, she not only extinguished the light, but overturned also the candlestick. Every one seemed glad that the meal was finished; and when the large old bible was brought, and Mr.

Chester proceeded to read a chapter, every one wondered why he had selected so strange a one, and why he read with such unusual earnestness.

The reading of the chapter was finished, the bible was re-closed. In accordance with the custom of the family, all fell upon their knees to offer up the evening prayer. Hitherto in performing this duty Mr. Chester had made use of one form of words. On the present occasion, however, he departed from that form, and praying with more than his wonted fervour, adopted a strain that was unfamiliar to the ears of his children, while the requests which he solicited Heaven to grant were such, that the children of farmer Chester wondered why their father prayed so strangely, and in such solemn words. This act of duty concluded, however, all rose up to retire for the night. Gerrard and his sister having parted from their parents in the usual manner, proceeded to their chamber, and Mildred and Marion were about to follow their example, when they were detained by Mrs. Chesier.

"Stop, my good children," said she. "Take your seats again, for Mr. Chester, I believe, has something to say to you."

Why was Mildred pale, why did poor Marion tremble as she resumed her seat?

"The key had better be turned in the lock, dame," said Mr. Chester, addressing his wife.

"It is turned; and the children have closed their bed-room doors," replied Mrs. Chester.

For some minutes there was most profound silence in the room. Mr. Chester sat with his head bent down, and resting on his hands; while his wife seemed to be scrutinizing poor Mildred with sundry direct, oblique, cursory, and penetrative glances. At last, Mr. Chester poked up the fire, and desired Mildred to change her seat to one that was opposite to him.

It was the thirteenth night of the month; six months had passed away, and Marion, as her heart beat convulsively against her chest, remembered the gipsey's prophecy.

"Mildred, child," said Mr. Chester, in a deep serious voice, "six months have gone by, or nearly so, since I offered to you and your sister a home under this roof. Mrs Winnerley and my dame here were always on friendly terms, and perhaps there was no person living in this village half a year since that both of us respected more than we did your good grandmother. Well, she died, and her death was sad enough, but she is now in Heaven, and all the suffering which she had here is forgotten there. When I heard of her death, and thought how you were both left in the world, 'Dame,' said I, we must make a home for the two poor lasses, we must take them in and be kind to them now, when they are nothing better than orphans, and have none to look up to,' I didn't think so much I was doing a kindness, as I was a duty when I made the proposal to dame; and she agreed to it at once. So when your poor grandmother was put in the earth, and after I had seen the cold clay put down on top of her, I took your hands you know, and I told you—I told you I'd got a home for you; and that you could come to it, and be good lasses, and never want for anything so long as I lived and had a roof of my own. Well, you came, you know, and we did all we could to make everything comfortable for you; and I wanted to make you feel as if I was a sort of father to you; and dame has done all she could to be a mother-like. So here we are; and you've both been good lasses, and you've never wanted for anything that I or dame could get you— have you?"

"Never, dear Mr. Chester," answered Marion, her eyes swimming with tears of gratitude.

"Aye, and you say the same as your sister—do you not, Mildred ?"

"Yes—indeed, yes !"

"And you've been quite good and contented, and never done anything that you need blush to tell ?   You'll answer me that, Mildred?"

"I hope neither I, nor sister ever have so done," replied Mildred,   "Sister will speak for herself."

"Yes, yes, to be sure.   And there's been a little acquaintance between you and Mr. Hargrave up at the Manor.   Mr. Hargrave sees that you are a good lass, and it's no wonder that he should take notice of you as he does.   But there is a sort of respect we should all have of ourselves in such matters, and I hope you've not been pressing Mr. Hargrave to marry you because he's a baronet's son, and is likely to have large estates of his own bye-and-bye—I hope you've not been forgetting yourself so as to do anything of that sort?"

"No, Mr. Chester ; it is not likely that I should do so," answered Mildred, in a weak voice.

"Of course not — of course not, child.   There is no reason why you should want him to marry you too soon — not for some years ; there is no reason, I say—is there ?"

"None," stammered Mildred, faulteringly.

"And you do not wish him to, yet, you have never asked him—never asked him yourself ?"

"My sister would not so far forget herself as to do so," said Marion.

"To be sure she would not—to be sure. But let her speak and say if she has. Come, child, say—say."

"I—I never have, Mr. Chester—never."

"And you have never wrote to him in a letter anything of that sort, eh, child—have you ?"

"No, Mr. Chester—no."

"Yes, yes to be sure—to be sure you would not do so. God is hearing you now, child ; and you can tell Him that you have never behaved so foolishly—so wickedly. Come, Mildred, child, say—say."

"I have not, Mr. Chester—indeed I have not."

"Aye, to be sure — to be sure ; and you will call God to witness it — eh, child ?"

"Yes ; I—I do, Mr. Chester."

Fearful was the change which the countenance of Mr. Chester suddenly assumed.   He fixed his eyes upon the face of Mildred, he gazed at her with a searching, withering look.   Plunging his hand into an inner pocket of his coat, he drew forth the missing letter, unfolded it, threw it upon the table, and ex-claimed—

"Liar ! You have appealed unto your Maker, and that letter gives proofs that you have spoken his name with a lie upon your lips."

With cheeks that were blanched to very whiteness, with lips that quivered as they tried to utter sound, with hands that shook like the leaves of the trembling aspen ; with a look, an action, a demeanour, that all proclaimed her guilty, Mildred fell upon her knees at the feet of Mr. Chester, and burst into tears.

"Sister—my dear, sweet sister! what—what is this—what does it mean—what—what?" ejaculated Marion, as she threw herself upon the floor beside her sister, and clasped the neck of the weeping and accused girl. "Answer me, my only sister—answer me!"

Mildred wept more bitterly.

Marion moved aside upon her knees, and grasped the right hand of Mr. Chester.

"Tell me, sir—oh, tell me, I implore you—what has my sister done? What was the meaning of your words? I—I am sure my poor sister has done nothing wrong. Oh, no, no, no!"

Whether at that moment the accused or her accuser trembled the worst it would have been difficult to say. Mr. Chester endeavoured to speak, but his emotion appeared to be too great, and the words which he was about [to uttter died away upon his lips Still, however, Marion continued clinging to his hand; still she besought him to say why he had spoken so harshly to her sister, and still she prayed him in piteous accents to make known the crime of which he supposed poor Mildred to be guilty.

"She has deceived us all," replied the honest farmer, a choking sensation preventing him from speaking with distinctness, "she has deceived her friends, and worse still, she has deceived herself."

"Oh no! it cannot be, sir, it cannot, I assure you. My poor sister deserves not that you should say this."

"Listen!" said Mr. Chester, resuming his seat, and taking the hand of Marion in his own; while Mrs. Chester had drawn Mildred towards her, and was whispering in her ear, to urge her to a confession of her guilt—"Listen! Heaven intended us all to be content with our situation, and when we are not so some ill is sure to follow. When a young lass forgets her own station, and endeavours to get a sweetheart beyond her rank, it seldom happens that all things go rightly in the end. Now, for some time past, I and dame have kept a watch upon the behaviour of Mr. Hargrave Manners and our Mildred, as I may call her. Well, we saw that they were often together, and we knew that Mildred was no match for the 'squire's nephew. Dame and I have told the lass so, and pointed out to her that Mr. Hargrave is a wild young man who is not very likely ever to be a good husband for any girl. Well, things have gone on, and how they have gone on as they have, with the counsel the lass has had, is wonderful enough. She has reckoned upon her fine face and her beauty to do great things; but a fine face is often the greatest curse a poor lass can have. Neither dame nor I suspected how far things were gone, nor knew anything about it hardly, until I took this letter out of the hand of little Jessy to-day. The child had taken it to play with; and when I asked her for it, I supposed it to be one of my own. On looking at it I saw it was in Mr. Hargrave's handwriting, and reading some of it, I found it had been sent to our lass here. Give me the glasses dame, and we'll read the letter again.

Marion listened, and Mildred continued to weep. The letter ran thus.

"MY DEAREST LOVE,—Your very affectionate favour has just reached me in London. Nothing can equal my vexation at being so far from you at the present moment. You say that at times you almost doubt my love. Can such be possible, can such a thought enter into the mind of my charmer for a single instant? Surely you do but write in banter; you cannot doubt the devotion or the fidelity of a heart which is all your own. You cannot suspect the sincerity of one who loves you to madness—to distraction. Wherefore should I otherwise than love you? Where or when could I expect to meet with moments of happiness like those that we have passed together, when rambling through the silence of the deep green wood, or sauntering in some secluded meadow? Never, never, never, can the memory of those happy moments be effaced from the tablet of my mind. Oh, for the coming of that time when I shall enjoy such bliss again, when I shall once more clasp my sweet idol to my heart, and hold it there, for ever. Dearest, no words can adequately express the passion which binds me to you; it is not mere love, it is not mere adoration; it is something deeper, holier far—the devotion of the soul—the religion of affection.

"And now with respect to our mutual situation. When, dearest, I shall be able to quit London it is impossible for me to say; but it will not be long. As to our union then, nothing shall cause the least delay—nothing shall interpose to prevent the completion of our bliss. At present your situation is not such as will excite suspicion, the ceremony which you desire shall be performed. Remember! should our sweet infant live when born, how many blissful reminiscences will it recall to us of past joys, when we shall be more formally allied than we are now, but when it will be impossible for me to love you more as your husband than you are now devotedly beloved by him who being your husband in the sight of Heaven is even your adorer upon earth. Once and once again let me insure you how sincerely and passionately I am your faithful and ever-affectionate lover.   HARGRAVE MANNERS."

"Sister—dearest, dearest sister!" exclaimed Marion, again flinging her arms around the neck of the weeping girl, and pressing her affectionately to her heart. "Why, why have you hidden so much from me—why have you not told me that which I have now heard?"

"Forgive me, Marion! forgive me, sister—pardon me!" stammered poor Mildred.

"You will pardon my sister—you will forgive her for not having told you that she is to be the wife of Mr. Manners so soon?" implored Marion. "Even to me—her sister—she has not told the secret."

"Not for keeping the secret, not for that, do I blame her and beg God to pardon her," answered Mr. Chester; "but it is the lie—the lie just uttered that I can never forgive."

"Oh, say not that! do not say never—never forgive!" exclaimed poor distressed Marion. "My sister has done wrong; she has been foolish—very foolish; but you will pardon her, you will say that you will pardon her, you will, Mr. Chester; her sister asks it—begs it—prays it; and Mildred will pray too; she will ask your pardon—she will beg your forgiveness, she will tell you all, and will never deceive you again. Oh, pardon her, say that you will pardon her!"

"It is her God who must pardon her; let her ask pardon of him. The fault was committed, what need there of doubling it with a lie?"

Mildred continued to weep. Once or twice she attempted to speak, but sobs prevented her utterance, and the excess of her grief almost amounted to hysteria. She grasped convulsively the hand of her sister, hid her face so as to conceal her confusion, and rested her fevered brow upon the lap of the farmer's wife. Poor Marion grew afraid that the greatness of her sorrow would induce delirium in her poor sister's brain.

"My sister will die unless you pardon her," said she again, passionately appealing to Mr. Chester. "Hargrave loves her, and he will marry her, he has promised to do so, and my sister will be happy then—quite happy."

"It is my hope that the poor lass will have come to be so," said the farmer, "but if she trusts to Hargrave Manners making her his wife, she is more likely to find sorrow than happiness."

"Sorrow ! Mr. Chester," ejaculated Marion.

"Ay, lass. Even if young Manners did marry her, there'd be little chance of anything but sorrow coming of such a wedding ; but there's no likelihood of such an event as that coming about."

"No likelihood—no likelihood !" repeated poor Marion in a breathless voice.

"I do not see that there is," continued Mr. Chester. "In the letter which we have here, he says that he is in London, and that he is coming down to the village very shortly. Now when I read these words to-day I had my doubts as to there being truth in them ; so to know the rights of the matter a little more, I just stepped up to the manor-house, and made a few inquiries. Mr. Hargrave and the 'squire went up to London as we heard, but instead of thinking about coming home quickly, they have both gone to France, and are going a travelling for some months to come. Whether the young 'squire will ever return to the village at all, isn't quite certain, but it isn't likely that it will be for a year or two, even if he comes then."

Words cannot easily, cannot faithfully describe the effect that these revelations produced upon poor sorrowful Mildred. When the honest farmer told of Hargrave's absence from England, the weeping girl started up, and stared earnestly at him with an expression of terror ; when he prophecied that the absence would be long, the listener breathed heavily, and her countenance assumed a look of wild affright ; as he continued speaking, her breathing became heavy and short, and when he came to the concluding assertion, declaratory of his belief that years would elapse before Hargrave Manners returned, the eyes of the terrified maiden glistened with a look of madness, as she sprang forward—threw herself at Mr. Chester's feet—grasped his hand—clung to his arm, and exclaimed,—

"He will—he will come ; Hargrave will come soon !"

In vain did the good farmer endeavour to undeceive poor Mildred, in vain did he reveal to her, so far as he was able, the true character of the man who had betrayed her with lying promises, that were never to be fulfilled. Again and again the deluded girl repeated to herself, "He will come—he will come !" And when Mr. Chester produced another letter which he had borrowed from the old steward at the manor-house, which the squire himself had written, and when he read to Mildred the words of Hargrave's uncle, to the effect that neither himself nor his nephew were likely to return for many months, the poor girl still continued to mutter—still repeated to herself, "He will not be so cruel, he will come—he will come !" Gradually, however, the false hope seemed to die away ; gradually, yet with fearfully increasing conviction, the presentiment gained strength in Mildred's mind, that she was deceived—deserted—abandoned—ruined—betrayed ! And as the fear grew stronger, and the hope diminished—as the suspicion deepened into certainty, and the delusive dream dissolved away, a look of blank despair, an expression of unutterable woe gathered upon the countenance of her who was so haughty in her beauty, yet now so helpless in her misery. Then it was that the gipsy's words recurred to her mind, then it was that Marion, as she saw the pallor of her sister's cheek, recalled too well to memory the scene in the chamber of death, six sad long months ago. How vividly that scene presented itself to her now! And Mildred who was so haughty in her beauty then, how did she now behave in the misery of despair? No shriek escaped her lips, she did not utter exclamations of misery, nor give vent to her feelings in tears. But as the conviction deepened, as the sense of desolation increased the despair, as clearer and more clear to her became the misery of her position, a faint murmur fell from her lips, her eyes rolled to and fro until at length they became fixed on vacancy, her brain reeled, her heart ceased its quick pulsation; without a cry, without a moan, without a movement of hand or arm, she fell back upon the floor, senseless, motionless, and apparently bereft of life.

"My sister—my poor sister! She is dead—she is dead!" ejaculated Marion.

———

CHAPTER VII.

HOW PRIDE SET OUT WITH BEAUTY TO TRAVEL TOGETHER, ON A LONE ROAD, IN A DARK NIGHT.

IT was slowly, and not till a considerable period had elapsed, that Mildred Winnerley regained her consciousness. When she had recovered, Mrs. Chester proposed that she should at once retire to bed, and that nothing further should be said concerning the subject on which they had been conversing until the next day. Poor Mildred, however, was in no mood for sleep; and Mr. Chester had something more to say relative to the promised return of Hargrave Manners. After pointing out more minutely the improbability of that return taking place at an early period, the good farmer continued—

"The poor lass has done wrong, certainly," said he; "but the young 'squire is more to blame than she. We must see and write to him, letting him know that the lass has friends, and they are determined to know what his intentions are, as well as resolved to make him atone for the misery he has already caused. If writing to the young 'squire be of no use, we must let his uncle know about it, and try what can be done in that quarter. Meanwhile, you know, dame, we have children of our own, and we must not let them have a bad example before their eyes if we can help it. Besides, matters like these do not remain secrets very long; and the condition of the lass will soon be seen by all the neighbours. So to prevent there being too much talk and scandal about it, as well as to keep our own children from going astray themselves, through having seen others do so, we must contrive so that Mildred shall leave the village as soon as possible, and——"

"Oh, no! you will not do that—you will not turn my poor sister out of doors!" exclaimed Marion, throwing herself at Mr. Chester's feet. "Say not—oh, say not that you will do so!"

"Peace, lass. I have said that the poor thing must not stay here longer than can be helped. There is no time to-night for coming to any decision as to what shall be done ; but we must think to-morrow about it. I and dame will consult together, and see if we know any one to whom we can send her. It will be better for her to go anywhere than remain here."

"Yes, yes," returned poor Marion. "It must be so. Mildred will go, and her sister will go with her. We will go together ; I will be poor Milly's friend, if all others leave her ; and if the world blame my poor sister, I will comfort her, I will work for her, I will live with her, and never, never shall dear Milly have cause to say that her sister was angry with her for not having made her a confidant in her secrets, or for doing that which it had been better that she had never done. I will watch her; I will ever be her friend!"

So, to their one bed, silent and sorrowful, that night the sister's went; and far, far into the night did each lay awake, with the arms of Marion entwined round the neck of Mildred, and the head of Mildred pressed to the bosom of Marion; and as the grey morning dawned, and the light broke in gently through the ivy-mantled casement, wearied with weeping, and exhausted by mental distress, the two sisters fell asleep, to dream of the past that would never return, and of the lonely future where all seemed so dark, so drear, so wrapt in desolation and gloom.

A few days passed; and then Mr. Chester having made arrangements with a widowed sister of his, living in the vicinity of the metropolis, who promised not only to receive the two orphans into her house, but to procure for them employment in the way of needlework, Marion and Mildred were informed that when the coach passed through the village on the noon of the following day, they must hold themselves in readiness to bid adieu to the pleasant village in which so large a portion of their youthful years had been spent. Being prepared for such an announcement, they heard it with satisfaction rather than sorrow. Not but what each experienced a slight feeling of gloom at the thought of quitting a place were they had enjoyed so many happy hours; while presentiments oppressed the minds of both, that the fearful future into which they were about to plunge, was destined to be fraught with more miseries than ever yet in their young years they had known. For, still amidst her misery, still amidst her woe, Mildred Winnerley looked in her glass, and seeing that she was beautiful, ceased not to be proud.

Another day arrived, and in an hour more, the coach that was to carry the sisters to their destination, would stop at the gate. Marion was busily employed packing up the remainder of the small property; and Mildred was sitting alone in the apartment which during the last six months she had occupied, her head resting on her hand, her thoughts busied with reflections on the past, and conjecturings as to the events that were to happen. Suddenly, the door opened, and Gerrard Chester glided into the room.

Mildred did not immediately perceive the entrance of the young man; nor was she aware that any one besides herself was in the apartment until moving gently towards her, Gerrard fell on his knees, and seized her hand with a passionate clasp—

"Mildred—dear Mildred!"

The poor girl started, and endeavoured to draw away her hand.

"I have come to speak with you, before you go. I have much to say. Will you not hear me, dear Mildred?"

"I—I—it is almost time for the coach to be here, Gerrard. I and sister must be in readiness when it enters the village."

"Yes, dear Mildred, yes; but there is an hour yet, before it will be here. I have much to say that I wish you to listen to—that you must listen to."

"Not now, Gerrard—not now."

"It must be now. The time is short, and I have much to say, much to explain But come—come with me; let us both take a walk in the garden for the last time."

After expressing much reluctance, Mildred at last consented to Gerrard's request, and accompanied him into the garden. They walked together for some minutes in silence. Each wished to speak; but both felt the difficulty of giving expression to their thoughts. Turning into a shady walk, they at length arrived at a small summer-house, in which poor Mildred had been accustomed to spend much of her time; and which situated as it was at a remote portion of the garden, sufficiently secluded Gerrard and his companion from the observation of any one within the house or engaged upon the farm. Entering this retreat, Gerrard pressed Mildred to take a seat beside him; the poor girl, without uttering a word, complied. No sooner had she become seated, than applying her handkerchief to her eyes she gave vent to a spontaneous burst of tears. Gerrard pressed her hand, raised it to his lips, implored her not to weep so violently, and intimated that, as the interview could be but short, all that each had to say would have to be said without loss of time. He had scarcely finished speaking, before Mildred arose, and endeavoured to disengage her hand from his clasp.

"I must go," said she; "I must not stay here."

Gerrard Chester drew her back to her seat.

"Not yet, you must not go yet, Mildred, Listen! I have that to say to you which you must hear before we part this day. We have known one another for years, Mildred; we played together when children, we sat on the same form in the village school. Many years have passed since then, and during those years I have learned how dear you are to me,—how those who were playmates in their childhood cannot—ought not to separate when they have grown up together. I have loved you, dear Mildred—loved you as I shall never love any one else. There has been nothing that I would not have done to win a smile from you; there is nothing at the present moment which I would hesitate to do, if but requested to do it by Mildred Winnerley. I know, dear Mildred, that you are beautiful—that you are very beautiful; and I know that you are worthy of a better and a richer husband than I should make you. Still, dearest, none have loved you, none love you now, none would sacrifice so much for your dear sake, none to win this fair hand would do that which I would not hesitate to perform. You have never heard me plead as I now plead, Mildred, and yet you must have seen that my love has all been yours, notwithstanding you have refused to listen to me, notwithstanding you have always seemed most happy when I was farthest from you; still Mildred, I have continued to love you as deeply and as fondly as ever. And now—now, dearest, that love is still unchanged; let me tell you how true and strong it is; let me——"

"Not now, Gerrard—not now," said Mildred, applying her handkerchief to her eyes, and again attempted to leave the summer-house.

"Yes, now—now and in this place, dearest. Listen to me! I know all, Mildred, I know why you are about to leave us, and everything that has happened to yourself."

For a moment the poor girl gazed at the youth with a look of wild affright. Then, endeavouring to keep down a choking sob, and again turning away her face, she exclaimed in a trembling voice,—

"Have they told you? Have they let it be known so soon?"

"No one has told me, dear Mildred. Pardon me—pardon, and hear me! Last Wednesday night, dearest, when we sat at the supper-table together, I felt that something was about to happen. Never before had I seen poor father look so grave and sorrowful. I knew that something was oppressing his mind, and my heart told me that his thoughts were concerning you. I knew nothing, I had heard nothing. That you had listened to Hargrave Manners' addresses was all that had come to my knowledge, but I had a presentiment that in some way or other, my father's dejection arose out of that circumstance. When we rose up and bade each other good night, dearest, I felt still more deeply impressed with the idea of some impending sorrow being about to happen to yourself; and when we parted, and I heard my mother whisper to you that she wished you to stay in the room with them, I knew that they had some sad news to communicate. What it was I could not conjecture; in vain I endeavoured to do so. I went up to my bedroom, I closed my door, and threw myself upon the bed. Feeling no inclination to sleep, I lay for some minutes thinking over what had occurred in past years relative to myself and you. As I so lay thinking, it struck me that I heard my father making use of some harsh words. I listened, I heard your voice. There was a sound of weeping. My father was talking in an angry manner. I knew that you were the object of his anger. The thought maddened me, it made me tremble with fear and apprehension. Sobs—your sobs, dearest, fell upon my ear. I heard your sister pleading in an earnest tone, and I heard my mother using words of gentle reproof. Pardon me—forgive me, Mildred! I could not bear the anguish of knowing that you were in sorrow, without my being a aware whether or not it was in my power to console you. The staircase was dark, the door of the keeping-room was closed. I took off my shoes; I crept slowly down the stairs. My father was talking in a yet more angry tone; you were sobbing as though your poor heart was about to break. I listened, I heard every word that was spo ken. Pardon me, dear Mildred, for having done so! The perfidy of Mr. Manners—the letter—your situation—my father's resolution—the false promises —the lost note—the endeavour on your part to conceal—the reason for my father's anger—everything and all I know. Hear me, Mildred! do not attempt to go away; you must hear me. Listen! The cause of your sorrow is known to me, I know that you have given your love to another who has never loved you, I know that he has deceived—abandoned—forsaken you; I know that you listened to his lying words, and that he has brought misery upon you: of all this I have the most thorough knowledge— the most perfect information. Yet now—now at your feet, he whom you have treated with so much coolness, he who has loved you, and never been loved in return, offers to you his hand—offers to marry you—to hide your disgrace—to work for you—to support you—to defend you against the world. Everything that is past forgotten—everything that would bring torture with the remembrance, cast from memory—I offer you now and here, Mildred Winnerley, that love—that affection which hitherto you have so haughtily rejected. Tell me—tell me, dear Mildred, do you consent—do you accept the offer ?"

For a short time Mildred Winnerley preserved silence. At length, turning towards poor Gerrard, who still continued on his knees before her, and replying to him with a proud, cold, angry look, she said,—

" I thank you, Mr. Gerrard; I feel obliged to you—much obliged to you. Not till now was I fully aware of what cause I had for sorrow, nor how urgent the reasons are for my at once leaving this house. Your offer is as generous as your conduct. They who listen at doors, and learn that which does not concern them, are undoubtedly the class of people who know best how to insult those who through any misfortune become for the time friendless. If I had asked your patronage, I should then have had to thank you for your obliging proposals; not having done so, I know not in what terms to praise your conduct in having sought an opportunity like the present for showing the difference in position between a poor orphan girl and the son of a wealthy farmer. I thank you—thank you, much." ·

"Mildred!" exclaimed Gerrard Chester, "you have mistaken my meaning, you have misunderstood my words. You cannot—you do not think that I have said anything with the intention of wounding your feelings. Heaven witness that I have not! I know that I am no baronet's son—that no titles nor large estates will ever fall to my share; but I have offered to make you the wife of an honest man—of one, Mildred, who will never make a promise that he does not mean to keep, nor deceive the woman who chooses to accept his love. No dishonourable proposals have I made you, none that I fear to make to you before parents, friends and relatives. Far be it from me to wish that a single word of mine should occasion you the least sorrow, or that one sentence should escape from my lips, that in calling back the memory of the past, should be regarded by you as an accusation. For all that has gone by I forgive you, frankly forgive you. I knew that I was scarcely worthy of your love. The past forgiven and forgot, what reason is there that we should not be friends, dear Mildred, in the future? I am young and strong, I promise to be industrious, and therefore we shall never want for bread. It is possible that my parents would object to our union, it is possible that they would forbid its taking place; but much as I love and respect them, I would not hesitate to disobey their commands, if by so doing I should win the hand of her I love. Do not look so coldly at me, dear Mildred, do not turn your face away from me. Come, I will forgive you all; I will love you for ever."

"As I know not that I have wronged you in any way, Gerrard Chester, there is nothing for you to forgive; as I do not wish that this conversation should be continued, it will be as well that we both separate."

"Mildred—Mildred Winnerley—dear Mildred, will you not hear me—will you not listen to me this once?"

"I have listened long enough. Do not let this interview terminate by my having to call for assistance. Release my hand, sir, and let us part as friends."

Involuntarily, as if an electric shock had unnerved his whole frame, Gerrard Chester relaxed his grasp of Mildred's hand, while his own arm fell helpless by his side. For an instant he remained silent and motionless; then, as the haughty girl was about to pass by him, in order to leave the summer-house, he rose up, placed himself in her way, and in a deep, grave, stifled voice, said,—

"Be it so, Mildred Winnerley—proud Mildred, as I will henceforth call you. I know you to be proud, and knowing that pride works woe, I wished and still wish to save you from misery and sorrow. But your heart is cold and ambitous, Mildred; it will not let you love the farmer's son, but will rather be the tossed-away plaything of the baronet's heir. I cannot change your heart, Mildred; if I could do so, God knows that I would, in order that you should enjoy that happiness which otherwise I fear that you will never win. I shall still love you, Mildred. Proud Mildred I shall endeavour to forget, and remember only that beauteous and playful Mildred that once I gathered posies for in yonder meadow. We are about to separate now; we are about to be farther apart from one another than we have ever been since we were children. I shall not trouble you; I shall not offend your pride with my poor proposals, nor will I, without your leave, talk to you again on the subject which, though it so nearly concerns my happiness, shall never, with my permission, be allowed to cause you pain. Still, Mildred Winnerley, go where you may—go to what part of the wide world you choose, I will watch, I will follow, I will be there to protect you. Fear not that I shall trouble you. While you want me not you shall not see me, but if—if Mildred, dear Mildred!

it should ever happen in some lonely moment of sorrow you should need a friend, if in some hour of distress, you should need a comforter—a defender—a devoted being who would be ready to risk his life, or sell his happiness for you, then, at that time—at that moment—at that hour, expect again to meet with me. That time may come, Mildred Winnerley; how near it may be neither you nor I can tell. Till then, or for ever, we now bid each other farewell. God bless you, Mildred—God keep you from ever wanting such assistance from me! I hear the sound of a horn in the distance, the coach is entering the village, it will presently arrive at the gate. Come, Mildred, come."

Gerrard led the haughty beauty into the house. No word was spoken as they passed along together through the garden in which he had so often gathered flowers for her, and she had so many times sported when a child with him. They entered the house, they lingered for one moment at the door of that room in which the two sisters had been accustomed to spend their days together. Gerrard took Mildred's hand, raised it to his lips, kissed it, pressed it against his heart; then, without speaking a word, without uttering one adieu, without soliciting one promise, or venturing to express one wild passionate hope, he turned away his face, retraced his steps, and parted from her whom he had promised never to trouble again. There were more tears at that parting in the eyes of Gerrard Chester than there were in those of Mildred Winnerley; for the one was gentle in his love, while the other was haughty in her beauty.

The sisters took their places on the coach-top. Farmer Chester with his wife and daughters, kissed them, and handed to them their several presents. The villagers thronged round, and wondered why the two grand-daughters of old dame Winnerley were about to leave the village. The coachman gathered up the reins; the guard blew a merry blast with his horn; there was much weeping, much waving of hand-kerchiefs, much shaking of hands, and wiping of eyes; then, the horses threw up their heads, the wheels turned slowly round; there was a loud shout from the little urchins, and many " good byes !" from the elder folks; the dust flew, the poultry ran across the road, the maid at the " Green Dragon," looked out round the curtain, the old pike-man pushed open the gate ; and so amidst noise, and bustle, and weeping, and merriment, Mildred and Marion bade farewell to the village where their happy days of childhood had glided so pleasantly by. Though so many were around the coach, to bid the sisters farewell, Gerrard Chester was not among the throng; Gerrard Chester dared not to intrude himself there! He had given his promise, he had pledged himself not to trouble proud Mildred again. When, however, the sisters had fairly taken their seats, the guard gave into the hand of Mildred a nosegay which he said that he had been entrusted with to deliver to her. Was Mildred puzzled to know by whose hands those flowers had been gathered, or who had sent them to her? No, full well she knew whose gift they were, and so knowing, she placed them carelessly by her side.

And then, as the coach rolled onward, and Marion could no longer discern the spire of the old church, a gloom came over her spirits, and involuntarily the thought occurred to her, that already she and her much-loved sister had commenced their journey upon the lone road and through the long, dark night. Then looking up, poor Marion saw that the sun had become shrouded, and that in the distance, hastening forwards to meet them, were black clouds, burdened with thunder, and laden with rain.

Gentleness, pride and beauty on the coach; the dark night, the stormy sky,—and the louring cloud afar in the distance! What was to be the destiny of the journey?

CHAPTER VIII.

HOW MR. JOHN JACOB SMAGS DESCENDED FROM HIGH LIFE, INTO A VERY LOW POSITION; AND HOW THE SECOND SIX MONTHS CAME TO AN END.

GOOD Mr. Chester having felt the necessity of dismissing poor Mildred from the shelter of his roof, had exerted himself to the utmost in finding out some acquaintance to whose care the erring girl might be committed, and who would not only be willing to shelter her for a while; but feel interested in putting her in the way of earning her own livelihood. Both Mildred and her sister had received every instruction from their grandmother in the use of the needle, and they could not only stitch and sew, and knit, and make dresses, but they were also able to embroider, and to do various other kinds of fancy-work with neatness and dexterity. Now the Chesters had a relative, living in the outskirts of the metropolis, who was a widow, and who had once in her life been in business as a milliner somewhere in the great city of London. An application to Mrs. Cheriton—for such was the good woman's name—resulted in an agreement on her part, not only to receive the two sisters at once into her house, but to procure for them immediate employment if she found them to be skilful and industriously disposed. Such a proposal, and from an individual whose character Mr. Chester had good reason to appreciate, was considered by the honest farmer, as the most fortunate occurrence which, circumstanced as the two sisters were, could possibly happen. The arrangements were readily completed, the journey was commenced.

Don't you wish, dear reader, that the world still had stage-coaches to journey by? Would you not willingly have a single one of the real, old, genuine sort replaced upon every road in the kingdom? Railways are very well for those who hate to look at green fields, or who see no pleasure in journeying through a beautiful country. A train is certainly a well-adapted affair for those to travel in who, having become wearied with life, wish to dispel their *ennui* by trying the exhilarating effect of falling through a bridge into twenty feet of water, or a roll down a bank into ten feet of mud. Then, there is the chance of getting rid of a leg on the journey, which is a comfortable consideration to a person afflicted with the gout; and, moreover, there is the probability of having the two sides of your head jammed together by coming in collision with a coal-truck; not that such an accident is in any way disagreeable, since it is likely to produce the very good effect of radically curing the head-ache. A railway carriage is particularly well suited to those who are fond of inhaling smoke, or sniffing the odour of burnt oil, or who have any other pleasant predilections in that way; but give us, say we, the inside of a stage-coach; let us travel by starlight, and let us have some pleasant, bright-eyed, slender-waisted companion for our fellow traveller on the same seat. Then, with the said bright eyes twinkling upon us through the gloom; with the said slender waist heaving within our clasp, and the prospect of having our shoulder converted into a pillow for the convenience of some sleeping beauty, let us roll on slowly, and a fig for all the railways that have ever been laid down. No maxim is more true than that a person who is fond of railway travelling must be, an necessarily is, an unsociable, sour-tempered, disagreeable, dull, priggish, gooseberry-tarted sort of being; one who would rather pray for you than do you an act of kindness, and who would shudder with very horror if her most gracious majesty were to publish a proclamation to the effect that a kiss should always accompany change for a sovereign, and that every man found without a sweetheart should have fourteen days at the nearest treadmill. We have heard of many pleasant acquaintances having been made in a stage-coach, but who has ever heard of a man winning a wife in a second-class carriage, we should like to know?

Then there is something handsome and spirit-cheering about a four-in-hand. There is the jolly old gentleman on the box, with his red nose, and his sprig of lavender in his mouth, ready at all times to tell you whose great house you are passing, or what little village you are getting into; and then again there is the pleasant guard, who speaks so blandly and looks so kind, that you feel him to be conferring a perfect favour upon you when he holds out his hand for half-a-crown. Further more, there are the nice sleek-skinned, well-conditioned horses, with real legs and proper bones and muscles, looking very different in appearance to the queer things you see tearing along the railroads which though they seem to be great warm-blooded animals of some kind, have neither legs, eyes, nor arms—nothing but a large mouth, which is always wanting to be fed, and a long nose which they do nothing but blow from one end of the journey to the other. Then again, there is something pleasant and intelligible in the neigh of an honest Dobbin; but who on earth can bear the screech of a high-pressure engine, without having their teeth remain on edge for a week afterwards, and a pain in their ears for a full month to come?

Well, it was a real old-fashioned, reputable stage-coach, that on which Mildred and Marion set out for their journey; and there was a real coachman on the box before them, and a real guard sitting by their side. Pleasant was the country through which they had to journey, for who is there that would dare speak otherwise of the scenery along the old south-western road? Every now and then the coach would ascend some gentle eminence, and the sisters saw huge chalk-hills skirting the horizon on one side of them, and patches of woodland diminishing away into large tracts of brown heath on the opposite side. Then driving down into some valley, they entered a neat village full of pretty cottages, with its church hidden among the trees, and its noisy children gambolling around the old well. Onward and onward, up the steep hill, down into the deep valley, over the open country, along the wooded road; through the cool air, surrounded by the scent of leafy hedge-rows, fragrant with the falling shower; so travelled the fair girl and the haughty beauty, towards their destination and their destiny.

Now it had so happened that in passing through the next town after Mildred and Marian had taken their seats, the top of the coach received another addition in the person of a little, squat, red-faced, light visaged man, who. seeming to possess a considerable share of humour about him, gave evidence also to having in his possession a very respectable stock of impudence and self-conceit. His hair was brushed back from the middle of his forehead, and heaped up on the top of his head, just as the hair of persons who think that they have more brains to show than have their fellow-folks always is; his cheeks were pursed out, as if their owner had contrived to excavate two commodious receptacles for impudence on the outer side of his gums; his chin was double; he wore

a very large ornamental pin in his cravat, the said pin of course being gold ,if judged only by the largeness of its size ! The owner of the pin was also the owner of a walking-stick with a tassel to it, and a heavy watch-chain, to which three large seals were attached and two watch keys, to make up for the absence of a watch. The traveller's hat was placed on one side of his head, and the corner of a red handkerchief peeped out from beneath. He wore very loose trousers, very clumsy boots, seemed to hold gloves in profound contempt, cultivated a small garden at the top of each finger-nail, and had a pair of very large salmon-coloured hands, the right one of which had two of its fingers ornamented with what appeared to be diamond rings of immense value, the diamond in each being so large that the jeweller had thought fit to place a piece of white tinsel behind it, so that no one should mistake it for glass.

The sisters made room for their new acquaintance, by taking their cloaks and baskets from off the seat. After calling for a glass of brandy-and-water, drinking half, and proffering the other half to the guard, the owner of the diamond ring and the watch-seals contrived to shake himself down into the place allotted for him; then, having pulled up his shirt-collar and stuck a cigar into one corner of his mouth, there was nothing left for him to do but to stare around and make friends with his fellow travellers.

Mildred and Marion were alone at the back of the coach with their new acquaintance, the guard having taken his seat on the box along with the Jehu, in order to indulge in some pleasant chat. It was not long before the little red-faced man took occasion to observe to the sisters that the day was uncommonly fine, qualifying the assertion, however, by remarking that there were some uncommonly large clouds away in the distance. Marion replied to these observations with expressions of courteous assent; but Mildred had turned away her face from the first moment of the little gentleman having taken his seat, and now sat with her head bent down and her features concealed from view. Incited by a laudable curiosity to know what his fellow traveller was like, the proprietor of the rings poked his nose under Mildred's bonnet, and by so doing obtained a slight view of her countenance. Satisfied that the beauty of his companion fully warranted his paying his attentions to her, he forthwith made bold to lay his fingers upon her hand in a familiar manner.

"Come now, I don't want to quarrel," said he, as Mildred hastily withdrew her hand. "I'm friends with you, and you'll be friends with me. My name's John Jacob Smags, Jacob they usually call me, and that's what you are to call me, too, my dear. Jacob's a nice name—isn't it? What's your name, my honeysuckle?"

Mildred was silent, feeling greatly annoyed by the conduct of her far from agreeable companion.

"Sad, that," continued the little gentleman; "you've got the toothache, I know you have. Allow me to look at the tooth. I'm the possessor of a secret for the cure of that distressing pain. I purchased it while out in India, of a black man. My servant comes in and says,—'There's one of the natives at the castle-gate, who wants to speak with you, sir.'—'Show him into the hall," said I,—of course I kept him waiting some time, and then I went down to see about his business. I saw he was a low feller at once. 'What do you want here, feller?' said I; remarking at the time to Lord Rowstenstorn, who was knocking about there just then, that there was only one way of dealing with all low fellers, which is, just to let them see that you know what they are at once. 'What do you want here, feller?' said I. 'Begging your pardon,' said he, 'I've come to sell you a cure for the toothache, sir, the one I cured the Great Mogul with just before he died.' I and the Mogul, you see, had been a sort of chums together, and the old chap had told me all about how he had his toothache cured by a native who came to the palace, and how he had wanted to purchase the secret but could'nt afford it at the time. So, remembering that, I said,—'What do you want for your secret, you black vagabond?'—Lord bless you! I spoke just like that, not a bit more civil, I assure you. 'Three thousand pounds,' said the black feller, 'that is what it must go for.' Well, you see, I hadn't three thousand pounds of hard cash in the house at the time; and them natives never will take bank notes. So I told him to call again the next day; and after I'd got the secret from him I tossed the money into his hand, and told him if he stayed in the castle a moment longer I'd kick him down the stairs. I've had fifteen thousand pounds down offered me for that secret, and I won't sell. It's no use their getting me to their dinners, and trying it on in that way. Georgey—the Regent I mean, came that dodge a little while ago; but it would'nt take you know—it would'nt take. Georgey is very sharp though, and does some queer things about the palace. Fond of a lark too. Only think, put his father's crown on my head, last time I gave him a call. Old man himself came in and saw it on. Said I looked well in it. Asked me what I thought of it. Told him it didn't look quite the thing—wanted the ball and cross taken away from the top of it, and a sort of a spire put. Old fellow slapped me on the back, and said he'd tell the parliament he must have it done. Know much of high life, my dear—not much, I suppose? Fine fun in high life—call anybody any names you please when you've got the wine before you. Plenty of fine women easy to be got too. Women uncommonly fond of me. Don't know how it is, and they don't know how it is—can't help themselves, that's it. Take a sort of liking to me yourself, my dear, I dare say. Well, we shall be good friends, presently. Take a lemon-drop, my love, real good sort these, given me by Lady Hatherly last time I dropped in to see about those estates she's trying to outbid me for. Take one, my pretty dear, two if you like, got plenty more. Lady Hatherly will give me as many as I like to ask for, anything to keep my good will. Don't be afraid of them. I keep them in paper, because they taste of the tin, if you carry them in a canister."

Mr. Smags pressed Mildred to accept a few of the drops, and ventured so far as to place the paper containing them in her lap. Indignant and offended, the haughty girl with a single sweep of the hand tossed them over into the road.

"Never mind, my dear, you don't like them, I see. Very well, their loss is not worth speaking about. Should have thrown them away myself. Throw away lots of them sort of things—oceans of them I may say. Haven't any thing else to offer you just now, unless you wouldn't mind a piece of this cheese. Very superior cheese, I assure you. The one from which it was cut, given by my old friend Napoleon to the Duke of Wellington. Called at Strathfieldsaye yesterday—the duke just sat down to luncheon, Couldn't stay, so he asked me if I'd take a bit of the cheese with me, just to eat going along. Allow me to offer you a piece of the duke's cheese."

"I really wish and beg, sir," said Mildred, refusing the proffered article, "that you'd dispose of what you have, to your own convenience, without inconveniencing those with whom you happen to be travelling."

"Inconvenience, my dear. Ah, I'd forgot. Toothache—cheese bad for the toothache, so it is. Very inconsiderate of me to offer it. Wish I had my cure for the toothache here. Know what the pain is; have had it myself. There's a draught on the top of this coach. See, here, my love, this neckerchief is very large and warm. It was given to me by Blucher when he was over here, or rather he and I chopped for it. One cold morning, you see, the general had to be present at a review. Biting cold wind that morning, he felt it. Saw me, I had a rough woollen comforter on, that the Countess of Norwich had given me. Blucher called me aside, 'Nice warm wrapper for the neck, that,' said he. 'Very warm,' I replied. 'The colour hardly becomes your complexion, I think,' said he, 'I have a neckerchief on which I think would suit you better.' Of course I saw what he was driving at. So I wanted to make him a present of the comforter, but he would give me something in exchange, and he gave me this. Allow me to put it round your neck."

"I thank you, sir," said Mildred, moving aside. "I do not feel cold, and when I do, I shall put on my cloak."

"Yes, pretty cloak—very pretty cloak. Pretty hands to handle it with too. Hands are very great points in beauty ; but fingers don't do without rings—diamond rings of course. It's a rule with me to set all fellers down for low fellers, who come anything under diamonds. My dear, I think we are getting very good friends—uncommon good friends, I may say. You'll excuse me, I know, for mentioning it, but should you feel sleepy by-and-by, you can rest yourself against my shoulder, and I'll see to it that you don't fall off the coach. Not used to travelling much, I suppose, my dear? nothing like being friendly while on the road. Can't say what such friendship may result in. Delicate waist—very delicate waist, yours, my love. I'm Jacob ; there's no harm in me —no harm in Jacob Smags."

So saying, Mr. Smags very gently attempted to place his arm round Mildred's waist, but met with a repulse in the way of a look of flashing indignation, that for the moment completely awed the eater of the duke's cheese, and the friend of the Prince Regent.

"If you will not conduct yourself properly, sir, I shall be under the necessity of calling to the coachman to stop," said Mildred. "There is certainly room enough upon the seat both for myself and you. Perhaps you will oblige me by keeping your distance."

"Certainly, my sugar-mouth. You're struck by me, I see; the girls always are. Jacob Smags was a favourite among them from when he was first a boy, always was fond of having a lark with them. Last time Honourable Miss Delamore asked me to accompany her to the marchioness's ball, said yes, and promised to meet her at the corner of the street. Did so. Got jolly drunk first, led her into the room, danced with her four times, swore I would'nt let her go, told her I'd fight for her, pulled off my coat, and offered to fight any one in the room. Life, that, my dear—touch of high life. Honourable Miss Delamore saw she had a man of spirit with her. You should see high-life, my love; its very improving, rubs you down as it were, and knocks away the rough edges. May be able to give you an introduction, I'm Jacob Smags—John Jacob Smags, as I always write it. Three names look well, don't they? Got three names yourself, my dear, eh? You're going to town, I suppose ; that's where I'm going. Must go to the bank and give a blowing-up to those scoundrels. Sent up some notes to them two days ago, and they said they could'nt cash them for want of sufficient hard cash. Jacob Smags won't stand that—do you think he will, my dear? How do you like the pattern of these trowsers— pretty isn't it? Exactly the same sort as the chancellor had on a few days ago. They looked well on him ; so I asked him just to cut me out a small piece from the inside of the waistband that I might give the pattern to my tailor. Chancellor a very obliging man, my dear, rose up instantly, unbuttoned his trowsers, and cut me off the piece with a gold handled knife—real gold, I assure you. Chancellor keeps nothing about him that isn't gold—knives and forks, chairs and tables, mahogany drawers and everything, all gold, my love. Permit me to wet my handkerchief, and wipe a small piece of black off your nose. Countess of Norwich very fond of my wiping her nose for her."

"I really cannot bear your impertinence any longer, sir," said Mildred, rising up, with the intention of calling to the coachman. "Were there any gentleman on this part of the coach, I am sure that you would not dare to be so insulting."

"Do not speak to him, dear sister," said Marion. "See, we are approaching a town in which, I dare say, the coach will stop. We will then change our places."

A few minutes passed, and then the coach rolled into the dull, old-fashioned, Sunday-like city of Winchester. Mildred having never before seen a cathedral, wondered at the size of the church, and thought that it would have looked much better if it had been surmounted by a steeple, instead of having a mere square and squat tower, looking as if some giant had sat down upon the top of it, and crushed it with his weight. As the coach had no sooner drawn up to the door of the inn than Mr. Smags dismounted from his perch, and as his seat was immediately taken by a middle-aged woman with a large bundle, the sisters thought that they were now secured from the troublesome attentions of their communicative acquaintance for the rest of the journey. Indeed, as the time drew near for the coach to start on the next stage, and no Mr. Smags made his appearance, they felicitated themselves in the thought that he would be left behind Just, however, as Marion was intimating this hope to her sister, the friend of the Prince Regent appeared, standing by the hind-wheel on the off-side of the coach, with two large tumblers full of brandy-and water in his hand.

"Like a drop of warm-with, I dare say, my dears. Real cogniac this ; just the same sort as I have got in stock at home. I told the rascals to put in plenty of sugar, because 'sweets to the sweet,' you know—Shakspere—not me. Try it my darling, just for love of me—for love of Jacob Smags."

So saying, Mr. Smags mounted upon the hind-wheel of the coach and endeavoured to force upon Mildred the acceptance of one of the tumblers, he having placed the other in the road beside the coach. At first Mildred simply refused, and made a movement towards the other end of the seat, Mr. Smags, however, seized her left hand, and holding her in that position, raised the tumbler to her lips. Instantly the watchful girl uplifted her other hand, and with one quick sweep of her arm dashed the glass and its contents over the head of the unfortunate Jacob, who immediately jumping backward off the wheel had the misfortune to come down with a plump upon the other tumbler, thereby not only communicating a disagreeable dampness to his nether garments, but receiving sundry small pieces of sharp glass into one of the most sensitive parts of his animal frame. Now this was very provoking to Mr. Smags, though it elicited much laughter from the lookers-on. The poor man having made his way into the inn, and having succeeded in extracting the before-mentioned pieces of glass, was next called upon to pay for the tumblers. To this Mr. Smags demurred, alleging that as he had sustained injuries from the glass, it was only fair that the said glasses should sustain injury from him. The landlord of the inn, however, having omitted to study moral philosophy in his younger years, could not perceive the ethical strength of this argument, and insisted upon being paid for his broken tumblers, without any allowance being made for the damaged person of Mr. Smags. As the horn was sounding, and the coach had began to move, there was no time for disputation ; so reluctantly putting down the sum required of him, Mr. Smags bolted out of the inn, and scrambled up that side of the coach which was farthest from where Mildred Winnerley sat.

Once more the coach rolled pleasantly along the road; it had not proceeded far, how-ever, before there was a cry of "Stop!—hillo there!—stop!" from some one at a short distance behind. The coachman drew up the reins, the guard looked round to see what was the matter, and in a few seconds the waiter at the inn which they had just left came up to the side of the coach, and in a breathless voice, exclaimed—

"Gent as broke the glasses has given two bad shillings."

"I!" ejaculated Mr. Smags.

"Yes, sir, you sir; nobody else, sir. Here they are; rig'lar Brummagims, made out of stolen pots."

"Indeed!" returned Mr. Smags, "I hope you don't suspect me of having stolen the pots they were made from. What a provoking occurrence, ladies! Here, waiter—here are two more in the place of them."

The man took the money, and was about to depart. Hastily turning round, however, he cried out—

"One of these is bad. How many more have you got of the sort, sir? See there, ladies,—I've bit a hole clean through it."

"That's those fellows at the bank!" exclaimed Mr. Smags. "They never can be trusted to give good silver, and they haven't a thought of the inconvenience they put people to. I shall represent the circumstance together with their conduct to the legislature. You haven't change for a sovereign—have you, waiter?"

The waiter replied that he had not.

"How very provoking. I wish Lord Stonners were here, that I might borrow a little loose silver of him. Ladies, you could'nt oblige me with the loan of a shilling—could you, any of you?"

"I think I can, sir," said the middle-aged lady, who had lately taken her seat.

"Thank you, my dear lady. Here is the shilling, feller. What do you want more?"

The waiter took the money, and made an insinuation to the effect that he had his doubts about Mr. Smags being a gentleman, or only one of the swell-mob out on a holi-day. Mr. Smags, having a natural abhorrence to conversing with low people, made no reply. When, however, the coach was again in motion, and the waiter was out of hearing, Mr. Smags observed—

"Demm'd insolence, that, for low fellers to bring you back bad money. Coachman wanted to be off, and there was no time to spare, or I should have given the vagabond a few smart cuts with this stick. There's only one way of treating such low scoundrels, and Jacob Smags knows what that way is."

Some miles were passed over, and Mr. Smags had refrained from saying a word to Mildred, since the affair of the brandy-and-water. Finding, however, that the woman, who had seated herself beside him at the commencement of the stage, was without a male companion, the friend of the Prince Regent thought fit to communicate to her that his name was John Jacob Smags, that he was fond of the ladies, and that the ladies in return manifested always an extreme partiality for him. Not content with affording his fellow-traveller this important and instructive information, Mr. Smags proceeded to demonstrate to her his qualifications for being a favourite of the fair sex, by offering to adjust her bonnet for her, and by placing a pin where he considered it to be wanted at the back of her dress. These officious attentions were at first received with words of thanks; but it was not long before the good woman discovered that she had a very troublesome acquaintance by her side. Mr. Smags at length, availing himself of an opportunity to slip his arm under her cloak, clasped her round the waist, but was immediately informed that his services of that description were not at all required, by having his arm pushed away in a very determined manner. Then Mr. Smags insisted upon sociality, and asserted that he and his companion should shake hands, after which he declared that he had fallen a victim to beauty, and must necessarily be recompenced with a kiss. But just as the amiable man was about to commit an assault upon the lips of his fair companion, the coach came to the end of another stage, and the woman started up to look about her and examine the faces of the people who were gathered around the inn. In a few seconds, a man came up to the side of the coach, and, handing a parcel to the lady-love of Mr. Smags, entered immediately into conversation with her. Mr. Smags seeing, therefore, that his company was not wanted for the time being, prudently dismounted and sought consolation in the inn.

Now it so happened that the woman who had been subjected to the impertinent civilities of Mr. Smags was journeying to London, and had agreed to meet her husband at the place where the coach had now stopped, in order that he should accompany her the rest of the journey.

"Brown," said the good woman, "I wish you'd take your seat beside me before the man who was sitting here just now returns. He has been making himself very disagreeable, and I have been wishing for you here, to talk to him."

"Making himself disagreeable—has he? Let me catch him at any tricks of the kind, and I'll give him a taste of the Yorkshireman. As for sitting at the back of the coach, you know, I never can do that, my dear. Keep your place, and I will go and take mine in front. If the disagreeable fellow should trouble you again, I'll have my eye upon him, and I'll let him know that Mr. Brown's on the coach."

This arrangement being made, Mrs. Brown folded her cloak about her, while her husband proceeded to take his place in front of the vehicle. The horn was again blown. Mr. Smags mounted into his former position, and amidst the shades of evening the coach rolled on its way.

Lowering clouds had long promised a shower, and scarcely had the travellers proceeded another mile along the road, before the rain pelted upon them with full force. Mrs. Brown put up the umbrella, and Mr. Smags finding the storm to be inconvenient, resolved to partake of the shelter afforded by that useful article. So, not having remarked that the man whom he had seen in conversation with his fair neighbour had taken a place upon the coach, and feeling inclined to renew his attentions, he insinuated his heard under the umbrella and observed,—

"Nice, this—very pleasant indeed. Fine large umbrella and fine face beneath it. I may say, umbrella courtship. Comfortable, very. Between ourselves though, that old feller who was talking to you—husband, I suppose? Disagreeable man, I should say. All the better to get rid of him so soon. Treat you well—eh?"

"Certainly, sir," replied Mrs. Brown.

"Yes, I dare say. Couldn't do otherwise with such a beauty as you. Very jealous though, no doubt. Wouldn't like to see us so comfortable as we are now. It's very nice 'pon my word. There are times when husbands are not wanted, my dear; not that I should be afraid of yours if he were here. By-the-bye I don't think I had that kiss you promised me. Always pay debts, you know. Allow me to help myself to the amount."

Now be it known to you, reader, that from the first moment of Mr. Smags having taken his seat, the eyes of Mr. Brown had been fixed upon him with a steady and observing gaze. Whether every word that Jacob Smags uttered, met the ear of Mr. Brown it is impossible to say, for the rain was beating down fast, and the coach was rolling over the road with rapidity. Not one action of Mr. Smags, however, escaped the glance of the watchful husband; and then, when the gallant Jacob laid the claim to the kiss—when he drew Mrs. Brown towards him to obtain from her the desired salute, and just as he was stretching forth his head to bring lip in contact with lip, Mr. Brown sprung upon the roof of the coach, crawled slowly towards his destined victim, and with a grasp such as only a Yorkshireman has the power to give, seized the unfortunate friend of the Prince Regent by the back of the neck. In vain Mr. Smags endeavoured to cry out; in vain he attempted to free himself from the clutch of the angry husband. Without saying a word, the Yorkshireman, still retaining his grasp, glided down between the two seats, quietly lifted up the astonished Jacob, and then without further ado, swung that unfortunate man over the back of the coach and deposited him with a plump upon the muddy road. It so happened that Mr. Smags had paid his fare, so—whether aware of the loss of his passenger or not, it is impossible to say—the coachman drove on, and Mr. Smags bellowed loudly but in vain.

Though Mildred and Marion were glad that they had got rid of their troublesome companion, they were sorry that the Yorkshireman had been so vindictive in his revenge. But leaving Mr. Smags to seek comfort as he could, the sisters found that it was expedient for them to do their best in shielding themselves from the inclemency of the weather. The wind was whistling wildly over the fields, the rain beat in torrents against the sides of the coach. The night was becoming cold as well as wet, and there were yet many miles of ground to pass over before the end of the journey was attained. The sisters placed themselves close to one another, drew their cloaks closely around them, and endeavoured to keep themselves awake by talking about the various events that had already occurred on the journey.

It was night when the coach drove into the village of Bagshot, where preparations were made for changing horses. Almost frozen with cold, and with their cloaks wet through, the poor girls were glad to dismount and place themselves before the fire in the large room of the inn. Some warm drink was procured, and a hurried supper was made, out of the various refreshments which the Chesters had given to the young travellers at parting. Willingly would poor Marion have paid a treble fare, willingly would she have spent one half of the small sum which she had in her purse, could she have procured an inside place in the coach for her sister; but the coach was full, and those who had warm and dry seats, were little inclined to change them for the coach-top, with the pelting rain, the biting wind, and the chill dark night. And oh! as poor Marion sat in the room of the inn, hearing the rain beating against the windows, the wind rumbling in the huge chimney, the sign-board creaking as it swayed to and fro, the stamping of heavy feet as one individual after another entered the house from the

the stamping of heavy feet as one individual after another entered the house from the wet roadway, how did she look back upon the pleasant room, the warm fire, and the curtained bed in that old house, where night after night, for many months past, she had retired to rest, only to meet again, in the morning, the kind friends whom she was destind perhaps never again to see! Flung upon the wide world like a plant thrown upon the waters, to reach some shore where the lot may be to flourish or to die; sent forth to engage in life's stormy struggle, like a frail vessel launched on some tempestuous sea—separated from the friends of youth and the home of childhood, to seek misery or joy, amid strange faces and unsympathising hearts:—such was the present situation of the two sisters, as they sat together at midnight in the inn. Though the fire burned brightly, and the logs crackled well, it was yet a cold hearth and a cheerless fire to Mildred and to

Marion. They spoke not to each other, for each had too much to say. And Marion fixed her gaze upon the glowing flame, endeavouring to trace pleasant scenes and friendly faces in the ruddy embers; and as she was so engaged, a bright cinder shot forth from the fire, and fell at the foot of her sister. Mildred pushed the cinder back upon the hearth; but as she did so, it was immediately picked up by the maid-servant, who, looking at it for a single moment, ejaculated—

"Heaven save us, my lady : it's a coffin, that it is !"

And as the girl made the announcement, a cold chill crept over poor Marion. She turned her eyes towards her sister, looked at her with a deep sorrowful gaze, remembered that the night was dark, while the road was lonely, and raising her handkerchief to her eyes, she burst into tears.

"What is it which causes you to weep, dear sister ?" inquired Mildred.

"Nothing, dear, nothing : only a feeling."

"You feel cold and damp—so do I, Mar ; but we must endeavour to wrap ourselves up as well as we can, and not think of it."

Had it been merely the chillness of the weather which Marion felt, she would not have wept because of that. Little could her proud, beautiful sister understand the feelings or comprehend the anguish of that poor, trembling heart, which was then beating so near her own ; for all its throbbings were for her, all its agony, its sadness, and its woe were concentrated in the thought of her. Marion would have laid down her own life to have secured the future happiness of her sister ; but that sister, in the haughtiness of her thoughts, failed to comprehend the depth of the love of that gentle being by whom she was beloved.

The horses had been changed, the coachman had finished his pipe, the lights in the lamps had been trimmed, the guard was ready to take his seat, and the time of starting had arrived. The sisters arose, and wrapping their cloaks around them, took their way out to face the cold and stormy night.

Assisted by the guard, Marion regained her former position on the coach. Mildred was about to mount also, when her right hand was suddenly seized, and she felt herself drawn across the road in the grasp of a stranger.

"Help !" shrieked the poor girl.

"Silence !—do you not know me ?" said the individual by whom she had been seized.

Mildred looked. The light from the lamp on the off-side of the coach fell upon the face of the interrogator ; and, glancing at that face, the terrified girl recognised the countenance of the old gipsy.

"Six months are gone," said the old woman, "and I have met you, my beauty, to tell you your fortune now. It is still the same : the lines on your white hand have the same reading—' Pride, misery, and death !' There is one word more, but that I will read to you when we meet again."

So saying, the gipsy released Mildred's hand, and, with a look of hideous merriment, suddenly darted aside, and disappeared in the shade cast by a clump of trees which overshadowed the road. In that shade, standing there in the gloom, Mildred fancied that she could discern the form of Pharold, the gipsy chief.

And now Mildred resumed her seat beside her sister. The guard again blew some merry notes with his horn, the coachman cracked his whip, the wheels turned swiftly round; and the travellers were once more on their journey along the dark and lone road.

When the sisters arrived at their destination, they found Mrs. Cheriton in waiting to receive them. On the road they had both puzzled themselves to decide what sort of a person they should find Mrs. Cheriton to be; wondering whether she was a thin faced, meagre person with a sharp nose and chin to correspond, or whether she was a stout blowsy-looking person, with a pompous demeanour, and a pumpkin of a face. Neither of these portraits turned out to be correct; for it was Mrs. Cheriton who inquired for the two young women from Roseham; it was Mrs. Cheriton who caught Mildred and Marion by the hand as they dismounted from the coach; it was Mrs. Cheriton who said how glad she was to see any acquaintances of her dear Sally Chester; and it was Mrs. Cheriton who appeared to Mildred and Marion as a rosy-faced, plump little woman, with a kind glistening countenance, a pair of very twinkling eyes, a clear musical voice, and the largest quantity of good-nature apparent in her demeanour that can be said with certainty to have been possessed by any woman since the days of that much maligned lady, Mrs. Eve.

"So you have come to see me, and stay with me awhile, my dear children?" said the little woman. "Well, Sally Chester has written to me all about it, and I am very sorry that things have gone with you as they have; but it never does to grieve about that which has gone by, nor fret about that which we cannot alter. As it is, my dears, it must be made the best of, and were it otherwise we should perhaps be able to make it better. Poor Mr. Cheriton whilst he was alive used to read books about philosophy. I am sure I don't know what sort of philosophy it was, for the poor dear man put himself out of the world at lest, because the world wouldn't agree with him. It was very foolish of him, and I cried for days after days about it; for where was the philosophy of doing such a thing as that? The world never did agree with him, but that was no reason why he should not have agreed with the world. Poor, poor Samuel! he was very rash, but very good. We won't talk any more just now about such distressing affairs, my dears. Come, I have a nice breakfast waiting for you, and a nice large fire, and everything else to make you comfortable. I'm an odd creature, my dears, and I dare say you'll find me so. Poor Samuel was always of that opinion, dear man! I don't know whether he believed that or his philosophy the most. You see, dears, I can't help thinking about him now and then, though it always causes me to cry. I hope he's happy new, notwithstanding that Dr. Dismal, our clergyman, says he doubts it very much, because poor Samuel was so rash in not coming to terms with the world. It's very hard for one to believe what Dr. Dismal says; and I don't, because I think his religion may be no better than my poor Samuel's philosopy, which I'm sure was never very good. For all that, you would have liked to know my poor Samuel."

Mildred replied that she should have so liked, but poor Samuel being out of the way at present, Mildred thought that she should like her breakfast so well that it would probably make up for his absence. So without further ado, the two sisters were invited to commence the meal at once, not even waiting for Mrs. Cheriton to untie her bonnet. And then when breakfast was finished, the good woman insisted upon her visitors taking a few hours nap to refresh them after the fatigue of the journey; and when they awoke there was dinner and tea ready together, with a nice bright fire burning in a comfortable little parlour, the kettle hissing on the hob, a pair of very alderman-like tabby cats reposing upon the hearth-rug, and Mrs. Cheriton seated beside the table engaged in writing a letter to inform her dear Sally Chester that the young women had arrived in safety; and that the memory of poor dear Samuel was still sacred to her whom he had in his philosophy left behind. So, first there was a short stroll in the garden, and then a look at the birds, and then a renewed attack upon the eatables. Mrs. Cheriton had a thousand inquiries to make about her dear school-fellow, Sally Chester, and a thousand kind words to say concerning Marion and her sister. By-and-bye the candles were lit, and Mrs. Cheriton had two or three of her friends drop in to see her, to whom, of course, she introduced the two orphans. There was a pretty dark-eyed woman from over the way, who could sing songs and laugh as merrily as Mrs. Cheriton herself. Then there was the dark-eyed lady's lord, and the dark-eyed lady's brother. And certainly it was very strange that Mrs. Cheriton should happen to be a widow, and the aforesaid lady's brother a widower. Still more strange was it, as Mrs. Cheriton observed, that the gentleman first referred to should have eyes exactly resembling those of poor, dear Samuel. Such a coincidence was not to be overlooked. And the dark-eyed lady said that nobody had ever resembled Mr. Cheriton more than did her brother Joe; and the dark-eyed lady's husband declared that brother Joe was by some strange freak of nature possessed of all the late lamented Mr. Cheriton's ideas; an assertion which, if true, was certainly very extraordinary, inasmuch as brother Joe's round, plumb-pudding face, did not by any means seem like that of a philosopher. However, induced no doubt to believe that he was Mr. Cheriton himself, brother Joe certainly did draw his chair very near to that occupied by the merry widow, and certainly did use expressions which only a suspicion of his identity with the late lamented could have justified him at using. Why it was that brother Joe, happening to wish for a pipe, should have been furnished with one from the widow's closet, and how it was that the widow and brother Joe happened altogether to be on such good terms of friendship, matters not to the present story. Perhaps it may reasonably be supposed that brother Joe had made a slight hole in the widow's heart, and without hazarding an improbability, it may be conjectured that when brother Joe was present, poor dear Samuel was rather a long way off, from being remembered. Such may have been the case, and appearances seemed to favour the supposition. At any rate, however, Mrs. Cherton had worn widow's weeds somewhat more than a twelvemonth, having demeaned herself also as widows should do during that space of time. What right had the ghost of any Samuel, or of Samuel Cheriton in particular, to expect or to desire more?

So the winter passed on, and the sisters having had work obtained for them, plied their needles industriously, and remunerated Mrs. Cheriton for her kindness. The more industrious of the two was Marion. As for Mildred, whether it was that she thought too much on the past, or suffered too much from silent grief whether it was that she fed upon her sorrows, nursed her beauty's haughtiness—the daily task, though performed, was gone through with reluctance, and the gay heart which had once delighted in merriment, now grew a grave, torpid, inpenetrable thing. Sometimes, as the white fingers worked slowly, so the compressed lips might be seen moving to noiseless mutterings; and sometimes as the fair hand was about to perform some delicate manipulation, it would suddenly become paralysed, while the bright dark eyes would flash with a strange unintelligible gleam. But at times Marion would turn her face towards her sister to see if she were happy, ever wishing her to be so, and ever seeing that she was not; for when the gentle sister thus did look, she beheld not the gay sportive companion of her childhood, she saw a pale and silent form, proud-seeming in the pallor of beauty, and darkly-brooding in the silence of a haughty mind. How often did the eyes of Marion swell with tears as she gazed upon that sister s downcast countenance, and how often as she gazed in the dusk of evening did her boding brain cause her to descry frightful phantoms standing around her sister's chair! Full well the mournful grzer knew that within the shrine of beauty, ambition burned with a self-destroying fire, while pride, working like a demon, fanned the passson-flame. And knowing that, and fearing that the proud heart would break and perish its pride, gentle Marion would place her arm around her sister's neck, and say—

"Do not work, dear Milly; it pains you, it causes you to weep. You are too beautiful, dear sister, to do hard work like this, which makes the fingers ache, the eyelids red, and the spirits dull. It is a torture to you, and you were not made for it. Do not let it trouble you, dearest; I will do it all. Let me see you happy, sister, and I will not care to work many, many hours more than I do now. I will work for you, sister, and earn money to keep us both. I will rise early and work late into the night. I will seek no pleasure, that you may enjoy it all. But do not weep, sister; do not let poor Mar see her dear sister look so sorrowful—so sad!"

Kind and gentle though such words were, they failed in being balm to the soul of Mildred Winnerley. Instead of their exercising a soothing effect, instead of their calming the strong surges of passion, they added fuel to the fire of madnes, they lent fury to the fierceness of the tempest. For she who listened to them in her pride felt that she was not that which she had dreamed to be—felt that to be seeking high, she had sunk so low as to form a subject for pity and for sorrow. She who would have had her sister envious of her greatness, she who would have had her sister a suppliant at her feet, now heard that sister promising to be her friend—now felt that sister to be greater than herself in the greatness of the soul's purity, and the nobleness of affection's beauty. Therefore was Mildred silent when Marion spoke so tenderly, therefore did she turn away her face when words of deepest love were whispered in her ear. Could it be that Mildred Winnerley had learned to hate her sister?—could it be that pride had revolted at the thought of pity, and the haughty mind become a hater of the loving heart? Oh, thou proud beauty, if so sad a change has come, tremble for the future of they destiny—shudder at that which will be thy doom! Heaven keep thee Mildred Winnerley, now!

Three months glided by, and Mildred became a mother only to be motherless again in the course of a few hours. Perchance Providence, which knew that woe enough was in store for the parent, deemed it best to rescue from it the child. No news had arrived of Hargrave Manners, further than that he was still abroad, and having entered into a life of thorough dissipation, had become entirely cast off by his father and relatives. That he would ever again return to his native land was uncertain, if not improbable; for the chances were that the outcast would die in exile, and would perish either by the pistol of the duellist, or the rash hand of unbearable remorse. The promises he had given were as worthless as the promiser; the one whom he had deceived had grown almost as reckless as her deceiver.   And now the second six months were fast hastening to an end!

Goodness does not always accompany wisdom, nor does wisdom at all times cohabit with goodness.   Thus it was with Mrs. Cheriton.   There never was a little woman who had a better heart, but there have been many who have possessed a wiser head.   The world is a very harsh, extortionate and exacting world; it would have every one to be a paragon of excellence, and is prone to look uncharitably upon the most noble acts of affection, if the head fail to guide the heart; it is a sour-tempered world, more fond of hunting for a blemish-spot in beauty, than for a redeeming point in ugliness; it is a queer, contrary, do-what-you-will-you-cant-please-it world, that will not give its praise when it can find nothing to grumble at, and grumbles at everything which is not wholly entitled to praise; it blames the close-fisted man because he will not give, and censures the generous man, because by giving he encourages laziness.   Mrs Cheriton had been working all her life to please the world, but it never would be pleased, not even if she worked all the flesh off her bones; it had something to say against her for sheltering naughty girls in her house, and it had something to allege against her because she made the naughty girls work too hard.   Not but what Mrs Cheriton deserved, in some part, the world's censure; for when she saw how proud and ambitious was Mildred Winnerley, and how the proud girl in her misery pined because she was not that which her heart panted to be, the poor woman became sorrowful, and even went so far as to reproach herself for having imposed any task upon one who had so haughty a spirit; so that instead of endeavouring to curb the impulses, and calm the fire of a heart which had already brought misery to its owner, she fostered the flame of ambition, and sympathized with the heavings of pride.   And when she beheld the eyes of Mildred red with weeping, and when she watched the bosom of the mournful beauty swell and sink with the tumult of passion, she would seat herself on an adjoining seat, and talk of dairy-maids having at last become duchesses, poor girls having been made peeresses, and recounter every romantic story that she had read of in novels, or heard told to her in the days of her childhood.   Mildred listened to such conversation with pleasure; it was of that which her own heart responded to, and it fed the fire which burned within her bosom.   So, at length, on one cold chilly evening in early spring, Mrs. Cheriton, having just returned from town, seized Mildred's hand, shook it warmly, and bade the proud orphan accompany her at once into the parlour.   Mildred saw that Mrs. Cheriton had some important news to communicate, and she longed to know what that news could be.

"My dear children," said the good woman, "I have wished for some time past to see you introduced to the world in such a way that you might have a chance of making your fortunes, which you certainly never will have here.   To-day I have been to London, and while there I thought I would avail myself of the opportunity to do what I could to assist you.   Well, I called upon one, and I called upon another, but all to no purpose.   At last it struck me that I would go and see Madame Pomparon, who is a very old acquaintance of mine, and who now keeps a large establishment at the West-end.   I told her about you both, and told her what clever girls you are.   Madame Pomparon's, my dears, is a very fashionable house, and none but the best hands are employed.   However, Madame has consented to see you both to-morrow morning, and, if possible, take you into her establishment.   I don't know anything that could be more fortunate; for Madame is intimate with all the great folks, she has some of them coming every day. Who knows what may happen if you once get into Madame's employ? I'm sure it's impossible for me to say. Such numbers of lords and ladies do go backward and forward that some of them would be sure to see you, and there's no knowing what proposals some of them might make. Besides, my dears Madame would no doubt send you to the houses of the great folks now and then. Of course, some of the young lords and baronets would catch sight of you, and something would be sure to come about out of that. It really is the most fortunate circumstance that could possibly happen. I don't know when I've been so delighted—that I don't!"

The heart of the poor, proud, foolish Mildred, rejoiced at the prospect which was thus so temptingly presented to her sanguine fancy; but far otherwise was it with gentle Marion. No craving for admiration, no wild thoughts of winning wealth or titles, actuated her meek and unambitious mind. She recoiled at the thought of quitting a quiet retreat, to mingle with a busy world. The establishment at the West-end, with all its aristocratic visitors, and immense advantages, had no attractions for her. If her sister went, then would she accompany her to some lone home in the large city, there to sit and work while Mildred was away, there to be ready to receive her on her return from daily toil. In vain did Mrs. Cheriton paint the prospect in glowing colours; in vain did she persuade gentle Marion to go with her on the morrow. It was now the younger sister's lot to weep, while Mildred—proud Mildred—built lofty castles in the floating air.

So, on the next morning, Mrs. Cheriton and Mildred Winnerley started on their visit to Madame Pomparon. Many were the sage counsels which the widow gave the orphan, as to how she should demean herself when admitted to an audience with the great lady to whom she was about to be introduced; many were the instructions which she communicated concerning the mode in which she was to frame her replies to every question that might be addressed to her; and many were the chances of good fortune which Mrs. Cheriton enumerated as likely to] result from a connection with Madame Pomparon's celebrated and aristocratic establishment. But even as the widow and her companion indulged their day-dreams together, the second six months were hastening to their close, though Mildred had almost forgotten the gipsy's prophecy.

Madame Pomparon, the great West-end milliner, lived in one of the select streets near Hanover-square. There was a brass plate upon the door, and a large stone in front of the house for the gentry to step upon in descending from their carriages. It was not without some degree of timidity that Mrs. Cheriton ventured to handle the knocker, while it was with considerable emotion that she smoothed down her gloves and so disposed her handkerchief that it hung half-way out of her reticule. Presently the door was opened, Madame Pomparon was said to be at home, and Mildred and Mrs. Cheriton were ushered into a back-parlour.

"There, my dear," said the good little woman, addressing her companion; "put back your curls so that Madame may see what a pretty face you have. It's all very grand, certainly, but don't be dispirited. We mustn't be timid, you know—there must be no timidity in coming upon such business. But hush! some one is coming."

A servant entered and announced to the visitors that her mistress would see them in the drawing-room. Proceeding in that direction, they ascended the staircase, and found themselves in the presence of Madame Pomparon.

Now whether it was the sound of the name which had led Mildred to entertain such an idea, or whether she had a sort of belief that all French ladies were of large stature, or whether Mrs. Cheriton's instructions had induced her to suppose that Madame Pomparon was a very majestic woman, matters not; but certainly Mildred did expect to behold a very magnificent person. Imagine her disappointment, then, when she was introduced to a short, shrivelled, middle-aged woman, with a very precise demeanour, very wiry ringlets, and very small grey eyes. Such was Madame Pomparon. There was certainly nothing to abash Mildred in being introduced to such an individual, unless it were that Madame's very large cap, and Madame's very sharp chin, and Madame's gorgeously ringed fingers, had something in them which approached to the sublime. Not but what poor Mildred experienced a feeling of awe as she gazed around the handsomely-furnished apartment, seeing herself reflected in large swing looking-glasses, feeling that she stood upon a carpet of exquisite texture, and inhaling the odour of a fragrant pastile which was then burning on the mantelshelf, in a china burner of the most tasteful design. Rich dresses were laying upon the sofas, superb materials of every description were displayed upon a table in the centre, while on other tables placed near the rose-coloured window curtains, were scattered fashion-books containing a variety of gaudily-painted figures. In a room to her left, the door of which opened from the larger apartment, Mildred discerned a number of young girls seated around a large board, and busily employed with their needles.

Mrs. Cheriton introduced her young companion, and Madame Pomparon, having told Mildred to close the door leading into the adjoining room, bade her to be seated. Then followed a series of questions, some of which perplexed the poor girl, insomuch as it was with difficulty that she could find appropriate answers; and while the interrogatory was going on, in came Monsieur Pomparon, who was a stout, though very elegantly-made man, possessing an idefinite amount of black whiskers, rejoicing in a moustache of extraordinary size, and fond to a fault of a deep scarlet dressing—gown, a flute and a Turkish cap. Monsieur Pomparon was a professor of music, and was, therefore, licensed to play a flute. He was the husband of a French milliner, and was, therefore allowed to wear large whiskers and an exuberant moustache. There were certain appearances about Monsieur Pomparon which were calculated to raise a suspicion of his being a dissipated man. The facts were, some years ago he had contrived to become deeply involved in debt while residing in his native country, and, in order to save himself from the inside of a gaol, had absconded to England, carrying with him his little wife. Monsieur, not knowing a word of English, nor being an adept in any art, save that of cheating, found it difficult to obtain his own living in a foreign land, and was, therefore, reduced to the necessity of relying for support upon the talents of his better, though smaller half. Madame Pomparon first commenced business as a teacher of her native language; but Monsieur not having anything else to do for amusement, mostly contrived to make the pupils unlearn in half an hour all that Madame had taught them in an entire morning; and, at length, became on such intimate terms with some of the young ladies, that his wife thought it prudent to box his ears, and then send her naughty pupils off with their boxes. The school being broken up, Madame Pomparon turned her attention to a business of another description. Having taken apartments in one of the fashionable streets near Burlington gardens, she exercised her talents in making bouquets and flower-wreaths for the adornment of aristocratic beauty. Monsieur having now to get up at five o'clock every morning, and accompany a boy-in-buttons with a

ket to Covent-garden market, there to purchase flowers for that day's consumption,
netimes Monsieur Pomparon allowed himself to be cheated, and returned home with
vers that were too full-blown, for which act of foolishness monsieur was generally
arded by being deprived of breakfast; at other times, Monsieur Pomparon having
n too late in the morning, failed in obtaining the best flowers, for which dereliction
uty, he was treated with a sound slap on the face, and an infinity of cross looks
his much aggrieved, though gentle spouse. However, Monsieur Pomparon on the
e, liked this sort of life very well, for the work was not exceedingly hard, and
ame made much money. Not only did she provide bouquets for such ladies as
about to go to balls and levees, but many an orange-wreath was woven by her for

the beauteous brides of the aristocracy, and many a rich garland for some enamoured nobleman to throw at the feet of the prima-donna, or the chief *figurante* at the opera. Indeed, madame had an engagement with the lessee of one of the larger theatres to supply him with a certain number of large nosegays every evening, and to get them thrown from the slips upon the stage just as the favourite of the night came forward to make her curtsey. By feeing the sweepers of the theatre, Madame Pomparon contrived to make this branch of her business pay exceedingly well; inasmuch as that having chief part of the bouquets returned to her the same night, she placed them in water and made them do duty on the next occasion. Gradually, however, Madame Pomparon had worked herself out of the bouquet business and taken up with the art of millinery. Monsieur too, had practised considerably upon his flute, and having composed a very touching melody which nobody but himself could understand, deemed himself to be a professor of music, and had some thoughts of taking one of the theatres and trying his hand at getting up an opera. No sooner did Monsieur Pomparon enter the room where Mildred was undergoing her examination, than he started as if struck with the beauty of the poor girl. Accordingly, being of a very pale complexion, and having been up rather late on the preceding night, he posted himself beside the rose-coloured window curtains, that Mildred might see him to full advantage, and be able to survey her through his handsome eye-glass. By the bye Madame Pomparon owed half her business to those same rose-coloured curtains; for when some pale sickly girl, or some worn and shrivelled dowager, came to confer with her concerning some new adornment, madame took care so to dispose the cheval-glass in relation to the said curtains, that when age and pallor looked expecting to see the likeness of themselves, they saw the tint of health and the bloom of youth on countenances which they still knew to be their own; so they liked the flattering lie and spent their money with the cunning *artiste*. And behind those curtains others were concealed, which were of a bright blue tint, and which were only drawn when madame awaited the arrival of a customer who might be possessed of more natural colour than accorded with the rules of fashion, or who was likely to be flushed with the anticipation of some happy event. Madame Pomparon was too well acquainted with the world not to know that flattery, deceit, and cunning, are three of the most useful partners to unite with, in the carrying out of any business where the dealings are of necessity with human frailty, human folly, and human self-esteem.

"Victor, my dear," said madame, addressing her husband, "I am thinking of taking this young woman into our establishment. What is your opinion on the subject, dear?"

Monsieur Pomparon advanced, scrutinized the countenance of Mildred through his eye-glass, and then replied,

"Well, Adele, my love, your Victor thinks you would do very right. A good-looking girl decidedly, so far as I have the power of judging; and a deliciously soft hand."

"Go away, sir! I am ashamed of you, Victor," exclaimed madame indignantly, as she observed her husband squeeze Mildred's hand rather more tightly than was proper. "You are a naughty, wicked man. Go away, sir, and play your flute."

"So he will, my heart's love; so your Victor will," returned Monsieur Pomparon; but instead of playing his flute, he went and peeped through the crevices in the adjoining door, to wink his eye at the young girls at work in the next room.

Some preliminary arrangements had to be got through, and then Madame Pomparon came to the decision that Mildred should be employed in the establishment. But, as the poor girl, was not sufficiently advanced in the art to do any very difficult work, and as she had a good figure and small white hands, it was decided that for the present she should stay in the show-room with madame, and assist in waiting on the ladies who honoured the establishment with their custom. In order, however, that Mildred should be installed in this situation, a certain Miss Spiffins, who had hitherto occupied the post, had to be deposed; and as the said Miss Spiffins was listening at the door when the arrangement was come to between her mistress and Mrs. Cheriton's *protegee*, the whole state of affairs became known to her, and digging her nails into the palms of her hands, she declared to herself that from that time forth there should be eternal enmity and unmitigated war between Florinda Spiffins, and the daring usurper who had laid claim to her rights and privileges.

"I'll see how long the impudent minx stays here," muttered Miss Spiffins outside the door. "I wonder what next, indeed!"

Business being now concluded and Mrs. Cheriton being somewhat of an old acquaintance of Madame Pomparon's, the head of the establishment desired her dear Victor to touch the bell, that she might beg her visitor to oblige her by taking a glass of wine. The obedient husband did as he was bid, Miss Spiffins retreated from her post of observation, and in a few moments the door opened, giving entrance to a servant attired in a superb suit of livery, radiant in all the glories of scarlet plush.

"Some wine, John," said Madam Pomparon.

"Yes, madame," replied the servant.

Mildred Winnerley thought she recognized the voice of the last speaker, and turned round her head to see whether or not she was mistaken. For a moment she almost doubted the trustworthiness of her senses; but, continuing to gaze, she saw that she had made no mistake, and that the gaudily-attired individual before her was none other than——

CHAPTER IX.

THE SORROWS OF JOHN JACOB SMAGS, AND THE SPITE OF FLORINDA SPIFFINS.

YES, the fact stared Mildred in the face—the scarlet plush, the silk stockings, and the white neckcloth, were worn by no less worthy an individual than Jacob Smags, It was doubtles very extraordinary that Mr. Smags—the friend of the Prince Regent the visitor at the Duke of Wellington's the favoured friend of the Countess of Norwich, and the man whose influence was so great with the legislature—should be found occupying so strange a position in society. Mildred was somewhat surprised, and Mr Smags appeared disconcerted to an equal degree; for the recognition was mutual, and Mr. Smags fully remembered the conversation which had occurred on the coach-top. The wine was brought, and as Mr. Smags put down the tray, he winked his eye at Mildred in a very mysterious manner. Mrs. Cheriton prolonged her stay for a short time in order to indulge in a little chat; then, it having been settled that Mildred would commence performing her appointed duties on the following morning, Mrs Cheriton curtsied to Madame Pomparon, Madame Pomparon returned the compliment, and " dear Victor" kissed the tips of his fingers to Mildred. The interview of the morning was concluded.

Mildred was about to follow Mrs. Cheriton out at the door, when she felt a tap on the shoulder, and looking round perceived that Mr. Smags was desirous of saying something to her.

" Mum's the word," said that gentleman in a low voice. "All right—don't know who I am—doing it for a lark—surprise them one day or other—jolly house—plenty of fun—keep all dark, eh?"

Before Mildred had time to say a word in reply, her arm was seized by Mrs. Cheriton, who drew her away, and when they had got fairly into the street, gave her a little gentle reprimanding for having so far demeaned herself as to have had anything to say to madame's servant. Mildred was about to confide to her friend all that she knew concerning John Jacob Smags, when a slight hubbub in the street arrested their attention, and the incident of having met with Mr. Smags was for a time forgotten.

And now, having arrived at home, Mrs. Cheriton took upon herself the task of relating to Marion all that had occurred during the day. It was not with any feeling of pleasure, poor Marion heard that her sister was taken into the establishment of Madam Pomparon, but seeing that Mildred was elated at the event, Marion thought it was but proper that she should assume the appearance of joy, and counterfeit an expression of satisfaction. So she shook her sister's hand, and congratulated her on her errand having turned out so favourable ; albeit she feared that misery and not happiness would result from the occurrence, and albeit she had a presentiment that her poor sister in obtaining the gratification of her ambition was but winning to herself fresh cause for sorrow. Marion knew not why she had reason to think so, but the thought was more like a conviction than a supposition or a fear.

Three days had to pass before the arrival of the time appointed for Mildred Winnerley entering upon the performance of her new duties. Much had to be done in those three days. In the first place, Mildred required newer and better clothes to go in, and in the second place, as she would not have to sleep at Madame Pomparon's, it was requisite that she obtained a lodging somewhere near the establishment in which she was to be employed. Marion was determined to accompany her sister; and accordingly after some trouble, Mrs. Cheriton discovered a nice cheerful apartment at the west-end of the town, where the sisters could at once take up their abode. Now came the difficulty about the clothes. What was to be done ? Neither Marion nor Mildred had sufficient money to make the required purchases ; and Mrs. Cheriton was herself so deficient in pecuniary means that she could render but little] assistance. In this dilemma Marion remembered that she had in her possession a pair of gold earrings, and a brooch set with a few precious stones, both of which articles had been given to her by her grandmother. Marion valued her trinkets very much because of their giver, but she valued her sister still more, and she therefore determined to dispose of them in such a way that she might be able to furnish her sister with the sum of which she stood in need. Without saying a word, poor Marion, put on her bonnet and shawl, took the trinkets in her hand, and proceeded to the nearest pawnbroker's shop. Fortunately she found the pawnbroker willing to lend her the sum she required, so that it was not necessary she should sell the articles outright. Leaving them with the man, and having obtained the desired loan, she hastened away, purchased such things as her sister needed, carried them home, placed them upon the table, and telling Mildred that they were her sister's gift, refused to say how she had gained the money to make the purchase, until at length the secret was extorted from her by dint of persevering inquiry.

To their lone home in the large city the sisters went; and now indeed they were fairly thrown upon the world. The people of the house were utter strangers, and in crowded street the orphans found themselves isolated and alone. And as they drew down the blinds on the first evening of their having taken possession, they looked at each other, and felt that they were shutting out all of the world which belonged to them—the sight of busy crowds, and the light of the twinkling stars. There was no one for them to converse with, no kind friend to beguile them with cheerful talk. Life lay before them; the dreary road on which they had to travel stretched away from their feet into a dark and illimitable distance. What were to be the adventures of the journey, how were they to travel without a guide?

And far, far away into the night they sat together. Mildred brooding in her haughtiness, and gentle Marion thinking to herself how often she should have to sit before that fire waiting at evening for her sister's return. So the candle burnt itself out, the fire died away, the sisters fell asleep in their chairs. And still, as she slept, Mildred dreamed of riches and titles bowing the knee to her beauty; while loving Marion dreamed that trouble was coming to her sister, and trembled lest she should not be near to assist her. The dark room; the silent sleepers; the dreams of ambition and of affection's gentleness! Let the night pass away, the morning dawn, and Mildred Winnerley proceed to her new employ.

Madame Pomparon behaved very kindly to her unpractised assistant, and proceeded at the expense of much trouble to initiate her into all the duties of her office. Monsieur was no less polite and assiduous in affording to Mildred all the information of which he was possessed—never a great deal at any time—concerning the business and the mode of its being conducted. So, the morning passed away very pleasantly. Mildred gave satisfaction to her mistress by a display of ready apprehension, while at the same time she won the good graces of her master by seeming inclined to receive his very polite attentions. Madame Pomparon and her "dear Victor" were at dinner, and Mildred was busily employed alone in putting some stitches into a magnificent turban, when the door opened, and Jacob Smags made his entry on tip-toe.

"Hush!" he whispered, re-closing the door, "I'm come to let you into a secret. Funny place this, and funny people in it—much to see and much to learn. Don't be surprised at anything; you won't when you have seen as much of the world as I have. All rascals, cheats, humbugs; you'll find 'em out. Dare say you wonder to see me looking such a figure. It's a game, you know—a trick I'm playing—a very clever trick; do you understand, eh?"

Mildred replied that she had no clear comprehension of the matter.

"I'll tell you then; but you must keep mum—mum's the word here. Knew this rascal Pomparon, you see, while I was out in India, he borrowed a lot of money of me, I was fool enough not to get his note-of-hand at the time. Scamp never paid me—sent me word from time to time he was poor and had no money. Didn't believe him—thought I'd see—determined to find him out. Pitched upon the plan of coming here as a footman just to see how things were going on. Told the prince of It—Georgey laughed heartily—correspond every day. Came here—offered myself—old rascal didn't recognize—turned footman—lots of fun—got my eye upon him—watching to know what the amount of the ready is.   By-and-by I shall pounce upon him—discover myself—say 'liar, pay me my debt or dread my exposure!'—frighten them a bit— have a lark—then cut—go away, and tell the joke to all the friends of the prince. Prime fun—isn't it ?"

Mildred answered by saying that she thought it most extraordinary conduct on the part of Mr. Smags, and hinted her surprise at being informed that Monsieur Pomparon should be a debtor to so large an amount, while his creditor was living in his house as a mere footman.   Jacob Smags smiled as Mildred spoke, and observed—

"Funny world, miss—queer, strange, unaccountable world—no judging by appear. ances—no taking people for what they seem—all turns—world turns and we turn—all turned topsyturvy by-and-by—I master, and master footman.   But mum—mum's the word!"

Jacob would have said more, had he not heard the footsteps of his mistress upon the stairs; so placing some things upon a tray, he threw a white cloth over his left arm, opened the door and carried out his load.

The first day of her new service had passed, and Mildred returned to the lone fireside of her sister, to tell about all that she had seen, and every adventure that had hap- pened during the short period of her absence.

Day after day passed, and still Mildred went to her employ in the morning, and returned in the evening to her home and to her sister.   Sometimes when the evening was fine, Marion would put on her bonnet and go to meet Mildred ; and sometimes when the labour of the busy day was over, the two sisters would stroll out together to enjoy a quiet walk, to look at the starlit sky, and to talk to each other of their happy rambles in their younger days, and the small prospect there was before them of the future ever becoming as joyous as had been the past.   But then, Mildred would hint to her sister some ambitious thought, or some foolish aspiration, and Marion would sink into silence, making no answer, but thinking deeply and sadly, such thoughts, as she knew it was best to keep untold.

Thus a fortnight glided by; when one morning, just as Mildred was about to go to her dinner, Madame Pomparon called her back, and informed her that she would have to find her way to a house in one of the adjoining squares, there to receive instructions from a lady concerning a head-dress which had to be made after a peculiar fashion.

"You must pay particular attention to the instructions which you may receive," said Madame Pomparon ; "for the lady is very difficult to please, is at present confined to her bed, and has been a customer of mine for some years.   I would rather displease any one than I would Lady Manners."

Lady Manners!   The words fell strangely upon Mildred's ears.   Who could Lady Manners be?   Was she the wife of Sir Walmsley—was she the mother of Hargrave? Pale as lifeless marble became the cheeks of poor Mildred ; her lips quivered as she asked in a trembling voice,—

"Did you say Lady Manners, madame ?"

"Yes, girl ; yes, child.   Why, what is it which frightens you—of what are you afraid ?"

"Nothing, madame—nothing, I assure you.   But—but do you mean Lady Walmsley Manners ?"

"To be sure, I do. You may call her Lady Walmsley, not that I know there are any other members of the family living near by. Indeed, Lady Manners herself resided at a much greater distance, while Sir Walmsley was alive."

"While Sir—Sir Walmsley was alive!—Is he then dead, madam?" inquired Mildred eagerly.

"Oh yes, Miss Winnerley. Sir Walmsley has been dead these five months. He was a very nice gentleman; and I'm sure poor Lady Manners must feel his loss acutely. But, *mon Dieu!* child, what are you crumpling up that piece of lace-edging for?"

So great was the perturbation of poor Mildred's mind on hearing such unexpected news, that she failed to observe the damage she was involuntarily doing to a portion of Madame Pomparon's property. Willingly would she have made further enquiries, and much did she wish to learn what had become of Hargrave, and how the property of his father had been disposed. She dared not, however, ask further questions on the subject; but quitted the room, pondering over the strange fortunes which had again brought her in connection with the family of him from whom she had received such deep wrong. And then as she sat at her meal, the thought entered her mind that if Hargrave had returned to England, it would be possible for her to gain an interview with him, and demand from him that justice, which she was entitled to expect from his hands. Wild visions floated through the brain of the musing girl. Hargrave Manners she knew must be Sir Hargrave now; and was there not a probability of his retaining a portion of that affection which he once professed for the beauty of the Hampshire village; was there not a possibility of his making her his wife? And with the thought that such might be the result, came the determination that such should be the result eventually, notwithstanding any obstacles that might occur to cause it to be otherwise. Every spark of ambition that had lain latent within the proud girl's breast, now shot forth to kindle a perfect fire.

"He shall marry me—he shall make me his wife!" ejaculated Mildred to herself; and having so determined, she concentrated all her thoughts upon the mode of accomplishing her great design.

A little diligent enquiry sufficed to make Mildred aware that Hargrave Manners had returned to England; but that having greatly excited the anger of his father, Sir Walmsley had left him an exceedingly small portion of his property. This was unwelcome news for Mildred; but she remembered that the Hargrave of former years bore a title now, and was Sir Hargrave Manners. Could she but become his wife, she also would bear a title, and there was more probability of such a circumstance occurring now that she knew how Sir Walmsley had treated his son. With thoughts wild as these were, and with resolutions wilder still, Mildred Winnerley meditated on her schemes of ambition and of vanity, though she refrained from disclosing them to her sister.

It was the morning of the next day after that on which the proud girl had had an interview with Lady Manners, when, as she was sitting in the show-room busy at work, in the company of Madame Pomperon, the door opened and Monsieur Pomperon entered accompanied by another gentleman. That something had occurred to rouse Monsieur Pomparon's ire was very evident; for his countenance which was usually of the palest possible tint, was now tinged with a red flush, whilst his eyes wore an expression of fierceness, and his moustache bristled with unusual vivacity.   He called his wife aside, and after conferring with her for a short time, the bell was rung hastily, and all took seats with great gravity as if intent upon the performance of some serious act of duty.

"Where is dat man, John?" asked Monsieur Pomparon in an angry voice, and the summons on the bell was replied to by a female domestic.

"Do you wish to see John, sir?" asked the servant.

"Yes, I do. Where is he. Send him here directly."

There was a dreadful pause, during which Monsieur Pomparon curled his moustache very fiercely, and shook his cane as if he was testing its capability of inflicting a smart blow.   Madame Pomparon, who also seemed much excited, now laid her hand upon the arm of her husband.

"Do not be rash, dear Victor—do not be too rash."

"I will be rash—I will be rash in my own house!—Where is de rasca', why don't he come?"

Jacob Smags entered the apartment. He was confronted at once by his master and mistress, but the countenance of the visitor was hidden from his view; the gentleman having got up from his seat to look out at the window.

"Come here, sare—come here, and spik de honest trud," said Monsieur Pomparon, his anger causing him to be very incorrect in his English. "What for do you mean, sare,—What for do you come into my house wid de great big lie. Tell me, sare—what was de gentleman's name you live wid last."

"His name, sir?"   replied Jacob—"his name was Sir Robert Foster."

"*Eh bien*, yas, Sare Robert Foster. And Sare Robert Foster was in de Garmany, when you came here—isn't dat right."

"Quite right, sir, I assure you."

"Oh, you assure me, do you? And Sare Robert gave you de character—de recommendation on de bit of paper you brought here—did he?"

"Yes, sir!"

"Yas, yas, and he pud on de bit of paper dat you were one good honest servant, dat had never told one lie, nor done one bad ting—Sare Foster said dat?"

"That was what he wrote, I believe, sir. I had lived with him a long time, and if it hadn't been for his removing abroad, I should have stayed with him till now."

Monsieur Pomparon rose from his seat, and seized Jacob by his collar.

"You are one demmed raskal, you one big villian!" he exclaimed. "What is dis gentilman. Look! see! vat—is he?"

So saying Monsieur Pomparon confronted Jacob with the gentleman who had hitherto stood with his face to the window. Immediately that he did so, the unlucky Mr. Smags recognized Sir Robert Foster, and falling on his knees, implored to be forgiven for having told so many lies, and for having forged a written character in the name of his late master.

"You must be a very wicked man," observed Madame Pomparon—"a very wicked man indeed, to have acted with such duplicity. I did not think I had such a person in the house, or else I should never have had an hour's sleep. Monsieur Pomparon must give you your dismissal directly."

"I would certainly advise my friend to do so," said Sir Robert Foster. "The fellow's audacity in having forged my signature to his paper of lies, is only equalled by the manner in which he cheated me while in my service. It was well for him that I kicked him out of doors instead of sending him before the magistrate. And as for my giving him a recommendation, the only one I could give him with any satisfaction to myself, would be one that would secure him a situation in the hulks. I chanced, my dear madam, to be passing your house on horseback yesterday, and seeing the rascal in your livery, thought you could not be aware of his real character; and therefore determined to apprize you of it at the first opportunity. Before you dismiss him from your house, I advise you to examine your plate-chest and wardrobe, to see that nothing be missing."

"Sir Robert is very hard upon me, and wishes to do me all the harm he can," blub-bered Jacob. "I don't deserve to be so treated, not if I were the worst man a-going."

"Be silent you demm'd scoundrel!" vociferated Monsieur Pomparon. "You came into my house to rob me; you vant to steal my tings, and tell me all the great big lies. I'll give you one lesson vat you do never forget."

Hereupon Monsieur Pomparon laid his cane over the shoulder of Jacob with a smart thwack. Madame Pomparon fearing that something sad would occur, again inter-posed,

"Do not demean yourself so, dear Victor; do not be so rash with the wicked man. He will beg your pardon, and you can then let him go."

"Bag my pardon, de demm'd rascal! I'll teach him one leetle lesson first. Give me my box wid the leetle pair of pistols in it, my dear; and I'll shoot de—de big tief, I'll—"

Mildred had hitherto been a silent onlooker to this very startling scene. Now, how-ever, feeling a dread that Monsieur Pomparon would put his threats into execution, and in reality inflict some injury upon Jacob Smags, she rushed forward, and throw-ing herself upon her knees grasped the cane which her infuriated master held in his hand.

"Oh, no, Monsieur Pomparon! you musn't do so; I am sure you will not. If John has never acted dishonestly since he has been in your house, you have no right to punish him; and I am sure you would not wish to treat him worse than he deserves."

Monsieur Pomparon paused; his eyes met those of Mildred, the soft pressure of Mil-dred's fingers was upon his hand; her warm breath fanned his face. The effect was magical. Those brows that had been so knit in anger assumed a sudden smoothness; those eyes that had darted such glances of fury now beamed with a look of the mildest sweetness. He put down his cane, threw himself back on the chair, turned away his face from Jacob Smags, and pressing Mildred's fingers with one hand, while with the other he motioned the friend of the Prince Regent to leave the room, said,

"Go away! You be ver bad man. You must leave my house. You are ver big rascal, I will have noting more to do wid you. Go, go!"

Jacob Smags left the room, and Monsieur Pomparon entered into conversation with Sir Robert Foster.

Now another person, as well as Mildred's mistress, had watched the whole of this scene, having witnessed not only the angry behaviour of Monsieur Pomparon, the disregard with which he had treated the requests of his wife, and the imminent danger of the detected Jacob, but also the conduct of Mildred in rushing forward to protect the guilty man, together with the wondrous influence that a few soft words from her lips and a few soft glances from her eyes had had upon Monsieur Pomparon. The individual who had witnessed these things was no less a person than Miss Spiffins, the young lady who had been deposed from her place in the show-room, in order that Mildred Winnerley might enjoy those rights and privileges which Miss Spiffins felt to be lawfully and indubitably her own. Florinda Spiffins had been blessed with a spirited mother, and the virtues of the elder Spiffins had descended to the younger. Florinda had made up her mind not to submit tamely to the degradation which she had suffered—not she indeed! What! allow herself to be supplanted by a country hoyden who was unable to discriminate between the crest of a duke and the crest of a baronet when she saw them upon the carriage panels. Certainly not! Florinda had a very firm opinion that the usurper was an impudent slut; and Florinda in the height of her indignation had ventured to express her opinion to that effect in the presence of the young ladies connected with the establishment. As, however, Miss Spiffins was no great favourite of the said young ladies, her indignation only served for a subject of merriment; and knowing that Miss Spiffins was particularly attached to Monsieur Pomparon, while the events of every day sufficed to show that Monsieur had latterly transferred his attentions to Mildred, the young ladies had enjoyed themselves by annoying Miss Spiffins with an indefinate amount of imformation concerning the progress which Mildred had made, and the various commendatory expressions which had been bestowed upon her by the two heads of the establishment. All this had served to rouse the ire of the Spiffins to such an extent that she only waited for a convenient place and opportunity in order to wreak her most signal vengeance upon the eyes of her detested rival. So now as she peeped through the keyhole of the adjoining door, and saw Mildred Winnerly interpose so successfully to save Jacob Smags she felt that the hour of retribution was not far distant. Jacob she had always hated while monsieur she had always adored. Miss Spiffins was not the young lady who could suffer such proceedings as she had now witnessed to pass without some more important result.

"Really," said Madame Pomparon, while conferring with Miss Spiffins in her own room, "I am very glad that we have found out the true character of that wicked John so soon as we have. To think of his impudent audacity in imposing upon myself and Monsieur Pomparon, with a forgery and a number of wicked untruths. I am sure if Miss Winnerley had not spoken in his favour, as she so good-naturedly did, Monsieur Pomparon would have done some injury to the naughty abominable man."

"Yes, madame," observed Miss Spiffins, "it was very good of Miss Winnerley to interfere as she did, and Monsieur Pomparon was very kind to listen to her; monsieur did not pay much attention to your entreaties."

"I do not wonder at it," replied Madame Pomparon; "his exasperation was so great that it prevented him, no doubt, from understanding a word I said."

"But he understood very quickly all that Miss Winnerley said, madame—did he not?"

"Yes, yes; he listened to her; he was more calm then."

"Monsieur is always very calm when Miss Winnerley is speaking to him," observed Florida Spiffins, with a peculiar expression of voice.

"What do you mean, child? I do not clearly understand you," said Madame Pomparon, her words seeming to quiver as she gave them utterance.

"Madame surely does not require me to tell her that Monsieur Pomparon always pays attention to anything which Miss Winnerley says, because it is so well known; indeed all the young ladies are accustomed to observe that half-a-dozen words from you, madame, are never so well understood by monsieur as half a word from Miss Winnerley is."

Artful Florida Spiffins! Clever as woman always is when placed in rivalry with woman. That which she had vowed to do she had now done, and she saw that by one happy stroke she had at once dethroned the usurper and avenged herself on him by whom she had been slighted. The countenance of Madame Pamparon had become perfectly pale;

her lips, which had lost their colour, trembled with a quivering motion; and her hand shook as she laid it upon the back of a chair preparatory to sitting down.

"Take a seat, Miss Spiffins," said the now jealous Frenchwoman, "let us both be confidential in these matters which we have been talking about. I—I think—that is, I wish you to speak plainly."

"What can madame wish me to say?" enquired Florinda, who was already exulting in her victory.

"All, my dear Mis Spiffins. I wish you to have my entire confidence, while at the same time I hope to enjoy yours with regard to Monsieur Pomparon, are you inclined to suppose that he and Miss Winnerley are perfectly—perfectly good friends?"

"There is no reason why they should not be, madame."

"Certainly, my dear Miss Spiffins. But—but they are very intimate, I suppose—Monsieur Pomparon often talks to that young woman."

"When he has opportunities to do so, madame, I dare say he does."

"Yes, yes; when—when he has opportunities. And that is——"

"When madame, they are left together, and you happen to be attending to the concerns of the establishment; just as happens to be the case at the present time, for instance——"

There was a pause of a single instant. Then, quickly rising from her chair, Madame Pomparon said,—

"I must entreat you, my dear Miss Spiffins, to remain here a short time. I will see you again presently. There are some instructions which I should have given to Miss Winnerley this morning, but which have only this mo ment occurred to my recollection."

Madame Pomparon hastily quitted the apartment; and did Florinda Spiffins remain there? Not she. Full well was the errand known to her on which Madame Pomparon was now gone; and so knowing, she followed her at a distance, and on tip-toe down the stairs.

Now it so happened that Monsieur Pomparon having parted from his visitor, and not knowing how to amuse himself until dinner-time, had taken his flute, and wended his way towards the room in which Mildred was engaged.   Seating himself beside the beautiful girl, and having gazed at her for some minutes as her fingers busily plied the needle, he observed,—

"My little charmer seems to have much of de melancholy to-day. What shall I play to her dat will please her?"

"Nothing, thank you, Monsieur Pomparon. I have a slight head-ache."

"My pretty pigeon has some of de head-ache—has she? Poor leetle head. Let me feel de leetle pulse of de leetle pretty hand. It is a ver pretty leetle hand indeed."

So said Monsieur Pomparon, as he laid down his flute and took the white fingers of Mildred in his clasp.   Mildred moved away her chair, and endeavoured to free her hand, but Monsieur Pomparon had now obtained so firm a grasp of her wrist that her efforts to rid herself of him were useless.

"De leetle pulse of de leetle hand beats ver quick, quick. Me must know if de leetle heart beats de same," said Monsieur Pomparon, placing his arm round the waist of Mildred.

"This is a most unwarrantable liberty, Monsieur Pomparon!" exclaimed Mildred, endeavouring to rise from her seat. "I beseech you to take away your hands. Only suppose madame were to come in and see you!"

"What would she say to me for feeling de leetle heart of my leetle pigeon. Oh! she would say ver much; but she is not here to say dat. I must feel my leetle pigeon's heart, and look at her leetle face, and her black brilliant eyes, and her pretty cheeks, and—and—oh! *quelle jolie!*—one leetle kiss from de rosy lips—one leetle, leetle kiss."

Monsieur Pomparon had so wound his arms around Mildred, that she could not escape from him, while he was just about to press his lips to hers, when the door of the room opened, and Madame herself entered. So noiselessly did the door turn upon its hinges, and so gently did the angry wife tread upon the carpet, that Monsieur Pomparon having his back to the door, did not perceive the intrusion. Mildred, however, saw the entrance of her mistress, and vainly endeavoured to apprise the amorous Frenchman. At length having drawn back her head, she exclaimed,—

"See, see!"

"See—vat am I to see—what else is dere for me to look at when I have de face of my leetle pigeon before me—vat more can I see?"

"See me! Unfaithful, false-hearted man!" replied the voice of Madame Pomparon, as that lady laid her hand upon the right shoulder of her lawful spouse.

Monsieur Pomparon, quailed at the awful words, and turning round gently, fell upon his knees at the feet of his wronged and wrathful wife.

"Don't be angry with me, Adele. Mademoiselle Winnerley has de bad headache, and —and————"

"Be silent, sir! I—I suspected this; I know now why Monsieur Pomparon thinks this to be the best room in the house for practising his flute in. We will come to an arrangement, sir, presently, and in some more convenient place. As for you, girl, I give you warning that you quit my establishment at the close of the present week. I will have no intriguing cunning hussies under my roof if I know it; endeavouring to inveigle any one that falls in their way. I am ashamed of you, and if I have cause for sorrow it is to see that you have no shame yourself—no shame at being detected in your wicked arts."

"Madame Pomparon must pardon me for saying that she is very much mistaken; and that she has used expressions which have been untrue. If monsieur be a gentleman he will support me in that which I have just said."

"You impudent creature!" returned madame. "It is not enough for such designing minxes to be caught in their wickedness; but they must endeavour to shift their own misdoings to the account of those poor weak things—" and here madame cast a withering look at her liege lord—"to those weak things, I say, who are foolish enough to allow themselves to be inveigled and drawn away by such practised cunning. My opinion of you is, that you came into this house with certain intentions, which certain intentions I am happy to think are entirely defeated by the little incident which has now occurred."

"You think as you say, Madame Pomparon?"

"I do. But I have no wish to bandy words with you, miss."

"Nor I with you, madam; but having so fully expressed your opinions, it becomes me to reply to them. You have thought as I have never given you reason to think, and you have spoken as you know that you have had no just cause to speak. There has not been one word of truth in that which you have said. For explanations I refer you to

Monsieur Pomparon, who, as I have already told you—if he be a gentleman, and if he have any one generous feeling, will do me the justice of denying every accusation which you have made against me, and will confess that not through any fault of mine has this most unpleasant occurrence taken place."

"Monsieur Pomparon will do no such thing," replied the head of the establishment. "If he has not the wisdom to take care of himself some one else must teach him how to guard against the intrigues of any artful hussy who may wish to make a simpleton of him."

This was no doubt particularly gratifying to Monsieur Pomparon. That gentleman, however, hearing Mildred's words, and seeing the poor girl looking at him with a piercing glance, took the hand of his spouse in a reverential manner and tremblingly said,—

"Will Adele listen to his Victor—will de heart's love listen to de heart that loves her? Mademoiselle Winnerley spik de trud; she has not——"

"Hold your tongue, sir! I will not hear a word. Miss Winnerley understands the arrangement which I have come to respecting her."

"It is madam, that I quit your service on Saturday next. Permit me to say that it will be more agreeable to me that we should part to-night."

"If you dare leave before the expiration of your time, you insolent creature, you shall not receive one penny of your salary."

"But, Madam——"

"Silence! I have said what my determination is. As for this silly man I will take care that he shall not fall again into your toils. Come, sir, follow me!"

Monsieur Pomparon obeyed, and Mildred was left alone. Silent, thoughtful, with a swelling bosom, and with tearful eyes she sat musing over that which had just happened. An hour passed away, and then the door again opening, Jacob Smags once more entered the apartment.

"What is it you want, sir?" asked Mildred, as Jacob, without being asked to do so, took a seat beside her.

"I'll tell you, Miss Winnerley. All's right. The head—that's madame, and the shoulders—that's the guv'nor, are at it fire and tongs up stairs. I've been packing up my boxes, and I've heard all about it. Head and shoulders have fallen out and got you into the mess. But you won't stand it, of course not."

"As we have nothing to talk about, sir, further than to bid each other good-bye, we will do that, and you will oblige me by leaving the room."

"There now, don't be foolish. Head and shoulders won't interfere with us, and we can just talk matters over. Of course you'll hear what I have to say"

"I have no such wish, sir; there is nothing that you can communicate which will have any interest to me," said Mildred, moving away her chair.

"Yes, yes, there is Miss Winnerly. What I want to tell you is I've been coming the humbug, I know it, and I confess it. But to all you heard the shoulders and Sir Robert say about me, that's all humbug of their own. Of course I have a great many acquaintances among the gentry, owing to the number of families I've been in. As to that Sir Robert, the truth is, he borrowed a little money of me when he was hard up, and wants to shirk payment by giving me a bad character. Same's the case with the shoulder's here. It's good fun for them, but it don't take with Jacob Smags. It's the way the world serve those who want to oblige them. The world treats us all very ill—dont it, Miss Winnerley?"

"I have no opinion to offer on the subject, sir."

"Just so. That was the sort of answer the Prince Regent used to make when I observed the same to him. The prince, you know, did talk a bit to me, because you see I was not exactly his friend, or any intimate acquaintance, but groom you know—second groom. Its all very well to say nothing against the world, that's the plan I adopt myself, but there is a conclusion which we must come to, viz., it treats us all as badly as it can. Now its been treating you badly, Miss Winnerly, and Jacob Smags has heard about it. Jacob knows it, and Jacob always takes part with them that isn't friends with the world. You wont be angry with me. I'm Jacob, you know. What I've come to say to you amounts to this. We're both of us going to make a start in life. I'm an old hand at that fun—you are not. Now we'll settle it this way. I have a sort of liking for you, which I dare say you have for me back again. Well, we clubs it. we do the kind offices—the Hand-in-hand, or the Union; or give heart for heart, and make it the Royal Exchange. You understand that. I Jacob, you Mrs. Jacob. Two of us together will fight the world well; Jacob Smags hasn't done it badly by himself. Just think about that, two minutes."

"This is unbearable!" ejaculated Mildred, bursting into tears, and rising from her seat in order to leave the room. She was detained by Jacob.

"Come, come, Miss Winnerley. Jacob Smags isn't the man to say a thing that would wound the feelings of any young woman. Jacob is a humbug—he knows that; but he's kind—kind to the backbone; trust him and try him. You mustn't mind his telling you, that he's heard you are not so well off in the world as you ought to be, Jacob thinks he knows that. Well, the head's turned you off, and the shoulders cant help you, but Jacob will, Jacob can. I didn't mean to propose anything just now, that I thought would distress you, but what Jacob did think was, that if he could do you a service he would, and so he thought he'd make you a fair offer. You'd never want anything so long as you lived, if you had Jacob. He knows the world—seen it through and through—humbug all—biggest humbugs win—therefore Jacob. However, if Miss Winnerley, you've not the inclination to join hands, I'll tell you what. I dare say you haven't much money, and Jacob has plenty. We've both turned off our guv'nors as we may say, and so we may as well take shares; If you want a pound or two, say the word. Jacob isn't humbugging now. There's the money."

"Let me leave the room, sir, or I will call for assistance."

"Don't be silly; don't have any shamefacedness. Jacob never had any—don't you have. It never gives any one a lift in the world. Humbug's a good deal better. Trust Jacob. The last time I was at the Duke of Wellington's—groom, you know, groom of course—I saw a convincing proof of that. Never say you won't when you wish to say you will. There's the money. You want it, I don't. Say how much you would like, and have it. Jacob will never mention a word about it; Jacob will keep it mum. Mum's the word. Jacob hears them say you are poor, and that you try to keep it hid. Jacob knows what a person has to suffer when known to be poor, and tell's them all you're a young heiress waiting for a fortune. Humbug, you know, but they can't get over it ; it tells—humbug tells. Come now, can Jacob help you?"

"No, sir," replied proud Mildred. "Whether your intention is or is not to insult me, I cannot say; but if you remain longer in this room or attempt to detain me here, I shall consider your behaviour as an insult of the grossest kind."

"I'm sorry for that, and I'm sorry for you, because you won't mind what Jacob says. However. you may want Jacob's help at some time or another! so there's his address—Muggins's cottages; you don't know them, but the post does. There's the cart at the daor for my traps. Jacob's off. Good bye! There's some money. Jacob leaves it for you. If you don't pick it up, head or shoulders will. Put a stop to that. Don't be a fool."

Jacob Smaggs darted out of the room, and Mildred—proud Mildred swept the money from off the table with her hand, and allowed it to roll upon the floor.

And now the proud girl's trial had come. There sat she in the dusky room, as the evening shadows fell; there sat she in her haughtiness and in her sorrow. Upbraided, cast out by the woman whose servant she was; accused of intriguing—she whose proud soul could scarcely stoop to ask a favour; accused of cunning, treachery and deceit. Oh, this was galling to the haughty spirit, this was torture, this was agony! But there was cause for torture yet more exquisite—cause for agony yet more acute. She had been pitied—she, the proud b anty, pitied! And by whom? By one who was himself a servant and an outcast. This was worse than all. To have seemed an object of pity to him, to have had from him offers of patronage, was degradation most complete. So the shadows closed round, and lights were brought into the apartment, and Mildred Winnerley sat plying her needle in the lonely room. Pale was her proud brow, pale even to deadly paleness those exquisite features; and her eyes sparkled wildly, and her bosom heaved heavily; there was conflict in her soul, there was madness in her brain.

And when her work was finished, Mildred placed on her bonnet, drew her shawl around her, and passed out into the dark street. By the hearth of home, weary and afflicted with illness, gentle Marion was waiting for her coming. Not in that direction turned Mildred. The dark streets leading into the dim squares were before her, and onward that way she went.

Go, Mildred Winnerley, go! The six months want but one day to bring them to an end; and thou must work out the gipsey's prophecy!

Pride and misery—she had known them both. What were these six months to bring! "Pride, misery, and *death*," were the three words that the gipsey uttered. Aye, but there was another which she told to Gerrard Chester alone. What word was that?

Go, Mildred Winnerley. In the dark streets wander at your will. The gipsey's prophecy works fast to its fulfilment now!

——————

MILDRID'S INTERVIEW WITH HARGRAVE MANNERS, AT HIS CHAMBERS.—*Page* 107.

CHAPTER X.

THE MEETING AND THE OATH.

ALONG the dark streets, round the silent squares, and out towards the large gloomy parks, Mildred Winnerley strolled at night-time, sorrowful, wretched, heart-broken in her wounded pride. She passed down Piccadilly; she was about to enter Hyde-park. Suddenly she stopped, gazed earnestly at a figure which had just glided by her, and then retraced her way at a quick pace, in order to look again at the countenance of one whom she thought that she recognized full well.

Yes, Mildred had recognized truly, there had been no mistake; for as the gliding figure turned the corner of a street, the lamplight revealed to the view of Marion's sister the features of Hargrave Manners.

Should she stop him, should she speak to him, should she accuse him of having played her falsely? Her heart beat violently, her limbs trembled; she had not the strength to place her hand upon his arm; she had not the courage to utter his name.

On, to where thou art going, Hargrave Manners—be it to the scene of revelry, or to the lonely home, be it to the boudoir of beauty or the dark haunt of the reprobate, there is one who is dogging thy steps—one who will follow thee this night, go where thou may'st! It is she whom thou hast deeply injured, she who bears within her the proud soul, and the haughty heart, and who will never forgive thee the wrong thou hast done her, unless it be atoned for amply, fully, and to the extent of the desire of that proud soul. Go on, Hargrave Manners! Mildred Winnerley will follow thee!

And onward through the lonely thoroughfares—onward along the dark streets, the girl followed her betrayer. Nor heeded she how her gentle sister waited her arrival by the solitary hearth, listening for her footsteps at the door, and going every few minutes to the window in a vain endeavour to descry her shadow on the distant footway. Wait gentle Marion; watch at the window if you will. Mildred Winnerley, thy sister, cannot come home to thee yet; she is busy, working out the gipsey's prophecy!

So onward they went—he who had done the wrong, and behind him, following like a shadow, she who had suffered the injury. Street after street was traversed, house after house was passed by. At length Hargrave Manners turned in beneath an archway, passed across an open square, entered a gloomy-looking house, took his way up a broad staircase, and stopped before the door of his chambers.

Mildred Winnerley had followed him through the archway, across the square, into the house, up the staircase, she had followed noiselessly, shadow-like and well. There stood she in the gloom, there stood she as he turned the key in the door. And as the door opened, she sprang forward; and as it closed she stood in the room by his side. A moment's pause, and then she laid her hand upon his arm. A light was burning on an adjoining table. Hargrave Manners turned quickly round, and his glance fell upon the countenance of her who had trusted him too well!

" Mildred !"

" Hargrave—Hargrave !"

What need to tell the excuses that were made for past deceptions? What need to tell how the betrayer endeavoured to exculpate himself to the betrayed. They sat together in the solitary room, they talked of the days of happiness and love. But was the conversation pleasant, did it bring back recollections? Alas! no, it brought back remembrances of promises made in falsehood, and of vows that were uttered only to be broken. And then when each had listened to the other, when the bosom of the betrayed heaved heavily as she thought over the last words of her betrayer—then, when he had ceased to protest, and she to accuse, a moment of silence came. His face was turned from her, yet he felt her damp finger encircling his wrist with a firm clasp; he dared not look at her, and yet he felt that her eyes were fixed upon him.

" Hargrave," said she, in a deep firm-toned voice.

He did not reply.

"Listen, Hargrave Manners! You have never known the heart of her whom you have treated so lightly; you cannot tell what its impulses are. It has suffered and withstood much; it has loved and it can hate. Listen, man! you have brought degradation and shame upon me; you have made one who is prouder than her fellow-women feel that she is lower than the lowest, and more wretched than the most houseless wanderer. There are those who can wear their shame and turn it into their glory—Mildred Winnerley is not one of them; there are those who having been betrayed can sink lower still, and turn betrayers themselves—Mildred Winnerley would drink poison in preference. Months—long months ago you promised to make me your wife—you promised me that you would rescue me from shame. Those promises have not been kept; and now, if they are not redeemed, you know not what the result may be. You are Sir Hargrave Manners now, you are a baronet, and one whom the world calls a man of honour. Do then as becomes your title and your reputation; act as Sir Hargrave Manners, the man of honour should act. But listen! I have asked you to take my hand—to make me your wife—to rescue me from shame and infamy. Mildred Winnerley would once have thought herself too proud to have pleaded to you thus; but you have made her humble—you have taught her to ask favours from you. It is well. She who speaks to you now was on the way to the water when she met with you to-night. Another hour and she would neer have sat by your side, as now she does, begging justice from you. Deny her—deny me, Hargrave, and be a murderer if you will. I cannot live with the shame which you have brought upon me.—I can die, for it is proud to die when the world points its finger and laughs with the laugh of scorn. Oh yes; Hargrave, I can die. Be comforted man, Mildred Winnerley can die!"

"Mildred!" exclaimed the baronet, "why—why do you talk thus? You are rash—much too rash. Why this inconsiderate behaviour? It is true—quite true, that I have loved you; and true also is it that I once promised to make you my wife. But see you not why it is impossible for me to do so now, know you the circumstances in which I am placed? Heaven witnesses that were it not I am so situated I would make you my wife on the coming morrow!"

"Why—why can you not—what is it prevents you, Hargrave?"

"Hear me. You cannot but be aware that I displeased my father so much by thoughtlessness of conduct, that for some months before his death—for more than a twelvemonth indeed, I was denied his house. I knew not, I did not form an adequate idea of what his revenge would be. When on his death-bed I was not permitted to be by his side; and when he was dead, I found myself to be a disinherited son. His title which he could not otherwise bestow, fell to my share; but his property—that which should be mine—is enjoyed by another,"

"By who, dear Hargrave?"

"By Lady Manners. So long as she may live it will belong to her; but when her death takes place it will revert to me. While she lives I have nothing; and till she pleases to die I have to fight the world as I can. How is it possible for me to keep a wife, and who would wish to marry a beggar?"

"But—but, Hargrave, Lady Manners may die soon. She is now very ill."

"Yes; but inquiring this day of her physician, I learn that there is every chance of her recovering. What then have I to hope for? My father heard that I was abdicted to play, and disinherited me for a time, in order that I might be cured. There was little wisdom in that, Mildred. The man who was fond of play then, is a true gambler now. He wins his bread by his cards ; he pays for his shelter with the dice-box; he supports his honour with his tricks. What think you of that? Do you still wish to be his wife?"

Mildred answered not for some minutes. Then, grasping Hargrave's hand, she said,—

"I have heard you, Hargrave Manners, I have heard no more than I expected to hear. There is one question, however, which I wish to ask you, and which you must reply to in honest truth."

" Well, Mildred?"

"Listen ! You have told me that it is your poverty which prevents you from marrying. Were Lady Manners to die this week—were your late father's property to become your own before the present month comes to an end, would you then act with justice to her whom you have wronged—would you then recompense her for all the heart-ache of which you have been the cause?"

"I would."

"You would marry me—you would make me your wife?"

"Yes, Mildred."

" And nothing but change of circumstances is wanted on your part, in order that I should become your wife? Answer me solemnly, Hargrave Manners."

"Nothing but that, Mildred, upon my honour!"

Mildred took both of Hargrave's hands in her own, and looking fixedly at him, said,—

"Not that oath, Hargrave; it is valueless. On your hope of salvation tell me truly that were Lady Manners to die this week, I should be your wife."

"You should be, Mildred. By Heaven I make you that promise!"

"It is well," said the proud girl ; and before another quarter of an hour she was on her way to that home where her sister had so long waited her coming.

" What can have detained you, dear Mildred," asked poor Marion. " Oh, how anxious I have been!"

"I have had much to do, dear sister, and could not get home earlier."

" Thank Heaven, dear Milly, you have come at last! Oh, you know not how unwell I have been. My poor head has ached the whole day ; and I had such pains in my face that I could not bear them, and was obliged to go to the doctor's in the next street, and ask him for something to relieve them. See, dear sister, he has given me this to bathe my face with. It is laudanum, sister, and the doctor has put a label upon it to show that it is poison. We must be careful where we put it, sister, so that no accident happens, for the doctor told me that there was enough in the bottle to poison three or four people. See, I will place it at the back of the cupboard, out of the way."

And now that Mildred had come home, Marion sat down to partake of supper with her sister. The meal was soon finished ; very little conversation passing between the two orphans during its progress. At length, Marion, rising from her seat, said,—

" I am very—very sleepy, sister. Are not you coming to bed?"

" Not yet, Mar."

"But why not, dear sister. It is late very late, and you must be tired. Come, Milly, come."

"I—I have some work to do," answered Mildred, taking up her needle and part of

an unfinished dress. "I cannot go to bed yet, but do not let that hinder you, dear Mar·
I will come to bed by-and-bye."

"But the fire has gone out, Milly. Why sit up in the cold? Come, dearest, I will
do the work for you in the morning."

Mildred refused the kind offer of her sister, and persisted in sitting up. Wearied
with pain and watching, poor Marion sought her bed, and in the course of a few minutes
had fallen asleep.

Why had the elder sister refused to retire to rest? Why was it that Mildred Winnerley
continued to sit by that cold hearth, when the house was wrapped in silence, and the hour
of midnight had struck? It was not to work; for already had she laid aside the needle,
and suffered the unfinished dress to fall upon the floor. Her eead was bent down; her
hands were crossed upon her lap; she was gazing abstractedly at the cold fire-place, while
thoughts chased thoughts through her phrenzied and bewildered brain.

What are your thoughts, proud Mildred? Why sit you so moody at an hour so late?
Your sister is sleeping, and why are you not slumbering also? To your bed, Mildred
Winnerley! Think not those thoughts to-night. Remember! the second six months come
to their end to-morrow.

Still silent and thoughtful, still motionless and moody, the sister of Marion sits watching at the dead of night. She recals the various events of the day; she thinks over the
interview with her betrayer, and the promise which he has made, And Mildred Winnerley remembers that on the coming morrow she has to visit Lady Manners, to see her
in her chamber, and to be alone with her there. Why do you start now, fair Mildred? Why do your eyeballs roll so wildly, and why do your fingers twine round
one another, as if your mind was in torture, and your proud heart swelling with
pain. Lady Manners you must visit according to your appointment, and Lady Manners is the bar which keeps you from becoming the wife of Hargrave; but what of
that?

True, Mildred Winnerley; the lady is an invalid, and confined to her chamber; true
also, that with woman's vanity she will not have thee to see her in the daylight, when her
hollow cheeks are colourless, and her sunken eyes without a sparkle. You have to visit
her at evening; but what of that?

Yes; you will be alone with her in the room, that the trickery of the adornments may be seen by as few eyes as possible; and her medicines will be by your side;
and it is more than probable that she will ask you to hand her a cup or a glass; but
what of that?

Mildred Winnerly, why do you so? why creep you to the bedside of your sister? why
look you so carefully to see if that sister be asleep? What is it which you are about to
do that you fear your sister seeing you?

And now, why go you to the cupboard? Why take out that bottle? You know its
contents are laudanum; you know that it contains poison. Put it back in its place,
Mildred Winnerley, why touch it now, when all are sleeping? Your sister told you that
it held death within it. Put it back. What have you to do with death this dark and
silent night?

What are your thoughts now, proud Mildred? Why do you take the bottle
to the light, and gaze so earnestly at that which it contains? There is poison
in your hand. Put back the bottle in the place from which you have taken it;

put it back ere the tempter whisper further in your ear!—while your hands are yet guiltless—while your soul is yet unstained with crime, put the bottle back!

"No; not yet did Mildred Winnerley restore the bottle to its place. She held it before the light, she gazed at the dark liquid which it contained; she sought for another bottle in the cupboard from which she had taken that which was filled with poison. And now with trembling fingers she drew the cork, poured greater part of the contents of the full bottle into the empty one, and put in water to supply the deficiency, so that her sister might not detect that which she had done. Her hand trembled as she restored the bottle to its place in the closet; and still more did her hand tremble as she put the poison-phial in her pocket.

She turned, she looked upon her sister, sleeping so quietly by her side; she thought that she too would sleep if she could; but she felt that sleep was to be a stranger to her on that fearful night, so again seating herself upon the chair beside the cold hearth, she gazed at the dark embers, and mused in her own dark thoughts; and when in the chill grey morning Marion awoke, and finding her sister not to be sleeping beside her, looking round the silent apartment, she saw Mildred still sitting on the chair, with her head bent down, and her hands crossed upon her lap.

"Milly—dear Milly, why have you got up so early?"

There was no answer, Marion sprang out of bed, and hastened to the side of her sister, she saw that Mildred had never been to bed that night, she saw that gentle sleep had not visited her sister's eyelids. And Mildred's face was so very pale, and Mildred's eyes were so very strange in their expression, and Mildred herself trembled so much beneath her sister's touch, that Marion shuddered with apprehensive fear, knowing that something sad must have occurred to render Mildred so sorrowful, yet scarcely daring to inquire what that something had been.

"I sat thinking, dear Mar, till I fell asleep in my chair," was the only answer which Marion could obtain to her inquires, and she perceived that truth was wanting in that answer, for the countenance of Mildred told too plainly that through that lonely night gentle sleep had never once closed her eyelids.

And a mournful breakfast was that of which the sisters partook; for there was no pleasant talk, no merry laughter, no cheerful behaviour. Mildred was grave, and Marion felt a weight upon her spirits which not merely repressed all merriment upon her part, but even took away from her the power of entering into conversation. Then, when they rose up to part for the day, they bade each other farewell in a manner far different to their usual custom, and afterwards separated, not as they had been used to do, with smiling faces and mirthful words, but with looks of gloom, and sadly bidden adieus. Thus the sisters parted, the one [to remain in her solitary home, the other to wander forth with the poison-phial in her pocket. And often during that weary day did Marion rise up from her chair to gaze—she knew not why—through the window out into the busy thoroughfare; and often also did she lay aside her work to press her hand against the beating heart, wondering what cause it had to to beat so heavily, and why it seemed so oppressed with woe.

Slowly, gloomily did that day pass; and when the evening came, it found Marion sitting by the window, gazing forth along the dusky street, and still pressing her hand to her bosom to stay the aching there. Oh! how did she long for her sister's return, how did she pray for night to come. Still darker the shadows fell; still dusky and more dusky the evening became.]

Marion heard a knock at the street door, presently there was a sound of footsteps upon the staircase; and ere another minute had passed some one tapped lightly at the entrance to the apartment. Marion trembled as she rose up to see who her visitor was, while imagination whispered to her that it was some one who brought bad news concerning Mildred.

The poor girl opened the door, and a figure clothed in a dark dress, glided into the apartment.

CHAPTER XI.

THE MYSTERY OF MESMERISM.

"Be not afraid," said a voice which Marion had heard before. "Do you not know me?"

"I—I cannot remember. It is some one whom I have spoken to, but I forget who," stammered poor Marion.

"See!" said the visitor, as she advanced towards the window, and threw aside her cloak. "You cannot have forgotten the gipsey-girl who rescued you from the flames, when the cottage was on fire. You remember me now?"

"Yes. I do; I remember well."

"I am the gipsey-girl. I am Isis. See, I have found you out, because I wish to be your friend, to be more—much more than your friend—your sister. You will not be angry at the poor gipsey-girl calling you her sister?"

"No," answered Marion. "But now that you have come to visit me, let me procure a light, that we may see each other while we talk."

"Stay!" exclaimed the gipsey. "No light—no light! We do not want it. We must go, we must go soon."

"Go where?" asked Marion, with astonishment.

"I will tell you. Listen! You will believe the poor gipsey-girl? Oh, yes, you will believe me. I am very fond of you, I am ready to do anything to serve you. Isis has promised to love you, and Isis never, never breaks her word."

"I thank you—I thank you from my very heart!" returned Marion. No words— no thanks of mine can repay you for the kindness which you have already shown."

"What I do is not done for thanks, and for thanks alone I would do nothing," said the gipsey. "I can only serve those whom I love, and for them I would do anything."

"And there are many who love you, I hope, dear Isis."

The gipsy-girl was silent for a moment, and then made answer.

"No; there are few who love Isis, but there are many whom Isis is obliged to love."

"But how can that be, dearest?" inquired Marion.

"It is because there are some whom I dare not hate, and yet must serve. But do not let us talk any more about that. I have come here to tell you secrets."

"Secrets!" ejaculated Marion.

"Yes. Isis has promised to serve you; and whenever you want help Isis will be at hand. You have a sister—where is she?"

Marion trembled as she replied,—

"My sister Mildred has not yet come home."

"Not come home. Well, that is all the better. Your sister is very beautiful. Do not the people tell her so?"

"They have so told her," answered Marion; "and poor Mildred deserves every compliment which they can pay to her."

"Yes, yes; that is as you say. Well, listen! I am a poor gipsey, and our tribe has a chief who once loved your beautiful sister; but Pharold forgot he was nothing but a gipsey when he thought of loving one so beautiful and good. He is a true Zingaro, and where he does not love he is sure to hate. Your beautiful sister scorned him, and now he hates her more than he loved her before. I am afraid of Pharold. I am afraid when I see that he never forgets, and that he is planning every day for his revenge."

"For what—on who?" asked Marion, in a hurried voice.

"On her who would not love him," replied Isis. "Listen! I have much to tell you, and that is why I have come here. Do you know how the poor despised gipsey can do that which others cannot? Do you know that the gipsey has secrets which give him a power that none else have?"

"I have heard it so said," replied Marion; "but I am ignorant—quite ignorant of what that power is."

"I will tell you. It is a power by which one man can read the thoughts of another man, one woman penetrate into the heart of another woman. Do you understand me now?"

"No," answered Marion.

"Ah, then you have not heard of mesmerism; and yet the secret has been stolen from our tribe, and there are those who go about, thinking themselves wise in being able to do that which the poor gipsey could do three thousand years ago."

"But what is it which they do?" asked Marion.

"Watch! I will show and tell you. I will do as Pharold does, and you shall be Isis. As you sit in the chair I wave my hands before you, and look into your eyes. Were it Pharold that was looking at you, you would feel drowsy and go off to sleep. That is how it is when he does so to me. But then in my sleep I see things that I cannot see when awake; and as Pharold wishes me to do so, I describe to him what people are doing far, far away. I have dreams and I tell him what I see in my dreams; but my dreams differ from your dreams, because I see things that are really happening, and know what real people are doing, and what they will do. Pharold asks me, and I tell him all this in my dreams; but when I wake I have forgotten it all, and cannot recall it to my mind I have a faint remembrance only of who the person was that I saw in my dreams, and sometimes I know that my dreams have been very dreadful. Oh! how often I wish that I never had such dreams, and that no one could make me have them."

"And who is that that can make you, dear Isis?" inquired Marion.

"Pharold can. I must do as Pharold wishes. He is my master, and has the power."

"But does he use it often?"

"Yes; very often. Listen! he seeks to be revenged on your beautiful sister; and he often makes me dream about her. I do not know what it is I dream; but I am afraid I watch your beautiful sister at times when I would not do so if I could help it."

"This is very strange, and is more than I can understand, dear Isis. Why should you be sorry that you are compelled to tell your dreams when they are only foolish things that you see in your sleep?"

"Not foolish things. No. They are what people are doing at the time—at the very moment. Every act, every movement, every thought. It is strange, and you may not believe it; but Isis has come here to tell you truth, and to tell you that she would not have her dreams if she could prevent Pharold from making her have them."

"And why can you not—why not leave Pharold?"

"No. Isis dare not. I am afraid of Pharold. There is nowhere that I could go but he would find me. He is waiting for me now; and to-night I know that he is going to make me dream; and he will make me dream about your beautiful sister. What I want you to do is, to go with me, and I will put you where you shall see everything that happens, and hear everything which I tell in my dream. Then, afterwards, I can ask you what I have said, and I shall learn it from you."

"But why should I do so? Do you think that you will be able to dream what my sister Mildred is doing?"

"Yes; if Pharold makes me."

"And you think he will?"

"He is waiting to do so now. I have come to fetch you. You must come—come now."

"Where is it you will take me?"

"Isis will show you. Are you afraid to trust poor Isis because she is a gipsey-girl?"

"No. I am not afraid. I will go with you."

And impelled by an impulse which she could not resist, Marion put on her bonnet and cloak to accompany the gipsey to the strange scene which she was destined that night to behold. The moon was just breaking through the clouds as the two girls passed over the threshold, and emerged into the street.

Onward, along the noisy thoroughfares, and past rows of glittering shops, the gipsey and her companion directed their way. Their course was along Oxford Street, towards the western extremity. Hyde Park was soon reached, and Isis still continued to travel onwards in the direction of Bayswater.

"Have we to go much farther?" inquired Marion.

"Not now. Let us walk faster. We shall soon be there."

The two maidens now took their way along, beneath the wall of the park, and that of Kensington Gardens. They had proceeded to a considerable distance, when Isis turned towards the right, and led the way into some open fields which stretched out towards Paddington.

"I have watched you," said she to Marion, "and have followed you since you left your village. I knew that at some day you would require my assistance, and I wished to be able to give it you then."

"But what assistance can you give me now, dear Isis?"

"I know not. Follow me. Yonder, see, is the light of our camp—yonder, in the deep hollow. Come, we will steal round in the shadow of these trees that no one may see I have company. Softly—tread softly! They are sleeping—all save Pharold and Jasper. Give me your hand, and be not afraid."

Marion obeyed the instructions of Isis, and suffered herself to be led onwards to where a piece of old canvass was stretched over some staves stuck in the ground, so as to form a tent. The gipsey led her companion to the entrance of this tent and told her to enter quickly.

"You will be safe there," said she; "it is the tent of Isis; and none will dare enter it. Wait and watch. Pharold will bring me to the back of the tent and there cause me to dream. There is a small hole in the canvass; you will be able to see through that all which may occur, and you will hear also every word which I may say. Let nothing pass unnoticed, and let nothing be forgotten. I shall want you to tell me all that occurs."

Marion promised to do as she was desired; and Isis having seen her safe within the tent, parted from her, to seek those who were waiting her arrival.

And what was gentle Marion to see, what secrets were those which were to be disclosed to her now? She remembered this was the night on which the second six months came to an end; she knew that her sister had parted from her that morning in sorrow, and she had an impression that some evil, the nature of which she could not even imagine was about to befal that much loved and only sister. Could it be true, as the gipsey girl had said, that a human being had the power to cause one fellow creature to become acquainted with the doings of another at some remote place? Could it be true that by the mere exercise of his will, the gipsey chief could make one of his tribe so far subservient to his purposes, as to command her to reveal to him that which her own eyes could not see—which his own senses could not pierc? Impossible! And yet Marion Winnerley had heard what the gipsey-girl had said—had heard her statements concerning the miracles which mesmerism could effect, what was she to think?—what believe? She had a presentiment she had not come to that place in vain, and believing in that presentiment she waited for the revelations of that mystery.

Hush! there is the tread of feet at the back of the tent, there are parties approaching, they are drawing nearer—nearer still.

Marion applied her ear to the hole in the canvass, and discerned Isis in company with Pharold and Jasper, as she gazed at the countenances of the two men she trembled, and experienced a momentary fear, lest she had been betrayed, and led into some dangerous snare. But that suspicion quickly vanished from her mind; for as the light from a small lamp which Pharold carried in his hand, fell upon the countenance of Isis, Marion saw that she could trust that open brow, and felt that those dark, yet softly beaming eyes could not belong to one who was practising deception. She perceived that Isis glanced towards her as the party neared the back of the tent; and she feared lest her own beathing should betray her presence to the men by whom Isis was accompanied.

The moon was concealed from view by large dark clouds, the scene, and the actors were illuminated only by the small lamp which the chief now placed upon the grass.

"Jasper," said Pharold, "you have your book and pencil, place the lamp upon the ground beside you, and note down all that we learn to-night."

The instructions of the gipsey chief were attended to by his companion, and Isis prepared herself for the coming ceremony by taking a seat upon a small stool which had been placed for her, and by loosening her dress around her throat; the dull yellow lamplight fell upon her countenance, and Marion could perceive that her cheeks had turned of a deadly paleness, and then her lips quivered as if with fear.

"Are you prepared, Isis," inquired Pharold.

"I am."

"And you feel that to-night you will see well?"

"I do," answered the poor girl, trembling as she spoke.

The gipsey-chief advanced towards her, fixed his eyes upon her's with a steady gaze, and passed his hands slowly over her dress, carrying them downwards from her head towards her feet, and then making a curve, so as to repeat the movement in the same direction.

Marion watched; she saw that as the gipsey waved his hand the lips of Isis ceased to tremble; she saw that as the operator continued his mysterious operation the eyes of the maiden became heavy, and her eyelids drooped as if oppressed with an unwonted drowsiness. And the yellow lamplight fell upon the silent actors, flickering on the moving hands, and dimly resting on the closed eyelids. Heavily the bosom of Isis seemed to heave; listlessly drooped her slender arms by her side. Bound as if by the spell of an enchanter; motionless almost as carven marble, she sat before him whose mystical influence was so great, and by the exertion of whose power she had thus become a passive plaything in his hands.

" What say you, Jasper, does she sleep?"

The gipsey approached, and raising the left arm of Isis, held it in his grasp for a single moment, and then releasing it, perceived that it fell heavily against her side.

" She does," he answered.

Pharold moved nearer to the gipsy-girl and pressed the balls of her thumbs upon her eyelids.

" Isis!" said he.

A faint low muttering was the only reply which escaped from the lip of the motionless figure. The gipsey-chief drew his fingers over the closed eyes, then waved his hands around the sleeper's head, and finally breathed gently upon her face.

" Do you see now Isis?" he inquired.

The poor girl writhed, as if afflicted with sudden pain, and replied—

" Yes, I see now. I see to a great distance. But do not hurt me so; do not put such a heavy weight upon my chest."

The gipsy waved his hand twice across the chest of the sleeper, and her countenance immediately assumed an appearance of repose.

" Have you any pain now?"

"None."

Pharold took the right hand of Isis in his own, and directed Jasper to observe well all that was about to happen.

"Do you see the person I am thinking about, Isis," he inquired.

" Yes; I see a young woman whose countenance is very beautiful; she is sitting before a fire-place, and there is some one sleeping by her side."

" Look again. Is the same person sitting in the chair still?"

"No; she has just risen up; she goes to a cupboard, takes out a bottle, and holds it up before the candle."

" Is there any label upon the bottle?"

"There is."

" Read it then."

" I cannot. The letters are not clear."

The gipsy again pressed his thumb upon the closed eyelids of the sleeper.

" Read it now. Are there many words?"

" Only two."

" And what are they?"

" ' *Laudanum*' and ' *poison*' "

"Well, what more do you see?"

" The young woman has placed the bottle in her pocket; she has again sat down on the chair."

" Look again. What is she doing ?"

" She is still sitting in the chair, and the daylight is coming in through the window."

Pharold turned to Jasper and conferred with him in a whisper for a few minutes. Then again taking the hand of the sleeper in his own, he said—

" Look, Isis. Tell me what you see now."

" I see the same young woman."

" Where do you see her, and what is she doing ?"

" She is entering a grand house. I see her go up the staircase, and into a rooms where some one who seems to be ill is sitting up in a bed. It is a lady, and she is giving directions about a head-dress which is being tried on."

" What things are in the room ?"

" Many. There is a table with a lamp burning upon it, and on another table there are many bottles of medicine."

" See you nothing with a crest upon it. Look well, and be certain before you speak.'"

" Yes; I see a handkerchief in the lady's hand, and there is a crest at one corner.'"

" What is it ?"

" It is a bird holding a sword with its foot."

" And the young woman—what is she doing now ?"

" The lady has asked her to pour out something into a glass. She is doing so—she takes a bottle from her pocket—she pauses to see if the lady is looking—she empties the contents of the bottle into the glass."

" Well ?"

" She gives the glass to the lady—her hand seems to tremble—the lady has drank that which was given her."

" What did that look like which you saw poured from the small bottle into the glass?"

" It looked like that which was taken out of the closet in the bottle that had the label."

" And what do you see now ?"

" The lady in her bed appears to be taken suddenly unwell. There are many people round her; but the young woman is no longer there."

" Look, farther, then; look as I now wish you to!"

" I cannot. It is all dim. I am in pain—great pain."

Pharold drew his fingers across the forehead of the sleeper, and Isis awoke from the sleep of mesmerism. For a few minutes she gazed wildly about her. At length, perceiving that the two men had moved off to a distance, she arose from her seat, crept across that portion of the green turf which intervened between the tent and the place where she had been sitting, and was in the course of another minute kneeling by the side of Marion.

And Marion was trembling with fear, and her head was bent down upon her knees, and when Isis called her by name, she did not answer.

"What have you seen, dear? What has Pharold made me tell in my dream ?"

" I know not—I do not understand."

" But you saw, you heard, and you remember ?"

" Yes; all—everything."

"Then you must reveal it to me—you must tell it to poor Isis. You will do so, and then poor Isis may be able to assist you. But let us leave this place now. I will go with you to your home, and you can tell me all as we are on our way.'

And recalling to mind all the particulars of the scene of mystery, Marion endeavoured to inform Isis of the various occurrences which she had witnessed through the aperture of the tent. The gipsey-girl listened with the utmost attention; and as Marion finished her story, grasped her hand warmly, and said,—

"Oh, how glad—how glad I am that you can tell me this. I knew there would be something take place to-night; and there was but one way in which I could learn what it would be. It is well that you have been able to tell me all."

"Why well, dear Isis, and what does it all mean?"

"The meaning is not worked out yet. That must be waited for. But Isis will help you now."

"How help me, dearest? Who was it you saw in your dream? Was it my sister?"

"It was."

"And why was it that you dreamed about her!"

"Pharold made me "

Marion asked no further questions, save than as she parted from the gipsey-girl, at the threshold of her own home, she desired to know when and where she should she Isis again.

"I will be near you when I can assist you," replied the gipsey girl; "but when I cannot do that I shall be watching for you at a distance. Perhaps you will want me soon; I think you will. Isis will be ready. You shall see her again then."

So saying, the gipsey girl pressed Marion's hand, and without uttering another word, parted from her, and quickly disappeared in the gloom which enveloped the lower portion of the street.

And why did Marion shudder as she ascended the stairs towards her own apartment? Why did she now and then pause to place her hands against her pale forehead, and to hold the banister with so firm a grasp? She feared to enter that lonely room— she feared lest she should fail in finding her sister there.

Marion's fears were not groundless; she opened the door, and found the apartment to be as when she left it. The moonlight was now falling in through the window; but no Mildred was there—no Mildred had yet returned to her home.

Trembling and breathless, the younger sister crept towards the cupboard, and felt for the phial of poison which she had placed there on the preceding evening. She found it—her fingers grasped it—she carried it to the moonlight—she saw that it was full as when she left—she pressed it in her joy—she fell upon her knees; and then she ejaculated,—

"Thank God, it was but a foolish dream, then; and my sister has not taken away this poison. It is here—it is here—it is here!"

Then going closer to the window, Marion threw up the sash, and flung the bottle down into the street. She saw it fall, and she heard it break to pieces upon the hard stones.

"It is gone now," she ejaculated. "It was fearful to have it in the house. It is gone, and Heaven be thanked. There was no truth in the gipsey's dream?"

Not so, Marion Winnerley. The dream of the mesmerist was true; the eyes of the mesmeric sleeper had seen too clearly and too well. You have thrown the one bottle into the street—you have destroyed that; but you know not of the one which your sister—your own sister—carried out with her in her pocket when leaving her home this morning.

And where is that sister? She has not been used to stay thus away from her home; she has returned to you, Marion! evening after evening, earlier—much earlier than this. But last night she came late, and to-night it is later still; yet she has not come. Wherefore does she stay? Why did she sit by the cold hearth through the whole of the last night? and how knew the gipsey girl that? Why was she so sorrowful on leaving home this morning, and why does she not return now? Hush, hush! there are footsteps upon the stairs. She comes! Go, open the door to her, Marion, open it quickly!

Fearingly and with trembling, Marion opened the door, and perceived her sister standing on one of the upper stairs. As Marion took her by the hand, Mildred started and shrunk back, as if she feared her sister's touch.

"Come, Milly, come, dearest. What has made you so late?"

There was no answer. Marion led her sister into the room, and placed a seat for her, believing her to be faint and tired. Then enfolding Mildred's neck with her arm, the poor girl said,—

"What has happened, dear sister? What can have kept you from your home? Are you fatigued? Have you had much to do, dearest?"

"Yes," replied Mildred, faintly.

"And you are cold—you are very cold. Let me place the chair nearer the fire-place and I will quickly light a fire."

"No—no. I—am not cold."

Marion looked at her sister's face, and saw that it was ashen white; she watched her sister's lips, and perceived that they muttered inarticulate words. The moonlight, was still streaming placidly through the window-panes; and it fell upon the pale face the colourless lips, the wildly-wandering eyes of Mildred Winnerley. Wonder not that your sister is so pale, gentle Marion; marvel not at that which you see. The second six months have come to their termination now, and the curse of beauty has worked to bring about the fulfilment of the gipsey's prophecy!

And Marion looked upon her sister; and as the strange scene which she had that night witnessed in the gipsey's encampment come forcibly to her mind, her sister's arm fell from its resting-place; and an empty bottle falling from her hand, rolled upon the floor.

Marion saw that bottle glittering there in the moonshine. No wonder that she remembered the revelations of mesmerism; no wonder that overcome by terror she herself sank helplessly on the floor, beside the chair on which her sister sat.

Be not far distant, Isis. Your aid will be wanted soon!

CAAPTER XII.

THE CONFESSION TO THE UNKNOWN CONFESSOR.

On the day following that on which the circumstances related in the previous chapter occurred, it was announced to the world that Lady Manners had died unexpectedly on the preceeding night. The physicians were puzzled to account for the cause of her sudden attack, and all their efforts at combating death had proved of no avail. Lady Manners was dead, and Sir Hargrave was now entitled to inherit his father's property.

Some there were who hinted that her ladyship had died strangely, and that the manner of her death had scarcely seemed to be natural. It was even said that had she been poisoned, her death could not have been more unexpected or more strange. But then who could have administered poison? who could have entered her cnamber with an intent to cause her death? No one. None but her own domestics were known to have been near her; and Hargrave Manners was a stranger to the house.

They buried her as pompous wealth is buried—in fringed and furbelowed drapery—in leaden easing—in mahegany coffins, adorned with crests and arms, and all the mockery of death. Nor was it strange that Sir Hargrave Manners paid attention to the gaudy funeral; nor was it wondrous that he took care to see the dead decked with flowing plumes ,and attended to the grave by a goodly company. Had he not reason to do so? Had he not cause to rejoice? The world has its customs in these matters; it knows not why it should be otherwise than joyful when the dead make way for the living, and the grave with kindly care clears away the obstructions to wealth, and title and honours!

So, when the funeral was over, when the mason received his orders for the tombstone, and the herald-painter had sketched out the hatchment, Mildred Winnerly departed from her home to seek this man who was now bound to redeem his promise; and who could no longer offer the same excuse for refusing to make her his wife whom he had so often sworn to love. He was wealthy Sir Hargrave Manners now; and Mildred went forth to remind him of his oath—to demand from him the performance of his pledge. She knew that he still resided in the same chambers where the last interview had taken place, and thitherward she directed her way.

Once or twice as she passed along the dimly-lighted streets she turned round and perceived a shadow following her at a distance; she saw that when she stopped it stopped also; and that when she altered her course, the shadowy figure did so likewise. At times the figure gained upon her as if it wished to overtake her; at other times it slackened its speed as if about to follow her no farther.

What was the figure, and who was he that was following Mildred Winnerly. He was a man clad in country attire; with a countenance which wore a mournful expression, and whose wish it seemed to be to speak with her that he watched her on her way along the dark thoroughfares. Never once did he suffer his eyes to wander from her; never once did he appear to look at any passenger whom he chanced to meet. Still gliding onwards, he followed Mildred as she hastened towards the chambers of Hargrave Manners.

And now Mildred passed beneath the arch, wended her way across the paved court, ascended the old stairs, and once again stood before the door of the room in which she had heard Hargrave Manners utter the last promise which he had made her. She had already laid her fingers upon the knocker when perceiving the door to be unfastened, she opened it, and entered the apartment.

The door of the chamber being thus left open, and there being nothing to impede her progress, the adventurous girl entering the gloomy room, passed on in the darkness, while the figure which had followed her up the stairs glided in after her and stole noise-lessly to her side.

Twice did Mildred faintly call Hargrave by name; but receiving no answer, she felt her way into an adjoining chamber, still darker than the former one, but where she fancied that she heard the sound of moving footsteps.

All was dusky and dim, there was no moonlight peeping in through the old massy window, and no twinkling star had taken its place on that night in the distant sky.

"Hargrave," called Mildred, faintly.

No reply was made, but a warm yet trembling hand was laid upon her own.

"You are here, Hargrave.—It is you!"

"I am here," was the answer, uttered in a smothered voice, while the hand tightened its grasp.

"And you know me, Hargrave? It is I—Mildred."

Still more tightly did the hand press her own fingers in its firm, yet nervous clasp.

"Hargrave—Hargrave Manners," said Mildred. "I have sought you here to-night that I may ask you a question and hear your answer. Listen to me! Months—many months ago you talked to me of love, and promised then to make me your wife. And I believed you, Hargrave; you know that I believed you then. I have had cause to doubt the truth of your promises, and the value of even your most solemnly-uttered words. But a few nights since, Hargrave, we met each other in this house. I then reminded you of your promises. I asked you to be just and honourable to her who once trusted you so much. I asked you, Hargrave, to redeem your promise; I asked you to make me your wife. Your answer was, that you still loved me, but could not make me that which I am already in the sight of Heaven, because—because, Hargrave, you were poor, and had to wait for the death of her to whom Sir Walmsley had left his property, before you could redeem you promise. That, you said, was the only barrier that stood between us and our happiness; that, you declared to be the obstacle which prevented you from doing according to you promise, and acting as honour dictates that you should act. And now, Hargrave, that barrier is removed—that obstacle exists no longer. Lady Manners is dead, and you—you are Sir Hargrave now. Tell me, then—for I am come to learn if you spoke truth to me the other night—will you redeem your promise—your solemn promise?"

"I will," replied the same low and suppressed voice.

"You will make me openly—you will let the world know me by the title which is rightfully mine—that of Lady Hargrave Manners?"

"No," was the reply, uttered in a hoarse, choking tone.

"Then—then—what am I to understand—what mean you, Hargrave?"

Deep silence followed this enquiry, and Mildred's question met with no reply.

"Again, Hargrave—I ask you again, will you be just to me—to your Mildred—will you redeem that promise which you so solemnly made?"

"I will."

"And I shall be your wife—I shall be Lady Manners?"

"No," was the answer returned in the same deep sepulchral voice, while the fingers of the speaker clasped tightly the cold hand of the agitated girl.

"No, Hargrave—not that word. Hear me—know me—listen to me! I am a woman with a proud heart and with a resolute spirit, Hargrave Manners. In time gone by you talked to me of love, and because you were of noble birth—because you were the late Sir Walmsley's son, I was willing to believe you—willing to listen to your words and accept your addresses. Understand me rightly—there must be no deception, no misunderstanding between us to-night; I did not love you, Hargrave; I wished to be your wife, and I wished to be so because I knew that on some future day you would be a baronet. I deceived you, Hargrave, if by my behaviour I led you to suppose that I had any real affection for you; and you deceived me by causing me to suppose that your love was as deep and as passionate as I believed it to be. So far, then, we have undeceived one another; so far, nothing is misunderstood between us. But lately—only a few nights since, Hargrave, you again talked to me of love—you again solemnly assured me that I should be your wife, and that the sole obstacle to our union was the existence of one who has now gone to her grave; you promised me that were she dead I should be your wedded wife. She is dead now, Hargrave Manners—your step-mother is dead. Do you guess how she died?"

"I do not."

"Have you no conjecture? Do you forget how resolute in her nature your Mildred Winnerley is? You cannot see my face, Hargrave, this room is too dark, if you could, you would guess how Lady Manners died."

The warm fingers trembled as they still retained their grasp of Mildred's death-cold hand.

"You make no guess, you are silent, Hargrave. Listen to me, and in this dark room, where you cannot look upon my countenance while I speak—where you cannot watch me as I tell the tale, you shall hear a story which interests you much. Why do your fingers keep moving over my hand? are you afraid to hear that which I am not afraid to tell?"

"No," was the reply, given in a low whisper.

"The story, then, is of a proud girl who won a promise from a man who had once deceived her; there was no love between them, and never had been; but the girl knowing that—knowing that love would not cause the promise to be kept, thought that gratitude would bring about its performance. And the man being poor and titleless, and there being one obstacle in his way to riches and nobility, the proud girl thought that if she could remove that obstacle—if she could bring the riches and the title to him, and he came to know that her hand had wrought the change, that then—deceiver though he had been—deceiver though he intended to be—he would think how much she had done for him, and seeing how resolute and how bold she had been, would keep his promise, not because he loved her, but because through her he had become a rich man and a baronet. Do you understand me now, Hargrave?"

The fingers loosed the grasp of Mildred's hand, and a quivering, agitated, hoarse voice answered,—

"No, Mildred."

"Must I speak plainer, man—must I tell you that I—I was and am that proud girl, and that through me—by my hand Lady Manners died."

"Mildred!" ejaculated he who had listened to the story.

"Ay, Mildred the murderess, Hargrave Manners, for I am one!"

"You—you?" returned the listener in a voice which sounding less muffled—less disguised than it had been, scarcely seemed to Mildred Winnerley like the voice of Hargrave.

"Yes, I—I can tell you how Lady Manners died, that Sir Hargrave might make another Lady Manners take her place. I have done it—I!"

"God! this is horrible: it cannot be true!" exclaimed he whom Mildred addressed.

"It is true, and——" but suddenly Mildred ceased from speaking as the thought struck her that the voice which she had last heard was one which seemed not like that of Hargrave. Terrible thought! Could it be that she had made a mistake, and in the darkness of that lone room told her fearful story to another, and not to Hargrave Manners? Was it possible that to the ear of a stranger—to the ear of some one of whom she had no knowledge, she had confided that fearful secret which she had allowed her lips to disclose. No wonder that in the terror of suspense, the agony of her suspicion, the anxiety of her doubt, the cold perspiration stood in clustering drops upon her brow, no wonder that her limbs trembled, and that her breathing became partially suspended. Some few seconds elapsed before she rallied, then endeavouring to get the better of her fears, and persuade herself into an amount of courage of which she was scarcely possessed, she moved, or rather tottered forward, and endeavouring to grasp the arm of him to whom she had spoken, she whispered—

"Hargrave! Speak—speak!"

"Not to-night," returned the individual addressed—"not to-night, Mildred." Then before Mildred could exert herself to detain him he glided by her in the darkness, and left the room.

Was it Hargrave who had quitted her presence, or was it some one else? The voice was scarcely his; yet the individual whoever he was uttered her name, had pronounced it as if it were familiar to him. "Yes," decided Mildred—"it must be he—it must be Hargrave." And no sooner did she feel reassured on this point, than groping her way towards the staircase, she listened but heard not the footsteps of any one descending the stairs; she looked over the balusters, but nothing could she see save one small flickering lamp that shed its feeble rays upon the lowest landing place.

"Hargrave!" she exclaimed as she descended the stairs.

There was no reply.

She had reached the story immediately beneath that in which the previous scene had occurred, when, observing a door to stand partially open, she looked in, and discerned a man seated in a chair, with a cloak thrown on a table before him, while his hat yet remained upon his head and his gloves upon his hand. There was a light burning in the apartment, and by that Mildred beheld the countenance of Hargrave Manners.

"Hargrave—Hargrave Manners, you must not try to escape me!" she cried.

Manners started from his chair, and in a tone of surprise exclaimed.

"Miss Winnerley—Mildred! Why are you here?"

"I have followed you—followed you closely down the stairs from the dark room."

"Followed me! Well it may be that you have so; but certainly not down the stairs; up them you mean, seeing that I have but this moment entered the chamber."

"But from where—from where?" eagerly inquired Mildred.

"From the street," was the reply.

At that moment the glance of Mildred Winnerly chanced to alight upon the boots of Hargrave; she saw that they were wet and soiled with moist dirt; she saw also that there were spots of rain upon his hat. A feeling of sickly faintness overpowered her, the blood seemed to desert her heart suddenly, and she caught hold of the arm of Hargrave to save herself from falling.

"Tell me," said she in a breathless whisper—"tell me, were you not with me a minute since in the room above?"

"Not I, indeed, I can assure you, my dear girl. I have had no such pleasure. My chambers are on this story, as you see, and I have nothing to do with the one above."

"And who—who is it lives there?"

"Well, save the rats and the spiders, both of which are tenants in reversion for habitations of this sort, I am not aware that any one has taken up his abode in those chambers since the demise of the gentleman who has left his name upon the door."

Mildred covered her eyes with her outspread hands, and was silent. What had she done? To whose ear had she told the tale of horror? She knew not, she could form no guess. A minute passed away; then clutching the right arm of Hargrave, she looked wildly in his face, and said—

"Hargrave, I am your wife. There is no other Lady Manners now."

The young baronet rose up; and leading Mildred to a chair, invited her to sit down.

"I know not what has brought you here at this juncture," he said, after a moment's pause; "but as I have something to say to you of importance, it may be as well that I should avail myself of the opportunity. First, however, as you appear a little fatigued and excited, I must beg that you will favour me by taking a glass of wine; and after that we will proceed to business."

Mildred hastily swallowed the proffered draught, and then, leaning forward as she spoke, said in a tone which almost approached to a whisper.

"I am ready, Hargrave—ready to listen."

"Just so, Mildred, I must request that you will listen calmly, and think dispassionately on that which I have to communicate; in the first place the death of Lady Walmsley Manners has released me from certain difficulties under which I laboured, and in the second the death of that lady has placed me in circumstances which, from their intricate and perplexing nature confine me to a very circumspect line of action. Now with regard to yourself, our acquaintance has caused very much nonsense to pass between us, and entailed some inconveniences; I propose to do so in a manner which while it is most eligible to myself is likely to prove most comfortable to you; it is very simple and I will explain it."

"I listen, Hargrave."

"Thank you. The death of my father you see endowed me with the title of baronet, but not with anything substantial by which that title was to be supported. People have pitied me as poor Sir Hargrave, at the same time supposing that on the decease of Lady Manners sufficient property would revert to me in order to maintain my position with respectability. Well, Lady Manners is no more, and it turns out that all the property which has now passed into my possession scarcely exceeds one tithe of that amount which popular expectation believed it would be. Under such circumstances wisdom dictates prudence. This is a world, my dear girl, in which it does not behove any one to take a rash step; foresight, caution and reflection are the qualifications which it is needful for every one to possess. Now what would result if I contented myself with the gifts that fortune has so obligingly sent me and were to marry some unendowed maiden—yourself, for instance? Why, such imprudence would amount to madness; and such folly would well deserve all the laughter that it would obtain. Suppose on the contrary, however, an opportunity presented for my leading some damsel to the altar, whose fortune might be sufficient to make my title something more than a mere name. In that case you perceive, I should be able to allow you a moderate sum, to make your way in the world with, and furthermore have the advantage of being able to confer a favour or two upon any one else whom I might wish to oblige. This is all prudential reasoning; all sober, calm, and practical. Well, it happens then, that having lost no time and disregarded no opportunity, I have succeeded in nearly accomplishing so desirable an object, and have the pleasure to be able to say that the lady to whom I now stand engaged, besides the high position which she holds in society, has the more excellent qualification of an ample and satisfactory dowry of the most substantial description. All things are arranged and —— but, good Heavens! my dear Mildred, what is the matter with you? Are you unwell? Do you find this apartment too close? Will ——"

"I—I am quite well, Hargrave. I am listening to you. Oh, I am so well—so very well. I—it is nothing. You are going to be married, I think you said, and your bride ——"

"Will be young, rich, and noble."

"Yes, yes. I—me—you will not marry me."

"Tush! my dear girl. Marriage is a matter of interest and money. If I wed so as to be able to give you money to make you comfortable, that will be to your interest—will it not?"

"Yes—certainly, yes," answered Mildred, in an attempted tone of playfulness; then drawing her chair nearer to Hargrave, she fixed her eyes upon his countenance, and in an earnest, but seemingly not angry voice, enquired,—

"Your lady is very rich and very beautiful—is she not?"

"Both."

"And—and she believes that you love her, I suppose?"

"I have used my endeavours, so far as lay in my power, to impress her with that belief."

"Yes—yes. And she is noble. Her name is ——"

"The Lady Henriette Bellayre—Lord Bellayre's eldest daughter."

"And does she live in town—in London, I mean, dear Hargrave?"

Had Hargrave Manners noticed more observingly the manner in which Mildred asked this question, he would have paused before returning an answer. As it was, however, he replied,—

"The lady elect is now staying with her family at their town-house."

Preserving silence for a few seconds, Mildred rose from her seat, and keeping her gaze still fixed upon the countenance of the baronet, said,—

"There would seem to be nothing that is likely to impede your marriage, Hargrave. As for myself, I believe you said—dear me! I have quite forgotten what you did say."

"That so soon as Lady Henriette's fortune becomes my own, Mildred, I will allow you out of it sufficient to keep you in comfort."

"You are in earnest, Hargrave Manners?"

"On my oath I am."

"Thank you. And now I must bid you good night."

The baronet was startled as those two words—"Thank you!" fell upon his ear; there was that in them which sounded so strange, so sarcastic, so full of a hidden and a deeper meaning, that he gazed with a look of astonishment and perplexity at the face of her by whom they had been uttered. But he could not read the book which was contained there ; he failed in perceiving how dark a demon lurked in the smile which accompanied those simple words.   And as the woman whom he had wronged quitted his apartment, and stood upon the staircase without, he did not see how her eyes glistened, how her bosom heaved, how her clasped hands—so tightly clasped that the nails indented the flesh—told, by the tightness of their clasp, the desperate vindictiveness of her feelings.   Did he think that she, the haughty-souled, ambitious girl, was to be the paid mistress of a man whom, by her own dark confession in the upper room, she had been instrumental in elevating to his present position ?   Did he suppose that she, who had dared—who had done so much to become his wife, was willing to be his pensioner ?— she, who had sought to be Lady Manners, consent to be Sir Hargrave's mere annuitant ?   She had heard, she had listened well ; and now—now as she descended that dark staircase—now as she stood in the shadow of that old doorway, she vowed to the winds of heaven and the gloomy night, that if Sir Hargrave Manners never took her hand before the altar, no hand of mortal woman should he ever press within his own before that holy place.   She whose hand had been thought so little worth, now resolved that the greatness of the slight should only be equalled by the intensity—the depth of her revenge.

So into the streets she went, unknowing with whom it was she had held conference in that dark room, and to whom she had confided the dreadful secret.   At times she was tempted to go back, re-ascend the old staircase, and investigate if there was still any one within that gloomy apartment.   Then again she paused in her part and was half disposed to believe that her imagination had deceived her, and that she had merely fancied the existence of a companion while in that lonely chamber.   But how could that be the case?   Had she not heard a human voice ?   Did she not touch a human hand ?   And whose voice—whose hands then, could they have been ?   Whose ear had listened, and who was it that had gone forth to the world, able, if willing, to proclaim the secret of her monstrous guilt ?   She had confessed that she was a murderess, yet confessed she knew not to whom !   And what if he who knew the secret should proclaim it to the world ?   Well might Mildred Winnerley feel her brain reel, her senses to wander.   Along the street she went, and knew not if he to whom she had told the story walked behind her ; down the gloomy lane she turned, and knew not if he who walked before her was in the secret of her guilt.   So with fear in her heart, anxiety in her bosom, and revenge in her proud spirit, she went in her wretchedness home.

Home ! how sweet does that word sound to the happy and the innocent, but what bitterness is there in it to the wretched and the guilty !   There is a home for virtue everywhere ; to the criminal there is no home where there is no forgetfulness.

Changing the scene of the story, the action of the drama passes from the lonely streets and crime-stained Mildred, to the mansion of Lord Bellayre, and the elegantly appointed drawing room wherein at the close of evening the Lady Henriette sat, surrounded by her lovely sisters.

"Most fortunate, Henriette!" said the youngest daughter of Lord Bellayre, " only three dull months to pass away, and then you are to wear the orange blooms and learn the behaviour of a bride !"

" Imagine—only imagine, dear Emmeline," said the sister next in age to the Lady Henriette, " how very funny it will sound to hear them talk of the Lady Henriette

Manners. It will sound so novel, so strange, so unlike anything we have ever heard before. And Henriette to have a husband too. I wonder how she will live with him, and how they will employ their time, and whether they will ever come to see us, and whether we shall ever go to see them. And, oh! I wonder too if Henriette will get her dear husband to hold a skein of silk for her, just as she gets her lover to hold one now. I wonder very much about that."

"And whilst you have been so wondering, dear Clara, you have positively done so wise a thing as to put green worsted into the parrot's eye that you are embroidering."

"Thank you, sister. I see that I have been foolish enough to do so, but be cautious, Henny, lest when you have your husband you too have nothing to do with green eyes. I think they say jealousy has them."

"They say so, most witty sister, but one advantage is that if the gentleman you mention have green eyes, like your parrot, he is not in any way disposed to prattle; but is somewhat of a moody dispostion, such as any parrot would be if it had so ungraceful a neck and so drooping a head as yours seems to have."

"Ah me, my poor parrot!" returned Clara, with a merry sigh "how true it is that when people are in love, nothing is beautiful in their eyes save and except the one object of their affection."

A burst of laughter from the younger sister of the Lady Henriette followed this remark; and the jesting might have been carried to a somewhat unpleasant length had not a servant at that moment entered the room and announced that Lady Bellayre requested the immediate presence of her eldest daughter in her boudoir.

"Go, Henny," said the younger sister "*Mere* is waiting to give you a lesson in housekeeping, dear."

Amidst a titter of merriment, the Lady Henriette left the room to seek the boudoir of her parent.

It was a handsome room in which Lady Bellayre was waiting the reception of her daughter. Magnificent mirrors, elegant work-tables, china ornaments of the most exquisite patterns, and hangings of the richest pink and crimson hues, composed the furniture and the adornments of her ladyship's apartment. As her daughter entered, Lady Bellayre rose from off a couch to meet her, and displayed a graceful and commanding figure, with a countenance that had in it an air of queenly beauty, which while it fascinated by its beauty, awed also at the same time by the dignity of its majesty. There were indications that the complexion of her ladyship was usually of a roseate hue, yet at the present time her cheeks were ashen pale, and her lips were absolutely colourless.

"Henriette—dear Henriette! I wish to speak with you alone, my child."

"You are in tears, dear mamma; you look terrified. What has happened? What have you to grieve about?"

Lady Bellayre led her daughter to the couch, and sitting down beside her, preserved silence for a few minutes. At length, after addressing her with a few introductory words, she said,—

"It has grieved me exceedingly, my dear child, to hear that which I have heard within the last hour; it grieves me still more that having listened to that which has proved a

PHAROLD ENCOUNTERS JACOB SMAGS.

source of the most poignant sorrow to myself, I should feel it necessary to communicate the cause of that sorrow to you.''

"Dear mamma; what do these horrible words portend. Tell me—tell me!''

"Let me tell you calmly, if it be in my power to do so. The subject is one which so deeply concerns your happiness that——''

"My happiness, dear mamma! Can it—can it be in any way connected with—with my relation to Hargrave ?''

"It is.''

"What of him, dear mamma—what of Hargrave ?''

"I know not, dear child—I know not, unless that which I have heard be true, and if so, the——

"You hesitate, dear mamma! you are afraid to tell me that which you have heard!"

"I would willingly—how willingly Heaven knows!—not have to make to you any such communication. I have heard within this hour, dear child, and I have received solemn assurance, that Sir Hargrave Manners has not acted towards you with that openness—that candour which should have characterized his behaviour when making proposals for your hand."

"Hargrave a deceiver, dear mamma! Oh no, you cannot—do not mean to say that he is that!"

"I have not said so, my dear child. But listen, while I tell you that which I have heard concerning him. It is said that some time since he promised marriage to a poor girl, and by that promise contrived to ruin her peace of mind, and bring her to dishonour. The poor girl applied to him in her trouble, but he left the country and paid no attention to her application. A child of which he was the father died some short time since, and to the mother of that child, he did not so much as advance the money for its burial. Latterly, my dear daughter—ever since having made his proposal for your hand—he has again promised marriage to the poor girl whom he deceived, and is at the present moment bound by that promise to wed her. I have heard even more than this; but Sir Hargrave must be called upon for explanations on the subject respecting which I have already given you information."

"Explanations! If Hargrave be that which you have described him—if he be guilty of such wickedness, I will never speak to him, never suffer him to stand in my presence again! But he cannot be so guilty, dear mamma, he is not as you have pictured him to be. It is you who have been deceived, dear mamma. Some enemy—some foe of Hargrave's has told you these untruths. The story, dear mamma is a fabrication. I will not believe it. It is a falsehood."

"I would wish to believe it such, my child."

"Then do—do until Hargrave himself confesses to it, or you see the woman whom he is thus said to have wronged."

"She is here," returned Lady Bellayre, and stepping aside, she unlocked the door of an adjoining apartment, was absent for a single second, and then returning to the boudoir, she presented Mildred Winnerley to the Lady Henriette.

CHAPTER XIV.

THE PLOTTERS IN THE CHAMBER.—HOW THE LOVER AGREES TO BECOME THE ACCUSER. —JACOB SMAGS AND HUMAN NATURE.

AGAIN the scene changes, and again at night time, Sir Hargrave Manners sits in that lonely chamber where his last interview with Mildred was held. His head rests upon his hand; his fingers are thrust into his tangled, disordered hair, his hat and cloak are thrown on the floor beside him, his features wear the expression of demoniacal rage.

"Curse her—curse her!" he mutters between his clenched teeth. "The deceitful, devilish jade. That she should have gone to their house and told them her cursed story in such artful words. D—n her!"

And as Sir Hargrave was uttering these execrations in the lonely chamber, a man clothed in a dark rough coat was entering the door way below, and advancing up the staircase. He had not proceeded up many of the stairs before he stumbled over something in the dark.

"All right," exclaimed the undefined mass over which the man stumbled. "I'm Jacob—Jacob Smags. I'll speak about it to the Prince."

"What are you doing there, you drunken fool?" said the man who had so unceremoniously aroused Jacob from his slum ber.

"Drunk—who says I'm drunk? Jacob Smags has never been drunk since the last time Lord Castlereagh filled up the glass and proposed for a toast—for a toast—hip, hip,—hip, I say, hurrah!"

Leaving Jacob to relate his anecdote, the man passed on, and arriving at the landing-place, knocked at the door of Sir Hargrave's chamber. The door was opened by Sir Hargrave himself.

"Sir Hargrave Manners, a word with you."

"What are you, sir—why come you here?"

"On business—business that concerns you much. Give me admittance and I will let you know why I have troubled you at this hour,"

Sir Hargrave hesitated. "I know not who you are," said he.

"That will be better known when we have talked more together concerning the disappointments of to-day."

Sir Hargrave looked surprised, but after some further hesitation, he gave admittance to the stranger, who unceremoniously availed himself of a seat.

"You wish to know who I am," he said, addressing the baronet, and at the same time throwing open his outer coat. "Look at me, that you may know me. They call me Pharold the gipsey.'

"I have not seen you before, so far as I can remember," observed Hargrave.

"You have. But that matters not to the business of to-night. It is the chief of a gipsey band who is called Pharold, and I am he."

"Why have you come here? what is your business with me?" enquired the baronet.

"This.—You were to have wed the daughter of Lord Bellayre, but that wedding has been baulked—is not that the truth?"

"It is, man ;but how know you that?"

"I am a gipsey. Think you my secrets are so few. Shall I tell you who has baulked this marriage— who has crossed your path?"

"Do you know her?"

"I do; her name is Mildred—they call her Mildred Winnerley."

"My curses on her, man! You have named the revengeful wench."

"Revenge is sweet," returned the gipsey ; "she has had hers, would you not like to have yours."

"Ay, man; by Heaven I would!"

"Nor more so than I would have mine. Come, we will plan together."

"Plan what—plan how ?"

"To be revenged. This same girl was once offered a gipsey's love—the love of one who was a prince in his tribe; she spurned it; and the gipsey never forgets."

"Say you so, man! And that gipsey—"

"Was myself The gipsey has not forgiven ner forgot ; he has waited for his revenge' and now—the time has come."

" How come ?"

" I will tell you. It matters not to you how I, a gipsey, happen to know such a secret; but what if I tell you this girl is a murderess, and that it is in my power to prove her such."

" You !"

"Pharold the gipsey. He it is who tells you that the girl is a murderess—aye, Sir Hargrave, the murderer of your step mother—the murderer of Lady Manners. You start, you seem doubtful ; but the gipsey knows what he is saying, and says no more than he knows. I have had means of watching that girl—of following her in her actions when at a distance from her; and I tell you that she is the murderess of Lady Manners —that she murdered her by poison—that she murdered her to give you wealth, so that she might be your wife."

" Is this truth—can it be truth ?"

"It can be, because it is. Hark you! This girl is a trouble to you; she has crossed your path once, and if you stop her not she will cross it again. You must prevent her, and in so doing you will have your revenge."

" But how, man—tell me your plan ?"

" It is very simple."

" But it is what?"

" This :—You lay an accusation of murder against the girl, and when her trial takes place let Pharold the gipsey be called upon to support the charge. No more is necessary ; no more is wanted."

" Accuse her—accuse her of murder !"

" So, man. Do you think she would shrink from the job if it was she who had to make the charge and you had done the murder ?"

" She—she would."

" Very likely, I should say, judging from how she has behaved already. Have you not lost the earl's daughter through her already, and has she not obliged you by publishing all she could about you to the world."

" Yes, yes."

" And would you not have revenge ?"

" I would."

" Then take it. What have you to fear—what dread ? You have only to lay the charge—I—Pharold the gipsey will support it."

A further conference ensued between the baronet and his visitor ; and it was that night decided that Sir Hargrave Manners should become the accuser of Marion's sister—the accuser of her whom he had once professed to love. When the arrangement was concluded the gipsey took his departure.

"She will remember that night now," he muttered to himself; "she will remember that night when she refused to wed one who is the chief of his tribe. Be it so; the Zingaro has his revenge."

With a smile of malice upon his swarthy countenance, the gipsey pursued his way. Leaving him to play his part, it becomes necessary to trace out the manner in which Jacob Smags had employed himself during the conference between the two men in the chamber.

Rolled, or rather coiled up in a dark bundle upon the stairs, Jacob had assumed that position in order to sleep off the overpowering effects of suudry potations in which he had that day indulged himself; he was roused from his slumber by receiving an unpleasant kick from the gipsey as the latter was passing up to the apartment of the baronet, and though feeling at first very angry at having been disturbed, Mr. Smags in a very short time suffered his anger to subside into curiosity, and he was seized with a strong desire to know who the man was that had passed him on the stairs, and what his errand was in the upper part of the house. Intent upon satisfying this spirit of enquiry, Jacob contrived to steady himself by the hand-rail as he crept up the staircase, following the steps of the gipsy.

Arrived at the door of the chamber which Pharold had just entered Jacob, with a movement which seemed natural to him, managed so to fall upon his knees that he brought the keyhole immediately in a line with his left eye. As this method of study was the one by which Jacob had gained the greater part of the information which he had picked up in his course through life, his position was perfectly convenient to him, while his well trained ear, by being applied to the wood work of the door, failed not in catching such particulars of the conversation as Mr. Smags more especially, deemed it requisite that he should become acquainted with. It was some few minutes before Pharold departed that Jacob quitted his post, and descended the stairs in silence. He waited till the gipsy had left the house; then, retracing his steps, he again mounted the staircase, and knocked at the baronet's door. Supposing that the gipsey had returned to make some further communication, Sir Hargrave flung the door open, and bade his visitor to enter.

"You see who it is," said Mr. Smags—"It's I—Jacob. I—I've come to have a bit of talk."

"Get out, you scoundrel!" exclaimed the baronet, endeavouring to eject Jacob, and to close the door.

"Now don't be in a hurry—don't; you are only doing harm to yourself," observed Mr. Smags. "I've got something to tell you about the French count that we fell in with when on our tour together in Germany."

"There is nothing that you have to say which I wish to hear," said the baronet. "If you do not leave the room I shall have the trouble to kick you down the stairs."

"Well, you never have done that more than once before; and once is as good as a feast in them matters. I'm out of place now; so I've come to do you a service by telling you the French count is in town and knows where you live."

"Ha! rascal!" ejaculated the baronet, "am I indebted to your kindness for such an announcement. Tush! you are at perfect liberty to tell the Count of Aaltois or any one else where to find me if you choose, only beware that you do not incur a horsewhipping for your pains."

"Jacob Smags never had but two horsewhippings in his life," replied that worthy, "as for the French count it is'nt exactly correct that he knows where you live, or what the name of the gentleman was who fleeced him at Wiesbaden; however, you know I've met him in the street, and it's just possible that he may find you out."

"Which is as much as to say, you scoundrel, that unless I pay you for not doing so, you will oblige him with the requisite information."

" Well I might do so—I might, Jacob Smags is nothing more than human nature, though he has mixed with the best society."

" Mixed with them, you impudent villain !"

" Yes, Jacob has; he's stood in the same room with them—with a tray in his hand; but he's human nature for all that; and it's best for you to keep down human nature if you can, Sir Hargrave."

The baronet mused for a few moments, and then addressing Jacob, said,—

" Let us understand one another, the Count D'Aarlois is in town, you say, and it is certain that were we to meet, or any one to give him information as to where I am, I should have the pleasure of being recognised by him as the gentleman who arrived so suddenly at Wiesbaden and departed so suddenly again, after having taught the count that there are more tricks than one in card-playing. Well, any such recontre would be very inconvenient. I shall do my best not to put myself in his way, while you, I suppose, set a price upon your tongue, which only requires to be paid to purchase silence."

" That's human nature, Sir Hargrave, and that's Jacob Smags."

" Just so. Well, here is a note which I suppose will satisfy you. Take it; and see that you act prudently."

A few more words passed between the baronet and his old servant; then, taking his departure, Jacob passed out into the street, and stopped under a lamp to take a glimpse at the note.

"A ten bits flimsy by jingo !" he ejaculated. " Well, I've managed the first part of the business very well, and now for the next. The flimsy goes into my pocket and can't be taken out again. As to the little plot I overheard, Jacob must have a hand in that. It's all very clean to be seen through. In the first place there's the old gov'nor under promise of marriage to Miss Mildred, and in the second place he wants to marry my lord's daughter. Well, my lord's daughter won't have him because his old sweetheart has split about him to her. Then the gipsey chap has been sweet upon Miss Mildred too, and owes her a bit of spite. So they agree between them to accuse her of having committed a murder, which is of course all moonshine; though there's no doubt, however, they'll swear black's white to make out the case—leastwise I'm sure the gipsey chap will, and I don't think the old gov'nor is over particular to a shade. That far so good. Stand aside there," said Jacob addressing the lamp-post; " let's look at the matter fairly. I'm a liking for that girl myself, though she's been too proud to have anything to do with me. Well I'm not quite myself just now; but I think I see how the thing 's to be managed. They accuse the girl and I let them. When a witness is called for in court I steps up and introduces the French count, who'll be safe to give the old gov'nor a knock down blow. None of his swearing will do after that. The girl will get off, and there'll be no human nature in her if she isn't friends with Jacob Smags after that. Mind your standings, Jacob, keep well up in your argument !"

And with this salutary advice administered to himself, Jacob wended his way through the streets to a house, where he was well aware that his brethren of the order of the plush unmentionables made their nightly rendezvous. Jacob and human nature were inseparable—they always kept company together.

Sir Hargrave Manners went that night to his bed, determined to be the accuser of Mildred Winnerley. Shall it be said that in his heart he did not believe her guilty of the foul imputation—that in his heart he believed the gipsy to be accusing her wrongfully and wickedly? Yes, he did so believe. Yet he was willing that the charg should be made—ay, and that the gipsy should prove it if he could. And that was the Hargrave Manners who had once vowed love to the sister of Marion!

———

CHAPTER XV.

THE CHAMBER OF THE CORPSE.—MARION RECEIVES A VISIT OF CONSOLATION,

LADY MANNERS had been dead many days, but the corpse was not yet interred; it had been placed in the coffin of mahogany, it had been consigned to the narrow shell in which it was to moulder into dust, not as yet, however, was it placed in the family sepulchre, for the leaden case in which it had to be enveloped was not completed by its maker.

And the bright moonlight sweeps downwards through the curtained windows into a silent room, where, supported on tressels the corpse rests in its receptacle, awaiting the day of interment. All is lonely and deserted in that gloomy chamber, there is pomp and magnificence around, but the pomp and magnificence which are attached to titled death. No sorrowing heart is mourning there for the cold dead; no fond one weeps beside the bier of her who has died without leaving a friend. The windows are left partially open that the breath of death may not annoy the living, but float out and mingle with the winds of night. They have left the windows open, not fearing that thieves will enter; why should theives enter there? what is there for them to rob? The great thief, Death, has been there already; and that which he has left behind who cares to steal?

Yet see! the window opens wider, the curtains are thrust aside; and silently, gently the head and arms of a man are protruded into the room. Watch him! he opens the window still more, he holds the curtain more widely apart, he is forcing his body through, and now his feet touch the floor of the apartment. The man pauses for an instant, closes the window, draws the curtain, steals across the room and tries the door, to find if it be locked, and finding it to be so, creeps back to the coffin, and pulls off the black cloth which has been thrown over it, but which he casts so unscrupulously upon the floor, what can his object be? He is no common thief, or he would look elsewhere for his booty. Is it possible that he is one of those reckless men who make a trade of stealing and selling the dead? Surely not; for if so, he would content himself with some untitled corpse, that the risk incurred might be less. Yet watch him; he has drawn a screwdriver from his pocket and placed it on the coffin-lid, while the manner in which he is scrutinizing the coffin maker's work indicates that he is about to unloose the screws and profane the sanctity of the dead. There is scarcely sufficient light in the apartmen the fears to ignite a match; but, that the moonbeams may better assist him at his work, goes to the windows, and again separates the curtains. As he does so the pale beams fall upon his face revealing the features of Gerrard Chester!

Gerrard Chester, the lover of Mildred, in the chamber of the dead! What can be his object there?

Gerrard Chester approaches the coffin, he takes the screwdriver in his hand, one by one he unclooses the screws, he with draws them without noise, he lays them aside, he feels the lid, it is still fast, there is one screw more, he takes out that, he lifts the lid—removes it from its place—deposits it upon the floor—puts the screwdriver out of his hand. And now Gerrard Chester separates the drapery which conceals the corpse, the pinked ornaments, the frilled edgings, the white shroud, all are removed from where they hide the face of death, and Gerrard Chester beholds the countenance of her who had been the wife of Sir Walmsley Maners !

Strange it is that the intruder has entered the room so stealthily, and stranger still that he has entered it on such errand. What can be his object—what his design ? He gazes at the face of the corpse, illumined by the pale moonlight, but his gaze does not linger there—does not dwell upon the dead. From an inner pocket, he draws forth a small bottle, and from another pocket a common syringe. There is a white fluid in the bottle, resembling flour mixed with water. He withdraws the cork, he shakes the bottle, he inserts the point of the syringe into the mouth, he draws the piston, the syringe has taken up the contents from out of the bottle, he re-inserts the cork, and restores the bottle to his pocket.

What design can Gerrard Chester have now ? What is it that the syringe contains? Poison ? not that—surely not that ! what purpose could it serve to give poison to the dead ? Yet see ! he uplifts the head of the corpse, he holds the syringe, he pauses—places the instrument on the pillow in the coffin—slips the bandage from off the head of the dead woman, and pressing the lower jaw tightly, causes it to fall. He now again takes up the syringe, and placing its point in the mouth of the corpse, presses down the piston with his fingers. The fluid gurgles as it is forced down the throat ; and now that the syringe is empty, Gerrard Chester looks around, espies a jug of water standing on a table, he goes to it, refills the syringe, again uplifts the head of the dead woman, and again forces the contents of the syringe down the throat of the corpse. He now deposits the head upon its pillows—re-adjusts the bandage to the lower jaw—disposes the drapery in proper order—fits on the lid—drives in the screws—throws the black pall over the coffin—moves towards the window—opens it—creeps through the aperture—shuts down the sash—descends upon the roof of the outhouse beneath—passes over the wall, and again the chamber of the dead is silent, no meddler is there.

And the man who had thus desecrated the sanctity of the dead was Gerrard Chester —the man who as a humble villager had professed his love to Mildred Winnerley—had vowed eternal affection for her, but whose love had been slighted and whose affection had been scorned. What can Gerrard Chester be now, that like a thief he enters at night-time the house which now belongs unto the man who was his rival—that like a vampire he seeks in silence the fast-decaying corpse ? How is it that Gerrard Chester is in London—in the vast city that is so far removed from his village home ? It is true that he promised Mildred to follow her, go where she might ; true also that he vowed to her—though she cared not to listen to the vow—that he would ever guard, ever watch, ever be near to protect and deliver whensoever or wheresoever she might meet with danger and with difficulty. He gave her that promise—he pledged to her that vow, in the village where he loved her, and can it be that to perform the promise to keep the vow he has followed her to the city where she has forgotten him ? Has

GERRARD CHESTER WITH THE CORPSE OF LADY MANNERS.

he not been able to blot the image of the proud girl from his mind? Has he not been successful in erasing the remembrance of the haughty beauty from his memory? Can it be possible that he still loves her—still adores her, earnestly, desperately, burningly, as he did on that evening, when, he led her to that village festival, as he did on that well-remembered night, when, supposing her to be seated by his side, he turned to speak to her and found she was not there? Have not her slights chilled his love— has not her scorn cooled his ardour? Beware, Gerrard Chester! Pride goes with beauty in her whom you so madly loved; she is fair but she is haughty; she has the face of the angel, but hast thou not heard that pride entering once into an angel's heart hurled that angel from his seat in heaven? Beware, man; if the heart be proud what matter if the face be fair. When beauty and pride are linked together, then the demon and the angel are incorporated, and in that pride you have the curse of beauty.

High in the broad heaven above rides in state the queenly moon, as Gerrard Chester leaves the house of death; and moonbeams and starbeams mix as they descend in softness on the silent earth, sleeping in its beauty and its quietness, though rude men desecrate its face. The moon glides on, streaks of grey light dart athwart the eastern sky, one by one the stars veil themselves in their shrouding, a thousand living things awake to life, and heralded by opening flowers, and rising scents, and tuneful sounds, morning—glad morning comes. Glad morning men have called it, and such should be its name, fraught as it is with hope to the weary-hearted, and cheering as it is to the worn spirit which goes forth to court its influence. So bright, and cheerful, and gladdening the morning broke; and it found Mildred preparing to quit her home, and Marion tending on her sister.

"Milly, dearest," said the younger sister, " I know not what it is that oppresses me this morning, but I feel so gloomy so depressed, so wanting in spirits that—that, sister, I cannot eat, I care not to take any breakfast."

"You are unwell, sister. It is a slight indisposition which you will doubtless get rid of in the course of the day."

"No, Milly; I am not ill—it is not illness which oppresses me. I do not know what it is; but it is like the feeling which came over me some mornings ago—the morning of the day, sister, when it was so late before you returned home."

"You were unwell that morning, Mar."

"Not unwell, dear Milly, but depressed—depressed as I feel this morning. It is the same sensation, and it seems to me like a warning that something very dreadful is about to happen."

"Happen to whom, Mar?"

"I cannot tell you, sister. Heaven grant that nothing fearful is about to befall you, dear sister!"

"Why, Mar! how earnestly you express your wish—what silly whim can have taken possession of your brain? It is very unsocial of you to make one take breakfast alone, merely because you have been troubled, I suppose, with some nonsensical dream."

Marion made no reply, but drawing her chair towards the hearth, seated herself, and gazed earnestly and intently at the bright fire. Her respiration was irregular and fitful, the colour had flown from her cheeks, the smile had deserted her countenance. At times a sudden tremor seemed to pervade her frame, and at times she glanced round with a look of terror to see how her sister was employed at the opposite extremity of the room. The breakfast was concluded, the church clock struck the hour of eight, and Mildred rising from her seat, placed on her bonnet, preparatory to departing for the day.

"Stay, sister—stay!" exclaimed Marion, suddenly seizing Mildred's arm and preventing her from leaving the apartment.

"What is the matter, Mar? Why do you grasp me so tightly?"

"I—I—do not go out to day, sister—not now—not this morning."

"Why not, Mar?"

"It is my wish—my request. I am unwell—very unwell, and I am afraid."

"Afraid of what, Mar?"

"I do not know.   It is you, dear sister—you that I am afraid of."

"Oh! sister, were anything to befall you—any evil to happen to you, how miserable—how wretched I should be!"

"But why have such a fear, Marion?   I am not afraid, wherefore then should you be?   Indeed, I know not what you mean, nor yet what it is that you are afraid of. Come, Mar, this is all most ridiculous nonsense, all——"

"Hush, sister!   Some one is coming up the stairs?"

The sisters listened; they heard the tread of men's feet.   Presently there was a knock at the door.

"Who can it be, dear Mildred?" inquired the younger sister, tremulously.   But before there was time for Mildred to hazard a conjecture, the door opened, and two men entered the apartment."

"'Morning to you, ladies," said one of the two intruders, at the same time scanning the sisters with an enquiring glance.   "We don't like, ourselves, being hurried about business quite so early in the morning; and I dare say it's unpleasantsome to you. Only, you see, business must be attended to."

"What—what is it you want?" asked Marion, quivering as she spoke.

"We wants a young woman what goes by the name of Miss Mildred Winnerley, which is the one, my dears?"

"Wants you, sister!" said, or rather shrieked Marion.

The man advanced, and laid his hand on Mildred's arm.

"So this is the pris'ner—is it?" said he.   "Sorry to do it, my lass, but must arrest you, and take you with us."

"Take—take Mildred?" breathlessly articulated Marion.

"Yes, we must take her, and she must go with us.   That's all plain and straightforward enough."

"No—no!   Sister—dear sister!   what does this mean?   They shall not take you from me!"

"Peace, Marion!" said Mildred.   Then turning from her sister to address the man who had claimed her as his prisoner, she enquired in a voice that betrayed no symptoms of emotion.   "Why am I your prisoner?—who has sent you here?"

"Well; as for the 'tic'lars, umph, you'll know all about 'em afore long; but as to the charge we apprehends you on, it's neither more or less than downright murder."

Mildred did not start, did not shrink, did not draw back, did not manifest any feeling of surprise more than was revealed by a sudden closure of the lips, a sudden pallor of the cheeks, and a momentary cessation from breathing.   Erect, unmoved, calm, beautiful and proud, she stood, while her sister crept to her side, sank upon the ground at her feet, clasped her hand and ejaculated,—

"It is false, sister—they accuse you falsely.   But—but there is some cause—some reason.   Speak, sister, tell me—tell me what you have done?"

"Murder," was the sole reply of the haughty prisoner, and she said it without a quiver of the lips.

There was no shriek from Marion, there was no cry of anguish from the sister of the self-confessed murderess.   She had asked the question, she had heard the reply; it had passed through her like an electric shock; it had struck inward to her brain and thence into her heart. Power, feeling, sense—ay, almost life itself, it had sent away; stopping the pulse's play, the heart's beat, the brain's power of eliminating thought. No eyes of statue cut in stone could have been fixed in more rigid gaze than were those of Marion Winnerley as she now glared, rather than gazed, upon her sister; no actress, however clever in her art, could have imitated that look of speechless woe, that expression in which astonishment, conviction, fear, hope, love, horror, anxiety, phrenzy and despair were all blended, intermixed and yet apparent. It was an expression such as would have fastened on the memory of a beholder, and remained there impressed until life's latest hour; it was an expression which Mildred Winnerley recalled to mind throughout the day, and which haunted her through the night; so piteous yet so terrible, so loving yet so fearful was that look which her sister wore. Gradually, however, a change came over the stone-like countenance, while, gently fading, the expression which the features had worn, vanished away. Marion had heard the accusation, she had heard the confession also—what more was there for her to hear? Nothing that the ear could listen to, nothing that the brain could bear. She sank upon the floor—on the floor at the feet of that proud sister; her eyes still fixed, her breathing suspended, her hands motionless and cold.

"Arn't you got no old 'oman anywhere in the house to look after the lass now she's turned so queer?" enquired the constable, addressing his prisoner.

"If the man who is with you will knock at the door of the] room below, and ask Mrs. Downes to step up, I will beg of her to take charge of my sister," replied Mildred in a calm manner.

The man did as Mildred had requested him to do. Marion was committed to the keeping of the kindly-disposed Mrs. Downes; and the constables, after suffering Mildred to make a few preliminary arrangements, accompanied her down the stairs into a coach, which was waiting at the door for her reception.

Already in the hearing of the officers, had Mildred Winnerley confessed her crime. She thought, that her previous avowal of it to the mysterious individual who had conversed with her in the dark chamber was that which had led to her apprehension; and she believed that individual to have been some other person than Hargrave Manners. Now, however, she learnt that Hargrave himself was her accuser, and learning that, she believed that none but he could have been her companion in the gloomy room. Astonished she certainly was when first this conviction forced itself upon her mind, but gradually her astonishment gave way to self-reproach; and self-reproach softened down into resignation. Then it was that in a moment of madness—in a moment when phrenzy held mastery in her brain, and desolation had gained empire in her heart that she called the officials of the prison to her, confessed herself to be a murderess, told them how that murder had been effected, and bade them bear her message to Sir Hargrave Manners that there was no cause for him to proceed further in accusing her, who was was willing to inculpate herself to the full. She comprehended how revenge for having been exposed to the family of Lord Bellayre, had led him to take this step, and in the haughtiness of her proud spirit she determined to foil him in obtaining his revenge to the full, by confessing to all that he could lay to her charge.

And as the turnkey closed the door on Mildred in her cell, she asked him what the day of the month was. The man answered her; and the thought flashed instantaneously across her mind that the third period of six months from the date of Mrs. Winnerley's death had now arrived at its completion.

A fortnight has passed away; it is evening; on the morning of the morrow the murderess is to take her trial.

It is the apartment which the two sisters occupied together, and which but one lone broken-hearted girl inhabits now. Marion is on her knees, her arm resting on a chair, praying to Heaven that the following day a humane jury will find her sister insane and thereby save her from an ignominous death. The door opens. Marion starts to her feet, and her gaze meets that of Gerrard Chester.

"Gerrard—Mr. Chester. I—I am glad to see you—very glad to see you now!"

"I trust you may have cause to be, Miss Marion. I have heard all, and know how much reason you have to be otherwise than glad at the present time."

"Heaven knows, Mr. Gerrard, I am miserable enough. My sister—my poor sister!" ejaculated the sorrowful girl, giving vent to a sudden gush of tears.

"It is of her that I wish to speak to you. Sorry should I be, however, if I thought that my visit, by bringing back any old remembrances, should cause you additional sorrow at a time when you have so much to make you sad."

"Oh no, Mr. Gerrard. You—you were always good—always kind to poor Mildred; and to see now any one that thinks of her or even has thought of her kindly is happiness indeed. She scorned you once, Mr. Gerrard; but you must forgive her, for now she is scorned by all."

"Not by all," answered Gerrard Chester. "I gave her my promise at our parting that if she should ever want assistance, in me she should find one who would assist her, and that whenever all others might become her enemies she should find a friend in me."

"Kind, noble-hearted man!" exclaimed Marion with enthusiasm, as she clasped the hand of Gerrard. Then, assuming suddenly a calmer demeanour and drooping her head, she murmured in a low despairing tone. "It is too late; you cannot assist her now."

"Even of that you are not assured," returned Gerrard, the tone of his voice inspiring Marion with new, yet vague hope. "It would have been vain of me to have promised help to your sister if I had seen no probability of my being at any time able to lend her aid."

"Probability—aid—then—then you can assist her! Oh tell me that you can!"

"I believe it to be in my power to lend her some trivial assistance. Possibly it will be very slight, and there is no certainty of its proving very efficient. It is to cheer you with this hope that I have visited you to night."

"But—but it is a hope—only a hope?" enquired Marion distrustfully.

"It may possibly be something more," was the reply.

Marion gazed at Gerrard and was silent. After a pause of a few minutes she again addressed him.

"I have been thinking," said she, "if I can do anything to assist dear sister. I know not what I can do, indeed I know not if it be in my power to do one single thing. If there were any sacrifice that I could make more then I have made—I have sold enough to procure counsel—I am sure it should be made at once. Even if I could give my life to save her, I would give it cheerfully and gladly."

"Has your sister then, been so kind to you?" asked Gerrard.

Marion was silent for a few moments; then looking earnestly at Gerrard Chester, she answered,—

"It is not for me to complain of my sister's behaviour, but I am sorry, Mr. Chester that she should have treated you unkindly. Oh, how much I was grieved to see my sister so distant to you when your father and yourself were so kind—so very kind to ourselves. It grieved me, it made me sad, Mr. Gerrard, and it makes me sad now when I remember it; but I did not know at the time how my sister was situated—I did not know why she treated you so coolly. But you will forgive Mildred—you will pardon my poor sister, Mr. Gerrard. Oh! she has suffered much, she has endured much misery, and—and if you have ever loved her as deeply as I have, if she has ever been as dear to you as she is now to me, you can comprehend my feelings when I say that if I could sacrifice this poor life of mine to restore happiness to dear Mildred I would not hesitate one moment to make it. Tell me what I am to do; show me what course I am to take! Your coming here to night—the words you have spoken—the expression of your countenance, all assure me that it is in the power of some one— I know not whom—to render help to my sister. Entrust me with that power. Oh! I will prove worthy of the trust, or, let me aid you—let me give assistance to yourself if there be anything in which I can give you assistance. To-night, too—let us proceed about it to-night; do not let us delay. You know how near to-morrow is, and to-morrow will be a fearful day. At once—let us do something at once, Mr. Gerrard. My brain burns, but my mind is strong; my heart flutters, but my limbs are firm. Come, what is there we can do?"

"We must be calm," replied Gerrard. "The accusation which has been brought against your sister is one which is indeed fearful. Think you that Mildred can be guilty?"

"I—I do not know; I cannot imagine. Oh! it is too terrible—too terrible for thought! And yet she has confessed—she has acknowledged all that has been laid to her charge."

"People before now have confessed themselves guilty of crimes which they had never committed. What motive do you suppose your sister could possibly have had to commit a crime so great?"

Gerrard Chester waited for a reply. At length, Marion answered in a solemn voice,—

"Her pride—her ambition—the wish to obtain the title of her who is dead. You know not how ambitious my sister is—you have never known it, but I have; and years ago dear grandmother knew and said that misery would be my sister's share."

"Pardon me, Miss Marion, for asking the question at such a time, but you have alluded to Mrs. Winnerley, and you have spoken of her by the name of grandmother, now it is from other motives than those of curiosity that I am led to ask you, if either you or your sister have any certain knowledge of your parentage, and the story of those with whom you are connected."

"We know not who our relatives are," replied Marion. "There is a mystery concerning them and ourselves. We have never been told anything as to who our father was; and when we asked dear grandmother at anytime to talk to us about our mother she was silent and would turn away her face. She told us, however, that at some future time we should be made acquainted with the cause of the mystery; and she was about to perform that promise on the night she was burnt to death. Oh! that fearful night! Do you remember it, Mr. Gerrard? Do you remember also the prophecy of the old gipsey-woman? I have watched that prophecy almost to its completion, Gerrard Chester. The eighteen months have expired, and every prediction which that woman made to dear sister has come true—pride, misery, and now—now there will be death."

"Not yet," said Gerard Chester.

"Why do you say ' not yet?' What reason have you for saying so? Ha! I remember. The old gipsey-woman whispered a word in [your ear which was not heard by me. What word—what prediction was that?"

"It was but one word."

"Yes, yes, but what—what?"

"'Murder'!"

"' Murder'!" repeated Marion in a whispered murmur. " Pride, misery, murder, and death! Then it is all true—it is all fixed. My sister is guilty. We have no power to save her."

"We have, Marion Winnerley."

"Have!—have, man. No, no—do not delude me; it is cruel to do that. Let the prophecy work it's end—aye, for it will work!"

"It spoke of death, Marion Winnerley; [but it said not that it was your sister that should die. Death there must be, but it shall not be the death of her you love."

"Then let it be my own. I am ready. Let my sister escape, [and with my life let the prophecy be fulfilled."

"No Marion, brave sister that you are. There is another who must die—another whose place it is to die that Mildred Winnerley may live."

"Another! Who, Mr. Chester—who?"

"On the morrow you will know. At present you must tell me who the counsel is that you have engaged in [your sister's defence, and where I may find him to-night."

"I will show you—I will accompany you."

"No. I must go alone."

And alone Gerrard Chester went—alone to the dwelling of the barrister, at the hour of midnight. And in one room he and the man of law sat together; in a small room by a smouldering fire they sat. A lamp shed its yellow rays upon the countenance of each, and the barrister listened to that which his visitor had to tell. Though daily toil and midnight studies had long since chased the hue of health from the cheeks of him who was the listener, and in some degree deprived him of the majesty of manhood, he was yet a strong and resolute man. As, however, he listened to the story told him at the fireside—the story whibh his visitor had compelled him to hear—his face grew pale with terror, his limbs were agitated with dread. He arose from his seat, he threw himself forward upon his visitor, he cried aloud for help, and that night Gerald Chester was made a prisoner!

But what man was that with whom Mildred had talked in the dark chamber.

CHAPTER XVI.

THE CURSE OF BEAUTY.

OUR story approaches its conclusion. It is early morning, and the scene is the interior of the court-house at the Old Bailey. Outside the court there is a throng of people, and the carriage of the judges have just arrived. The report is spread abroad that a young woman is to be tried for poisoning. There are hundreds of individuals who have longed for some time pass to spend a holiday in seeing such a sight, and they have now availed themselves of the opportunity. The doorkeeper is busy demanding half-a-crown from each as the price of admision to the gallery, and there are reserve seats to be obtained at a higher price. One would think that some play or pantomime was about to be represented, that so many were pushing forward to enjoy the sight; and imagination might suppose the place to be a theatre, so business-like is the way of taking money at the doors. Your common horse-stealers and pickpockets can be seen for a single shilling; it must be a murderer, and one of the worst description to yield the treasury the larger amount that is obtained by charging the half-crown fees! Oh! nice distinction! Oh, most profitable justice! So, outside there are people jostling at the doors, inside there are people scrambling for seats, and not far away in the cold cell, is the lonely, weeping, desolate mortal, whom all have assembled to see. But now the judge has taken his place, the counsels have their briefs in their hands, there is a call for silence, a few preliminaries, a slight bustle, and then all eyes are turned from regarding the judge upon his seat to gaze at the prisoner in the dock. The prisoner is Mildred Winnerly.

The accusation is read, the accused girl is called upon for her plea.

"That's him, there he is. I told him there was no mistake—Jacob Smags never makes any," says some one in a very audible voice.

"Silence in the court!" exclaims the crier.

"Don't stand that. Speak out. Let them know who he is!" resemmends Jacob Smags, as he pushes the foreign-looking gentleman into the body of the court, and points out to his notice Sir Hargrave Manners.

"What is the meaning of this interruption?" enquires the judge of an official near him.

The official thus addressed, makes his way towards Mr. Smags, and endeavours to expel that worthy from the court.

"Don't push me!" is the advice of Smags. "I know what I'm about. All's right Let me speak a word to the judge."

"Not now, it is out of order, you must wait."

"That won't do for me. Jacob Smags cant stand that. My lord, that is my friend the Count of Aarlois, who's come to———"

"Silence him!" commands the judge.

Jachb Smaggs is turned out of the court.

The accusation is again read to Mildred Winnerley, and the plea of the prisoner demanded.

"Guilty," she replies.

In this manner did the trial of Mildred proceed on the morning of that dreadful day,

THE TRIAL OF MILDRED WINNERLEY.

which was to seal her destiny.   And Mildred was proud Mildred still—beautifully proud as she stood in that dock, and threw a glance of scorn at her accuser—queenly proud as she turned towards the clerk while he read the accusation—madly proud, as, in the depth of her haughtiness, she owned to the charge which proclaimed her to the world as a murderess and a poisoner, while by so owning, she dared the doom of ignominy which she knew to await her there.   And when the word—that damning word had passed her lip—and ere its echo had passed from out the apartment, a feeble yet frantic girl burst from the grasp of those by whom she was held, rushed across the floor of the court, sprung to the railing of the dock in which the prisoner stood, and ejaculated in a loud voice,

"Say it not, sister—say it not. She is not guilty, good judge; it is my sister, and she is mad."

"Let that young woman be removed," said the judge. "The prisoner has pleaded guilty, I believe, to the indictment?"

"She has, my lord," answered the barrister, with whom Gerrard Chester had conversed on the previous night, "but I am inclined to believe that she has accused herself falsely."

"Accused herself falsely!" repeated every individual in the court.

"What grounds have you for making such a statement?" inquired the judge.

"Many, my lord. In the first instance, I appear here on behalf of the prisoner, and have to state my belief—a belief which I shall presently produce facts to support—that she is afflicted with lunacy, and is entirely incapable of understanding the position in which she is placed."

"My learned friend, will perhaps enter into some further explanation, and adduce some arguments in order to account for why this singular plea of insanity is brought forward at the present stage of the proceedings," said the counsel for the prosecution.

"I am prepared to do so."

"Proceed, sir," said the judge.

"The whole case, my lord, is one which is enveloped in extreme mystery. The prisoner now at the bar has been indicted for the crime of administering poison to Lady Frances Manners, widow of the late Sir Walmsley Manners. Immediately that the indictment is read to her, she pleads guilty, and so far the case is without perplexity. A strange and most important circumstance has happened, however, within the last twenty-four hours. There have been many instances where a person has been accused of murder—placed at the bar—a plea of ' not guilty' returned to the indictment—tried and convicted. Then, at the last moment, the real—the conscience-stung murderer has stepped forth—acknowledged his guilt—given evidence which has led to the pardon of the convicted person, and, by so doing, saved an innocent individual from an ignominious death. But,[my lord, the present case is one still more strange—still more singular. We have here the accused person returning a plea of ' guilty;' and yet, as I before hinted, a circumstance has occurred which justifies me in pronouncing it as my opinion and belief that the prisoner at the bar has never committed the crime, in the commission of which she avows herself to be guilty. Last night, my lord, I received a visit from a man who in the most extraordinary manner, and doubtless driven to it by the most agonizing pangs of a crime-laden conscience, declared himself to be the actual and sole poisoner of the lady whose death the prisoner in the dock stands indicted of having caused. The manner in which the communication was made— the circumstances under which the confession was avowed, were such that, while they offer the most convincing proof of the real guilt of the individual, whom I shall presently bring into court, read the most fearful lesson of how the memory of a guilty deed haunts the doer, and with the lash of a fury—a lash of scorpions, drives him to declare his deed of ill to the ears of his fellow-men. Before proceeding further, it will perhaps be as well that the person of whom I have spoken be brought into court."

The counsel ceased from speaking. A slight movement near the door broke the stillness with which the preceding words had been listened to, and Gerrard Chester was placed in the witness-box.

"Gerrard!" exclaimed Marion, in a tone of mingled surprise and terror, while her sister only regarded the entrance of the young man with a look of quiet astonishment.

"This, my lord, is the individual," resumed the counsel. "It is true that he is acquainted with the prisoner in the dock, and true that he has recently had communication with the family of the accused. But that he is guilty of the crime to which he confesses I shall presently bring evidence in proof."

There was now some little confusion in court, and when it had subsided, the judge proceeded to interrogate Gerrard Chester. To these interrogatories Gerrard replied that he had poisoned Lady Manners from motives of revenge, and that her death was owing to the poison administered by himself, without the knowledge, consent, or assistance of any other party. The counsel for the prosecution now resumed his enquiries.

"In proof, my lord, and gentlemen of the jury, that this man is guilty, and that Mildred Winnerley has accused herself falsely, you will give me leave to call upon one of the witnesses for the prosecution. Let the gipsey Pharold, or Phareld Morthwin as he is otherwise termed, stand forward.

The gipsey advanced to give evidence.

"Your name is Pharold Morthwin; you are a gipsey; you state that you saw the prisoner at the bar administer something in a cup to Lady Frances Manners on the day of her death, and that you know the contents of that cup to have been laudanum?"

The answer was in the affirmative.

"And how know you the cup to have contained laudanum? Can you state positively to the name and nature of the poison?"

"I can. The poison—the laudanum, I mean, was taken from a cupboard in the prisoner's own room, by her own hand. Let her sister be asked if a bottle containing laudanum was not kept there, and if she did not see the prisoner remove the bottle on the night previous to the death of Lady Manners."

Marion was placed in the witness-box, and with much difficulty confirmed the statement of the gipsey. She had scarcely answered the interrogatory which was put to her before she was interrupted by her sister, who said in a deep, grave voice,—

"The gipsey has said rightly. The poison was laudanum."

There was a minute's pause. Then again addressing the judge, the counsel for the prisoner said,—

"My lord, you have heard the evidence that has been given, and you have heard the prisoner distinctly say that she administered laudanum to Lady Manners. Now, my lord, Gerrard Chester avows and confesses that he poisoned the said Lady Manners by the administration of arsenic. You will allow me at this stage of the proceedings to call for the evidence of two medical gentlemen who have examined the body of the deceased."

The medical witnesses were called, and they gave in evidence that having examined the body of the late Lady Manners, they had discovered a large quantity of arsenic, and so large had that quantity been, that there was not the least doubt of its having been the immediate cause of death. Evidence so conclusive as this, coupled with the confession of Gerrard Chester, caused the court to proceed at once to issue an order that Mildred

Winnerley should be set at liberty; and that, the grand jury being still sitting, Gerrard Chester should be remanded till a true bill should be found against him.   On an order from the judge, Gerrard was immediately committed to custody.

And how did Mildred Winnerley behave, now that Gerrard Chester—the man whose love she once despised—had rescued her by self-sacrifice from death on the gallows tree?   What emotion did she exhibit?   What avowals—what protestations did she make?   None!   Haughty as ever—haughty as when first wooed by him who had thus saved her—haughty as when in that green bower, he had asked her for love, and had received the answer of pride in return, did she behave herself now.   She knew that because of his love he had thus accused himself; she knew that to retaliate upon her for her slight he had made so great a sacrifice; she thought that he meant to humble her by showing how he could forgive the past.   Therefore, still to keep her pride, still to hold her haughtiness, still to be the cold and soulless being she had ever been, she determined not to press her former confession, but to let him meet the fate which he had brought upon himself.   So she returned to her home, and she sat in that chimney-corner where her loving, tearful sister had thought never to see her sit again; and she spoke no word, she gave no greeting, she returned not one look of love.

So was it with beauty and its pride; but how fared it with gentle Marion?   Confused, perplexed, amazed, terrified, rejoiced, distressed, her mind was a chaos of contradictory emotions.   She knew that Gerrard Chester had accused himself of a crime which he had not committed, and she knew also that the guilty person was her own crime-stained sister.   Struck with astonishment as she had been when the gipsey-chief rose to give his evidence, she knew too well how that knowledge had been procured; she knew that it was by the fearful power with which mesmerism had invested the Zingaro chief.   And in a few days—in only two perhaps—Gerrard would be sentenced to die.   Oh! this was horrible!   Yet what was poor Marion to do?   She had gained her sister back, and yet she had no sister now; for that haughty thing which sat by the fire-side spoke not to her, looked not at her, seemed to have no sympathy—no relationship with her.   And they sat together in their room on the night after this strange scene, and as they so sat, the door opened, and there entered Isis, the gipsey girl.

"Pardon me—pardon me!" she cried, falling upon her knees.   "Pharold has learnt much from me, but I was compelled to tell him.   Oh! you know not what his power is; you know not the sleep he can throw me into—the spell he can cast over me.   I have done you much harm; but I can do you some good.   I promised you once that I would, and I come to keep my promise."

"How—oh, tell me how?" enquired Marion eagerly.

"You remember that night when your cottage was in flames; you remember there was a trunk in that room above, and that it contained papers; you know not, perhaps that one of our tribe stole at the time some of those papers, and that I rescued them from him.   Those papers told me much, they told me your name was not Winnerley —that it is Fanbourne, that your mother after she had borne two children to her husband, deserted him to seek the roof of another; that he sought out her seducer, challenged him to fight, and the challenge being accepted, shot him, then, supposing that he had committed murder, your father left all and sought a home in another land, leaving you to the care of the mother who had already cast you off; happily the woman who had nursed your mother in her infancy took pity on you, and with the earnings of many years devoted to your support, resolved to bring you up in her cre; that good woman was Mrs. Winnerley whose name you bear. As for your mother, her paramour not dying from his wound, she continued to live with him; and a report being spread abroad that your father was dead, married her seducer. The property of your father was seized by his brothers; but your mother was heiress to an entail which she inherited through the death of her father, an event which occurred some six months ago. Your mother is dead now, and the entail descends to her eldest daughter, who cannot become possessed of it, however, unless the certificate of your mother's marriage with your father be produced; that certificate, together with all the other documents I will now give you, and broad lands and good estates will be yours."

"Give them to me," exclaimed Mildred, "they are mine, sister—mine by right!"

"Take them," said Isis, "but know you who your mother was, and what name she bore at her death ?"

"Give me the papers, girl. Her name was—what?"

"Her seducer was Sir William Walmsley Manners, and Lady Frances Manners was she called at the time she died."

Without uttering a sound, without a cry or groan, Mildred Winnerley, as her fingers were about to close upon the papers, fell forward on the ground, struck as by a thunderbolt from Heaven. Assistance was procured, she was raised to her seat. All that medical aid could effect was done. The fit passed away, and the red flush returned to the cheek of beauty; but from that day forward Mildred Winnerley was a maniac—a dumb, drivelling maniac; she lived, but it was not life that animated her, for that was not life which glistened in those dull, rayless eyes, and caused those ceaseless workings of lips that were for ever speechless. And though she was told that on the last occasion of her visiting Sir Hargrave she had been followed by Gerrard, and that to him she had disclosed her secret in the dark room, she understood not what was told her, nor comprehended the fearful past.

And the following day Isis returned.

"Tell me," said Marion—"what know you of our father ?"

"He died in our camp last night."

"He! who ?"

"Jasper, the gipsey. None have recognised in him Sir Felix Fanbourne of Fanbourne Hall !"

Gerrard Chester was brought to trial, but when placed at the bar and called upon for his plea, he answered, "Not Guilty." The trial proceeded; the medical evidence was conflicting, and went to prove that the arsenic found in the stomach of the deceased woman could not have been the cause of death; but was placed there afterwards. Reports were spread abroad that the prisoner had inculpated himself in order to set at liberty one whom he had loved; and when the jury were called upon for their verdict, they returned it in such a manner as to set Gerrard Chester free.

It is but little that we now have to communicate, and it can be told in few words. We will not state how many years elapsed before Marion Winnerley became Mrs. Chester; nor will we say anything concerning the extent to which her husband loved her. As for that silent thing which sat day after day by the fire-side of one to whom it could not speak, and whom it scarcely seemed to know, it lived for months, bearing its curse upon its once proud and beautiful brow; then, unable to say farewell to those who had loved it, unable to express the wish that came with death, it died, and ceased to be that which was once called Mildred Winnerley.   But in the top room of that well-known house where the widow Chester still resides, the skeleton of beauty sits ever beside the looking-glass—ever casting its fearful reflection thereon, and ever reading the truthful lesson, that when beauty is joined with meekness, it is an honour and a blessing, but when united with pride it is a misery and a curse.   There is poison in the beauty that dwells not with gentleness; but when face-beauty and heart-beauty dwell together, happiness always rents a cottage close at hand.

Isis the gipsey girl wandered from her tribe, and no more secrets did she reveal to the mysterious Pharold.   It remains but to say that Jacob Smags contrived to get up a duel between the Count d'Aarlois and Sir Hargrave Mnners ; that in the said duel Sir Hargrave was killed; and Jacob having entered into the count's service, contrived to rob him before having been his servant for a month, and was sent to recruit his health across the water, where probably he now regrets having at any time been acquainted with the nobility.

THE END.